America the Desolate:
A Brief History of America's Second Civil War

By B.A. Davids

In honor of Gabrielle Giffords and in memory of John Roll, Christina-Taylor Green and those others murdered in Tucson, Arizona January 8th, 2011.

And to Bill Werner, the best English teacher I never had who passed away shortly before this book's completion. He was the epitome of the great Fieldston School, which gave me the drive to do whatever I wanted, such as become a sideline author.

Tremendous thanks to the following people for their help and input: Jennifer Hannon, Karen Lindsey, Jason Rosado, Melissa Spaulding and Marie Yaker (or as I usually call her, mom).

Thank you also to Kristina Thorstenson for her gorgeous cover photo, depicting the essence of this book. To see more of her work or to inquire about projects, please visit http://www.kvtphotography.com.

The Start of the Second Civil War: A Brief History

History, the age-old proverb says, is written by the victors. No truer example of this may exist than immediately after America's second Civil War. The U.S. government-sanctioned textbooks suggested the first meaningful shot of the war was fired on Wednesday, July 26th, 2017. It was that day when Conservative talk-show host Fleet Sussman was assassinated while on the air. His supporters say it was that moment when they realized they had to mobilize against the growing Democratic threat. Around the globe, there were other thoughts.

Most non-Americans seemed to believe as the losing side did. According to them, the first real blow of the war came the week before, on July 20th. It was on that day when Eduardo "Edward" Rodriguez, the President of the United States, was gunned down after giving a speech in West Virginia. The President had been inaugurated to his first term in office just months before, on the heels of Barack Obama's historic two-term presidency.

In its teachings, the Far Right didn't dispute the assassination happened, but rather downplayed its importance. The outsiders couldn't understand how the party could just gloss over this event. Numerous camera angles of the President's dying moments were filmed and available over the Internet. Some members of the eventual winning party said it was politics as usual, the unfortunate actions of one of its more zealous followers. Some even hinted the shooter had in fact saved America, keeping the Left from continuing its "subversive" agenda. But Sussman's death was cold-blooded murder, an attempt to destroy the Constitution by permanently silencing America's First Amendment. It didn't matter how many times the radio figure stopped just short of promoting the destruction of the President, he didn't pull the trigger, and therefore wasn't responsible for the shooting.

In the end, the causes of the war weren't important. All that really mattered was that the conflict brought the country to its knees. What had been the world's brightest Superpower had fallen into the greatest state of despair imaginable.

Part One:

Before the War

Meet the New Boss

January 20th, 2017 was a proud day for many in America, especially for staunch supporters of the Democratic Party and particularly for people of Latino decent. For the party, it was a continued stranglehold on the top seat in government for a third-straight term. Neither of the major parties had had such control since the first President Bush succeeded Ronald Reagan. What was remarkable to all though, as equally championed by the Democrats as it was despised by the Republicans, was that the Left had been able to maintain its control of the Senate over much of President Obama's tenure, even when President Rodriguez was elected. By the time of the 2016 election, the Democrats had also made significant gains in the House of Representatives after years of stalemate tactics used by Republicans. The House had swung very closely to the middle, with the GOP maintaining only a slight advantage. In order to save face and some matter of control in Washington, the Right only put roadblocks up against what they considered the most heinous of Democratic bills.

A working healthcare reform bill was the party's coup d'état over Obama's tenure. By the time Obama's second term had ended, he and the Democrats had narrowed the tax gap between the wealthy and the poor, opened new avenues for stem cell research, and passed a number of civil rights laws for homosexuals, including passing federal recognition of marriages of gay and lesbian couples.

It was that January day when Eduardo Rodriguez was sworn in as the first Latino-American President of the United States. The 51-year-old Puerto Rican descendant had grown up near Third Avenue in the Bronx. He had lived within a mile from the original Yankee Stadium and its almost equally majestic replacement. He would walk to games often during the summers of his youth with hopes a generous patron would give him an extra ticket. He was an above-average student through high school, and from his sophomore year on, took an active part in community affairs. Sometimes that meant dabbling in local politics and at other times that meant volunteering with community groups.

Eduardo was quickly accepted to Brown University. His grades and community work were large factors, but it seemed as though programs dedicated to the advancement of Latino-Americans may have been the driving force for his acceptance. Once he was in school though, that question didn't matter. He excelled in all of his classes while still finding time to work with community groups in the Providence area. He graduated with honors with a law degree. Immediately out of his undergraduate studies, Eduardo applied to, and was again rapidly accepted to, Yale University to pursue his Masters. He maintained his excellent performance at the Connecticut institution, even as he took whatever available free time he had to continue pursuing his political and charitable efforts back in the Bronx. Even with his extracurricular dedication, Eddie made grad school look easy.

Once his formal education came to an end, Eduardo returned to New York and the Bronx. Many local organizations were eager to have him back. Mr. Rodriguez quickly found a job as a civil rights attorney, and strengthened his bonds with the political people around him through his professional and personal work to help and protect others. Soon he decided to enter politics on a greater level than being just an activist. Because of his reputation, charisma and his youth, Eddie easily won a seat in the state senate. He spent two terms representing the Bronx in Albany. He was considered one of the main forces behind getting a number of high-profile issues resolved. His push for funding helped get the on-again, off-again Bronx Convention Center finally built near Yankee Stadium. The project included a brand-new hotel right by the new park, which was an economic boom for the area thanks to a handful of rooms which offered partial views of the field. He helped revitalize the Grand Concourse and Fordham Road, making the areas very attractive for big businesses to set up shop back in the Bronx. Yet through it all, he still fought for - and won - many benefits for people who otherwise would have been left to rot in what had been one of the poorest districts per capita in the state and county.

During his second term upstate, it was suggested he run for the congressional seat of his native 16th district. He was sent to Washington in a landslide victory. He spent another three terms in the House of Representatives, towards the end of which an advisor suggested Rodriguez run for President. It was a novel idea, one which made many in the Democratic Party nervous. Nobody had ever succeeded in making the jump from that House to the White House. The closest such instance was Gerald Ford, but he had been Vice President before being anointed Commander-in-Chief after Richard Nixon resigned. Still, it was suggested that Eddie give it a try. He had become a Congressional star in his time in the nation's capital, and was a well-balanced mix of youth, charisma, strength and compassion. In his history of serving in elected offices, he had a solid record of winning by tremendous margins. Those who suggested him said his positives were in line with those displayed by some of the candidates the Right had rolled out unsuccessfully in recent years. Many of those people were also young and relatively inexperienced. However, those the GOP and the Tea Party had settled on often turned out to be laughable candidates. The base of the parties voted for their selections, but the undecided voters before Election Day were unwilling to cast their ballots for those candidates. In exit polls, people in the middle of the political spectrum said they didn't feel comfortable with candidates they perceived as being intellectually inferior, and who showed some major deficiencies when it came to discussing major topics.

Initial canvassing about Eddie however showed he was considered respectable when it came to political issues. He had made some eloquent speeches during the healthcare debates, and was never at a loss to talk about any major topic that came up. He also showed a willingness to compromise, a trait candidates from the Tea Party suggested was a weakness. Sometimes begrudgingly, members of the other side of the aisle admitted Rodriguez was well-liked and easy to work with. So, months before the first primaries, Eddie announced he would run for the presidency.

At first, the Democratic rulers tried to persuade him to drop out early. They were certain he had no chance. Then Rodriguez won the primaries in New Hampshire and Iowa. Exit polls suggested voters liked the fact he had a proven track record in politics, while still being a somewhat fresh face in Washington. He demonstrated acceptance of bipartisanship while still promising to push for Liberal platforms. This was a factor Democratic and unaffiliated voters seemed to like. Some pundits stole the term Maverick, used years ago in the fight against Obama, to describe Rodriguez. He was very charismatic, with a wide smile which he flashed often. Soon, the Democratic think tank started to take the youngster seriously. He was on a roll, and he hadn't even hit the states with large Latino populations.

The anti-Rodriguez engine also started getting fired up after Eduardo's initial victories. They were angered that the Left stole the maverick metaphor, first pointing out the term was unoriginal. When the moniker stuck, the Rodriguez detractors suggested the "Maverick" character was actually a swindler and somewhat of a thief. However, few in the second decade of the 21st century remembered 1950s television shows, or Mel Gibson's theatrical take on the character.

Next the spin masters of the ultra-Right started questioning Rodriguez' upbringing. They stated Rodriguez wasn't really U.S.-born, nor was he truly of Puerto Rican descent. One activist was able to produce a Mexican birth certificate of a man with the same name, born on the same day as the presidential candidate. The family of the other Eduardo Rodriguez, which had moved to California in the 1990s, said their "Edward" had died in a car crash in 2007. Despite government-certified documents showing the birth of one Eduardo in the Bronx and the death of another on the West Coast, the fanatics against Rodriguez were certain the candidate was actually an illegal alien, unfit to rule the country. Few took this claim to heart, and many were angered at the way the accusers showed a blatant disregard for the family of the deceased Eduardo, calling the Mexican Rodriguez family members liars. Those who believed the two Eduardos were one and the same said those refuting the claims would do anything to make sure one of "their kind" won office. Once Rodriguez was in office, his detractors stated, he would tear down the border walls and let any and every Mexican come to the U.S. without prejudice. They would then force hard-working Americans out of their jobs because of their willingness to work for low wages.

The candidate would at first laugh at the claims during his time on the campaign trail, before seriously addressing the situation. First, he'd point out how his opponents were trying to drive a spike through the country, by using the terms "us" and "them." "We are a 'we!'" Rodriguez proudly would state, and his supporters would cheer enthusiastically. He'd then give his condolences to the other Rodriguez family, for both their loss and the way they were being treated by the opposition. The California Rodriguezes appeared on occasion for the candidate on campaign stops on the West Coast. Their part in the campaign helped unify the Latino vote, where people of different nationalities hadn't always seen eye-to-eye.

The unified Latino base powered Rodriguez to wins in a number of states. His success in New York gave him an easy victory in his home state, as well as in New Jersey and Connecticut. His connection to the Mexican Rodriguezes was a driving factor in securing nominations in California, Arizona, New Mexico and Texas. In Florida, the Cuban faction joined with the growing community of other Latinos to help their candidate to another state's delegation. However, other Southern states rallied hard for various other candidates.

It was shortly after Super Tuesday when Fleet Sussman started to assail Rodriguez any chance he had. The Ultra-Right leaning radio personality started to warn his listeners of the dangers of electing Rodriguez. Sussman more than any famous figure kept the Mexican myth alive and he continued to state how scared Americans should be. He'd laugh when others would suggest Mexicans were Americans too, saying that term should only be used to describe people from the United States. The fact that Mexicans wanted to be Americans was one of his scare tactics. He used that notion to state Rodriguez would eliminate the border with Mexico altogether, so his "brothers and sisters" could take jobs away from "real" Americans and help destroy the U.S. economy.

Rodriguez tried to ignore Sussman's suggestions while campaigning. His listeners called themselves the "Susspicious Minds." They vocalized their unofficial moniker with an emphasis on the second "s." Sometimes they would crash Rodriguez' campaign stops to heckle the candidate, maintaining their claim that the Presidential hopeful wasn't truly who he said he was. Rodriguez would ignore the calls from the hecklers, then say the people causing the interruptions were indeed suspicious. This would get a chuckle and ovation from the others attending the rallies.

Media and Sussman critics said the broadcasting superstar went over the top in June, 2016, with one of his satirical commercials. The false ad was for the cleaning detergent Spic and Span, and emphasized the first word of the item's name as the Latino derogative. The fake commercial featured the voice of a stereotypical Mexican woman, making comments that she was going to "clean out" American houses under the guise of a maid. The woman also threatened to "sweep all the jobs away from American citizens." Rodriguez did respond to the commercial, calling it unfortunate and racist. Despite the criticism, Sussman refused to apologize. The Susspicous Minds stood by their leader, and a pro-Sussman website started selling T-shirts, depicting the cleaning product's familiar orange box with a Mexican woman dressed like Aunt Jemima prominently on it.

The issue of the false ad came to a head later in the month, at a high school in San Angelo, Texas. A student of Mexican descent was banned from summer classes for wearing a Mexican National Soccer Team jersey, while a Caucasian student went unpunished for wearing one of the Sussman shirts. The school's principal said he sent the Mexican student home for his own safety, while the White child was just exercising his freedom of speech. The school director said he was concerned because of a recent Olympic warm-up between the U.S. and Mexico which was more aggressive than the usual atmosphere that surrounded the rivalry. The school official suggested the American students were still angered about the loss. The principal would not answer questions from local reporters when they asked if there was really that much interest in the sport at the school. The institution hadn't had a soccer team for years, citing a lack of interest among its (Anglo) students. The principal eventually was forced to resign when the students went against his stated goal. The situation he created separated the Caucasian and Mexican students, and large fights took place in the school as well as around the city soon afterwards.

Rodriguez all but took a stranglehold on the nomination on Super Tuesday, and soon after President Obama endorsed the candidate as his hopeful successor. The two would appear on campaign stops together, attracting people of various races, colors and religions. Eddie's nomination acceptance speech at the Democratic convention was considered one of the great orations of the early 21st Century. To try and appease people in the middle and on the Right, he focused on unity and cooperation, while he also espoused upon the successes of President Obama and all the government had done for people of all backgrounds. He also reminded the world the U.S. would continue to defend itself from its enemies, such as terrorist organizations in the Middle East, but also said there could be room for peaceful resolutions if the dissenters were willing to disarm. His speech was considered hopeful and uplifting, while his eventual GOP rival's speech was viewed as bitter and angry. The Republican candidate used his platform to assail Eddie and Obama and to insist he was the man to win the country back.

In the end, Rodriguez and his optimism won out over the GOP's stubbornness. Rodriguez took the traditionally Blue states with ease, and a number of swing states. What threw him over the top though was the Latino vote, which gave him stunningly large wins in Florida, Texas, Colorado and Arizona. Cries of voter fraud rang out from the Right, saying many of the votes came from illegal aliens. The Left countered by saying not only were the votes legitimate, but the GOP had turned away thousands of registered voters and did its best to reject voters from minority precincts, pointing to the recent swell of Voter ID laws, many of which were held up in court by the time of the general election. In the end though, there was nothing the Right could do to nullify the results. Eddie was the President-elect, and many celebrated the fact.

As Rodriguez put together his cabinet, some complained about the number of holdovers who were invited to stay on from the Obama administration. Indeed, the soon-to-be President's transition team offered most of the lower secretaries the option to retain their positions, and most who were offered the opportunity accepted. In cases where cabinet members weren't asked to stay or decided to step down, Rodriguez made a number of offers to politicians from the other party. In most of these cases, the people rejected the offer, often calling it a ploy from the Left to remove a Republican voice from Congress or a state's governorship. In the end, Rodriguez' cabinet was almost entirely full of Democrats or Left-leaning Independents.

Inauguration Day brought a huge crowd to the National Mall, with many Puerto Ricans and Dominicans traveling from the New York-Tri-State area to witness history. Since it was a Friday, many decided to make it a three-day weekend, with many families breaking their kids out of school a day early for the historic events. Rodriguez was sworn in and gave another highly-revered speech. To many, it seemed like a glorious day. Then Sussman hit the airwaves the following Monday.

The talk show host was relentless in his opening monologue, unleashing a five-minute racial tirade about the President and the people who showed up in the nation's capital to support him. Sussman stated outside of the steps of the Capitol where the ceremony took place, there was not a single White face to be seen in the area. He suggested crime for the day in the city hit an all-time high, and that this had been the first

Inauguration Day at which more "visitors" from other countries attended than U.S. Citizens. Before going into his first commercial break that day, he called the previous Friday the lowest point in American history, and alluded to the notion it would have been a perfect day for terrorists to attack Washington. "They could have helped us clean this country of a lot of unwanted trash," Sussman said of a potential terrorist strike.

People who didn't listen to the show on a regular basis were appalled at Sussman's suggestion. The opening of the show was a disgrace, and his critics questioned how he could consider himself the great patriot he always claimed to be. No true American, they insisted, would wish for an attack on U.S. soil. His network suspended Sussman immediately the next day. Originally, they announced a three-week ban, but the Susspicious Minds not only initiated a campaign to save their hero, but said they would boycott any sponsor that would pull its advertisement from the show. Without publicly stating whether they agreed with Sussman's words or not, the most vocal of his supporters said companies which pulled support from his show would be proving themselves to be enemies of the First Amendment and therefore un-American. Tea Party types had made such claims before about the unconstitutionality of media outlets limiting the speech of their employers, either ignoring or ignorant of the fact that the First Amendment was about laws made by Congress. In the end, no sponsors pulled out, and Sussman was back on the air the following Monday.

On his first show back, Sussman "apologized." He said he was sorry for making Americans think he would condone an attack on Washington D.C. He then went on another tirade, saying he never truly said he wished for such an atrocity, and played back part of the segment, saying he hinted at a possibility of a similar event. He then attacked his detractors, saying it was another attempt to discredit him and to assail the rights of free speech. To address his words about the Latino majority in the crowd, he said he wished no harm to any people from other parts of the Americas and the islands, especially those who were in the United States legally. He then hinted once more that the new President may or may not be a legal resident of the country.

President Rodriguez tried not to discuss the situation. His spokespeople would only say their boss was "disappointed" in the talk show host. They said the President was so busy making sure the transition between administrations went seamlessly that he didn't have time to pay attention to a flamboyant talk show host.

The shift from Obama's tenure to Rodriguez' went very smoothly. The fact that there were so many holdovers from the previous administration made the transition easy. Rodriguez' main concern in his first days in office were his actions as the Commander-in-Chief of the nation's armed forces. As Obama drew U.S. forces out of Afghanistan, the focus of the war on terrorism shifted to Pakistan and Iran. Terrorist factions from Al Qaeda and the Taliban had had very little success in their attacks on the Western world during Obama's second four years, but in the final three months of his time in office, there were near-simultaneous deadly bombings outside the U.S. embassies in Egypt and Ethiopia, which Al Qaeda took credit for. The 200 deaths, 132 of which were American citizens, made the two-pronged terrorist attack the deadliest on the U.S. since 9/11. Obama ordered, with the blessing of Pakistan's government, U.S. troops into the mountains of the South Asian nation. There were a few attacks on militant installations, resulting in reported heavy casualties among the terrorist's ranks, with few fatalities on the American side.

As a demonstration of his vow to try for a peaceful resolution to conflict, but to stand at the ready to fight, Rodriguez stationed more troops back on bases in the region while offering negotiations if the terrorists immediately stopped their military operations. When Al Qaeda's response came in the form of an unsuccessful car bomb attack at a popular resort in Bali, Rodriguez ordered the U.S. forces back into action, and to escalate their push. Many of Rodriguez' opponents stated they were impressed by the President's willingness to use force if necessary. Sussman, on the other hand, said the escalation was nothing but pandering to the Right.

Rodriguez and his Left-Wing powerhouse in Washington were quick to pass a number of environmental initiatives left over from the Obama administration. By the time February came to a close, the U.S. had approved a number of federal-run alternate energy farms. A number of new solar farms were approved for the deserts of Arizona, New Mexico and southern California, while wind farms were to be created in most states and offshore on both coasts. Most energy experts praised the plan. They said the new renewable energy sources could provide anywhere from 45-to-85-percent of the electricity used by the country. The bill also included a system of car recharging stations, to help facilitate the growing number of electric cars on the road. The new energy production stations would power all of the recharge points, and the government worked with local municipalities and privately-owned energy companies to run them. The oil and coal lobbies were livid. Especially the oil industry, where the new electric car grid was concerned. The rise of the hybrid had been bad enough, but now, with the encouragement of the federal government, more and more vehicles that didn't need gasoline at all were cropping up all over the country.

Rodriguez and the Democrats spent much of March and April strengthening the government's ability to regulate Wall Street. It took all of Obama's first term and even much of his second for the nation to fully recover from the recession that had begun shortly before his tenure. The Democrats vowed to do their part to keep such a downward spiral from happening again. The majority of the party said the lack of oversight in the Bush years had led to the recession, and noted how little the government had done during that time to watch how financial institutions conducted business. Now, the FTC would be expanded, creating more government jobs to try to keep businesses from running amok.

All the items the Democrats passed angered the Right tremendously despite the fact a few people on the side of the aisle had been forced to vote for them. Rhetoric from the GOP, the Tea Party and sympathetic pundits claimed the Left was monopolizing the energy industry and destroying free trade. The Democrats maintained the push for renewable energy and the increased regulation of big business were necessary because those sectors had been neglected for too long, resulting in extreme burdens on the majority of Americans. One of the biggest detractors of course was Sussman, who continued his Obama-era claims that the Left's sole desire was to create a Communist, Fascist state. The Right however no longer had the votes to stop or stall each bit of legislation in the House, and the Senate was as good as a rubber stamp for anything concocted by the President, so just about all the items passed. Sussman's show became the prime venue for him and his listeners to spout off on the evils of the Democrats.

After the restructuring of the FTC passed, The Democrats slowed down pushing their agenda. Although they wouldn't admit it when questioned by various media outlets, behind closed doors they admitted to probably setting any true sense of bipartisanship back ten years. The Left let May go by relatively quietly as far as trying to get any major items passed. At the start of June though, President Rodriguez said he wanted the legislators to start looking at raising taxes. For the first time in his Administration, he verbally disagreed with his predecessor, saying despite some minor success, President Obama hadn't done enough to even the tax ratio between the classes in America. While the previous President was credited for bringing all the tax brackets closer than they had been in generations, Rodriguez said there was still more that could be done. Obama had made a number of changes to federal spending to keep the deficit even, but it was still at a record high. President Rodriguez said he wanted to finally make one universal flat tax rate, by bringing the level for everyone up to where it was for people with lower incomes. The added tax money was necessary to pay for the items his party had passed, and still would leave some money to continue reversing the nation's debt.

In a somewhat surprising unified response, members of the House and the Senate from both sides of the aisle stressed their concern with the President's plan. Partially out of guilt for their actions helping divide the government earlier in the year and wishing to avoid a definitely unpopular topic, many Democratic legislators denounced Rodriguez' plan. Most of the stalwarts of the party sided with the President, where Democrats closer to the middle of the aisle actually went on the news talk shows with their Republican peers to state how bad the idea of new taxes were for the country. Many pundits on the Right welcomed those Democrats who broke from the party line. Even Fleet Sussman grudgingly praised the support from the Left.

The topic of taxes was a firestorm in Washington, D.C. Rodriguez' push was going to be an extreme uphill battle, and threatened to tear apart the Democratic Party. Even the pundits on the Left were at odds with one another. Sussman loved the internal battle happening among the Democrats. He claimed if they couldn't even work things out among themselves, they should just scrap the plan. Some of his listeners took the matter a step further, saying that if they couldn't cooperate amongst themselves, they had no right trying to run the country.

For weeks people on Capitol Hill and at the White House made their cases for or against taxes. Both sides ferociously argued their points. By the end of the month, everyone had practically forgotten about the topic. A new bombshell issue became the hot item in the nation's capital, an item that would change the course of American history. On June 26th, Supreme Court Justice Antonin Scalia suffered a stroke.

Went Down to the Crossroads

Justice Scalia had turned 81 that March. He was the longest-tenured active Justice, and had been for a number of years. He had battled health problems during the end of Obama's second term. Scalia and Justice Anthony Kennedy, both of whom were appointed by President Ronald Reagan and were months apart in age, had hopes of stepping down once a Republican took office. They both waited out Obama's time in office and had hopes of a change in power in the 2016 election. When that didn't happen, both Justices - and many of their supporters - became nervous that the men wouldn't be able to maintain their seats for another four years. If either of them had to step down, Rodriguez was sure to appoint a more liberal Justice, shifting the majority rule of the Court to the Left.

The report of Scalia's situation broke during the first hour of Sussman's show, at which point the Justice's condition was unknown. When the talk show host heard the news, he immediately called it devastating. He asked his listeners to pray for Scalia's return to health. Sussman said not only did a long-serving member of the Supreme Court deserve such attention, but the idea he wouldn't be able to continue serving in that capacity could be disastrous for the country.

It was quickly confirmed that Scalia indeed suffered a mild stroke. People all over Washington voiced their relief to hear the Justice was likely to make a near-full if not total recovery. Some Left-leaning talk show hosts seemed disingenuous in their appreciation, and a few were assailed by critics of both parties for pointing out Scalia's condition might not allow him to continue on the highest court in the country. Despite their apologies for being seemingly uncaring about Scalia's health though, the fact was nobody was sure if Scalia would be able to continue serving in his post.

With Scalia's stroke occurring on a Monday, it was Thursday by the time he released his own statement. He thanked the people of the country for their prayers, well-wishes and concern. The Justice confirmed the fact it was indeed a mild stroke, and that he was expected to make an almost complete recovery by the time he was done with rehab. However, he pointed out, he wouldn't know much about his rehabilitation for a number of days, and he still wasn't sure if he'd be able to return to the bench. The statement ended with the phrase "God bless the United States of America."

After the statement was made public, politically-minded people around the nation somberly waited for more news. Sussman would sign off each day calling for a prayer for Scalia and the country, asking God for a full and quick recovery for the Justice. By the end of the first week, no new news was available. People went into the weekend still unsure of what the future held for the Supreme Court of the United States. Guests on the Sunday news shows were careful to not sound overly confident about the Justice's return or departure. All maintained they just hoped the man would recover.

The Fourth of July came the next week. The day before, Sussman again suggested that all Americans should pray for Scalia's return to health. While he wouldn't say it on air, the media icon was getting more and more nervous that his friend wouldn't be able to return to his duties. During a media address, President Rodriguez offered similar well-wishes for the Justice, especially on the eve of the nation's most patriotic holiday. A couple of days after Independence Day, Justice Scalia announced his plans. In a statement read by a spokesperson, he again thanked the nation for its support. He said serving the country was a privilege, a privilege he was humbled to have held for so long and one which he felt it was impossible to give up. However, this was not a normal situation. Had he been healthy, stepping down wouldn't have even been a question, and despite the fact he was going to live a normal life after rehabilitation, he was still 81 years old. He had tried to gut it out for political reasons, but here he was at the start of a new, four-year cycle, and he had dodged a bullet health-wise. It was time for him to step down, and to enjoy his senior years.

On his show that Friday, Sussman did his best to hide his feelings. He congratulated Scalia on a tremendous career and thanked him for protecting the interests of Americans and patriots for years. The entertainer fought back the urge to say he felt betrayed, and did his best that first day to avoid mentioning the future that was in store for the Supreme Court.

That day, the President also thanked the Justice for a lifetime of service. He admitted to having disagreed with Scalia on many occasions, but that in no way discounted what he had done in the name and service of the United States. He wished the Justice and his family all the best for the future.

That Sunday, the talk shows were abuzz again. The day started off with tremendous speculation about who the President would make his first court appointment. Obama's last appointment was to replace Justice Ruth Bader Ginsberg during his second term, and as with his other selections, he picked a Liberal-leading judge. Rodriguez was expected to do the same.

The question wasn't on the table too long. One of the last guests on one station was the President's chief White House spokesman. The man said not only was the decision made, but told the show's host the President would officially nominate Judge Brian Payton of the Federal Court of Appeals for the Ninth Circuit to take Scalia's place on the Supreme Court. Payton was indeed very Liberal, and would likely be the furthest Left-leaning Justice on the panel if he was approved. Considering the composure of the legislative arm of the government, the White House spokesperson said that wasn't likely to be a problem.

It would have been enough to let the conversation die there, but the President's mouthpiece had another item to bring up. "The President also wants to remind people, especially those in Congress, about the tax bill he was working on before news of Justice Scalia's stroke broke. The President wants to move forward on his original plan."

Had the White House spokesperson been the first guest of the day, his words would have altered the course of the news shows on each network. Instead, he spoke as the shows were signing off and networks were getting ready for afternoon sports coverage. Discussion continued on the various cable news networks, but few viewers tuned in to those stations on Sundays. Instead, only the Monday morning talk shows had a chance to fully disseminate the information before the President officially commented on both matters.

At 11 a.m. Eastern, Monday, July 10th, Rodriguez held a press conference to confirm he was nominating Payton and that he wanted the Democrats in both parts of Congress to push for a new tax plan. Payton, the President said, had proven himself time and again as somebody who ruled by the law and not by his beliefs. As for the tax plan, the nation had been in the red for far too long. It was time to work towards a balanced budget, and responsible spending was only part of the answer. Although the government had made strides towards a flat tax rate, the President wanted to level the playing field.

After making his statement, when asked by reporters about Payton's political affiliation and how it would affect the balance of power in the Supreme Court, Rodriguez was careful to only just hint at the shift to the Left. As for his renewed push on taxes, he said in a Democracy, everyone should be equal both in say and the portion of income they had to give back. The media questioned Rodriguez about his apparent unwillingness to compromise with the Republicans. The reporters said his cavalier attitude since taking office didn't conform with the reputation he had made for himself in lower levels of government. Rodriguez responded that if one looked at all the Democrats had done during his short time in office, he thought the Republicans would find things to be happy about. The way Rodriguez spun it, the shift from fossil fuels to renewable energy would open so many new opportunities for big business, even if that meant a lesser role for Big Oil. Oil could profit too, Rodriguez said, if the industry refocused its business philosophy. As for the strengthening of the FTC, the President pointed out companies would be fine if they adhered to the rules as they hopefully had done all along and that jobs were jobs, federal or otherwise. Regarding the selection of Payton, that was his prerogative to appoint whoever he wanted, the way it had been for his predecessors for ages before him. Payton was a fine choice, hard-working and thoughtful. The President admitted it wasn't a selection which would foster bipartisanship, but it was something he felt he owed his supporters and party.

Fleet Sussman's show had already started by the time the President made his announcement, and he broadcast part of the press conference from the White House live. After hearing the announcement, the talk show host was livid. He went on a tirade unlike any before. He verbally abused the President, his party and the entire government of the United States for Rodriguez' plans. He called the President's agenda "back-handed" and "evil," and if both items became reality, it would be the start of the end for the country. He berated the Right for failing to stand up to the President, and for their poor leadership, which was about to let the Democrats take control of all three federal branches of government.

Sussman continually played soundbites taken from Rodriguez' presser. His producers had taken only the most inflammatory actualities from the session. They used over and over again the cut of Rodriguez admitting he was choosing Payton on grounds of his political background. The bite of the President praising the Judge for his ability to make decisions based on law and not politics was left on the cutting room floor. The producers also had saved a number of clips referring to the new tax plan, in which Rodriguez stressed the inequality of the classes. Sussman would play these cuts in particular and say it was more proof of the President's Socialist agenda.

Sussman's listeners were equally disturbed. Some called in saying they were frightened, that their country was being taken away from them. They brought up their concerns about Rodriguez' heritage, claiming it was still just a matter of time before he annexed Mexico as the 51st State and then they'd all be on the hook for whatever welfare programs Rodriguez was undoubtedly planning for their poverty-laden neighbors. There was plenty of anger among the Susspicious Minds as well and calls to take back the nation by any means necessary. For the most part, the host would only thank the callers for their time, and not comment on the apparent threats and calls for violence.

One call however caught his attention. A man from Upstate New York called, complaining about Rodriguez all the way back to his time in state government. The man claimed that even then, he had been weary about the current President. He had watched Rodriguez destroy his state and then his country for too long. Now, the listener was saying it was time for somebody to do something about the situation. "Wouldn't it be something," the caller said, "if some patriot shot and killed the President."

"Wouldn't that be something," Sussman echoed, and didn't say anything more about the issue.

Ten days later, the President would be dead.

The Death of Two Kings, Part One

Gary "Bull" Dukeman and Freddy Villanueva were in many ways polar opposites from one another. The two would never meet, and if somebody had asked them, they would have both said they were perfectly happy about that. However, the two would forever be linked with each other in the American history books.

Dukeman was born and raised in West Virginia. He was the second-youngest of four children, one of 21 cousins in his generation of his family. Like male Dukemans for ages, he went to work in the nearby coal mines after he graduated high school. The Dukeman family felt a sense of pride and tradition when it came to the mines and in their small town. Not including semi-frequent trips to nearby Pittsburgh, few people in the clan had ever traveled out of state. College was deemed an unnecessary luxury and considered wasteful to many of Bull's family members. There was a good living to be made in the mines, honest labor that powered America and was essential to the upkeep of the nation. Over the years, only a small handful of Dukemans had died in the line of duty. After an initial grief period, the surviving family members would praise the fallen as heroes of American industry.

Villanueva, on the other hand, was a first-generation U.S. citizen. His parents crossed the border legally from Mexico before he was born and each achieved citizenship before Freddy's birth. Shortly after becoming naturalized and just a bit before Freddy's birth, the Villanuevas migrated from San Diego to New York. They found a small two-bedroom apartment in El Barrio, known better around the nation as Spanish Harlem. Months after they settled in, Freddy was born. He would end up being the oldest of three children, and his parents worked hard for their children. At first, the elder Villanuevas had hoped to send Freddy and his siblings to college, but that ended up being a dream unfulfilled. It was a goal set for the next generation.

Freddy worked many jobs after graduating high school. Despite at times working three jobs at once, he still found time to get married and raise a family of his own. He and his wife went on to have two daughters, both of whom excelled in high school. Their hard work paid off, and both ended up with scholarships to the state University in Albany. The younger daughter, Meagan, was honored for her achievements at a highly-publicized media event. The function doubled as a campaign stop for then-Democratic presidential hopeful Edward Rodriguez. After congratulating and praising Meagan on-stage, the candidate shook Freddy's hand in the wings, congratulating the father for raising two magnificent children and saying he was proud of the Villanuevas as proof of the American Dream. Although he wouldn't admit it in hopes of avoiding a sibling rivalry, Freddy considered it the proudest day of his life. He was grateful for having two incredible daughters, who were recognized by the man who would hopefully be the next President of the United States. Months later, that hope would be realized.

Immediately after Rodriguez' election, Bull Dukeman became extremely nervous. His favorite radio personality, Fleet Sussman, had for months promised his listeners a Rodriguez win would mean the end of American civilization. After listening to Sussman's show just days after Election Day, Dukeman became paranoid that his time in the mine would soon come to an end. He was convinced in the near future he would be replaced in the tunnels by a Mexican illegal, who would do an inferior job for just pennies a day. He was just as sure the President-elect wanted to end all types of traditional fuel production, or outsource it all to other countries. It was on par, Sussman said, with how the Left preferred to give money to other countries for oil instead of using American crude. Even hostile nations benefited from the U.S., for the sake of land and wildlife preservation.

In New York though, Freddy Villanueva couldn't have been happier. Although he had always felt the plight of his family represented the American Way and Dream, he thought his personal experiences were nothing compared to the man who grew up just miles away and would soon become the most powerful man in the world. He no longer had to worry if he was giving his daughters false hope when he told them they could grow up to become anything they wanted. Freddy also hoped the incoming President would protect people's rights and benefits in the workplace, and raise the minimum wage. Villanueva was optimistic the government would help him find a way to pay for the rest of his daughters' education, picking up where the scholarships ended.

Both Dukeman and Villanueva were full of emotion as they each watched the inauguration. For the West Virginian, the day was filled with fear and despair. The New Yorker meanwhile cried as he watched the events in Washington, D.C. Bull's day ended with dinner with his family, which featured a bit less conversation than usual. In El Barrio though, Freddy and his family attended a block party in recognition of the day's historic events. The festivities ended about midnight, two hours before President Rodriguez left his final ball of the evening.

Dukeman was impressed slightly at first when Rodriguez ramped up the military's operation early in his presidency, and had hope for a brief while that the new Commander-in-Chief would prove his detractors wrong with their speculation. However, his hopes were crushed beyond all recognition towards the end of March. In keeping with the Leftist

29

tree-hugging mentality of the previous eight years, Rodriguez and his cohorts promised to continue their push for environmental protection bills. The first meaningful achievements of Rodriguez' tenure were in this domain. Dukeman's heart sank into his stomach when he heard about the passed items. Among them was a ban on mountaintop removal mining.

The push against the controversial mining procedure had grown over the previous eight years. The idea was to remove the top of a mountain, take all the coal out, then rebuild the peak with the rock and dirt that had been removed. The mining companies liked the ease and accessibility of the procedure. The environmentalists complained the tactic was overly destructive to the mountains, its indigenous wildlife and nature in general.

Word that the procedure had been banned was devastating for the Dukeman household and the other branches of the family. Bull and many of his cousins had moved out of the underground mines and to the mountaintops. Even though the mountaintop procedure had been under scrutiny during Obama's tenure, the actual ban still came as a surprise. Everybody supposedly in the know - managers, union shop stewards, local news reporters - had continuously assured the miners that the government was only interested in deterring oil operations offshore and in wildlife preserves. The talk in Washington seemed to suggest coal would be more important to the upkeep of the nation, and there would be little if any anti-coal mining legislation passed. It was anticipated that if the government did anything regarding coal mining the move would benefit the workers. Bull and his coworkers hoped perhaps stronger safety measures would be approved. Seeing the newest, quickest techniques made illegal didn't cross the minds of anyone Bull knew.

It hit all the Dukemans extremely hard. As one of the families in the industry the longest, they were afforded the first chance to leave the mines for the hills. The money was a little better and being above ground was near-luxury for the excavators. Despite the nature of the work, the air was still considerably cleaner up in the mountains, and there was no fear of mine collapses or getting trapped below ground. The fact that Washington seemed unwilling to act on mountaintop removal made everyone think there was nothing to worry about, so all the Dukemans in Bull's generation eagerly accepted the jobs with the project, leaving the positions below for the rookies and those few immigrants who had moved into the area. At the time, Bull sneered at those people, willing to work in substandard conditions for less money. He may have been offended, had they put him out of work, but since Bull was headed for proverbial greener pastures, he just laughed that the newbies were getting the crumbs left over from his previous endeavors.

The ban on mountaintop removal mining was put into effect soon after the bill was passed, even though the various companies involved were suing the government to overturn the legislation. The day after the moratorium began, Bull was called to his worksite. When he got there, he was surprised to see so many family members and friends there as well. That surprise was quickly replaced with shock as those assembled learned they were all being let go. With the site out of commission, there was no work for the assembled masses. Some of the miners started to protest, saying they deserved to return to their positions back down in the mines. The site supervisor though, surrounded by the location's security detail, pointed out that the mountaintop men had signed contracts in their new positions, saying the company was not obliged to return them to their former jobs under any circumstances. The people would all be able to apply for jobs, but without the tenure they had achieved.

Bull went home shortly after the meeting thoroughly depressed. He pulled out the contract he signed when he took the new assignment. Sure enough, there was the clause his former boss had referred to. He remembered when he signed the pact. It was one of the few times the company had asked him to sign anything, which he thought was odd. The company man who had given Bull the papers said it was because the new site was practically experimental, but there was nothing to worry about in the contract. All would be fine, the man from corporate assured Dukeman. The miner could take a moment to check out the paperwork, but there was no need to. Bull signed the paper at the businessman's insistence, excited to start in his new position. That was then, and now Bull wished he had taken a closer look. Truth be told though, he was unsure he would have done anything differently. It was the kind of legalese he would have glossed over in the first place.

A couple of days passed and Bull wallowed in self-pity at home. He had more time to listen to Sussman's radio show, where in the past he was only able to pay attention during his half-hour lunch break or when he returned to the mining site's base to use the facilities. Over the following days, Sussman started to address the situation, denouncing the President and the rest of the Democrats for crushing American industry in favor of supporting terrorists in the Middle East and their oil production. For the first time, Dukeman called the show, eager to make his point. After fifteen minutes of busy signals, Bull finally got through. A woman picked up, saying Dukeman had reached the <u>Fleet Sussman Show</u>. Bull said he was a miner from West Virginia who had just lost his job due to the new mining legislation. The producer told him to turn his radio down in the background and stay on hold. Bull did as instructed and waited for his chance to speak. He was surprised when it only took five minutes for Sussman to take his call. He'd heard other callers in the past comment about being on hold for 30 minutes.

Sussman addressed the expedited answer as he introduced Bull. "Ladies and gentleman, usually every caller has to wait his or her turn to get on the air with me, but we have a new caller from West Virginia on the line, who is living proof of the devastating path President Rodriguez is leading us down. Gary from West Virginia, you're on the air with Fleet Sussman."

Bull had given his proper name to the producer, and stalled for a second when Sussman used it, not being used to hearing anyone address him with it. He thanked the host for taking his call, and said he was a long-time listener but first-time caller. Fleet welcomed him to the broadcast, then asked Dukeman to tell his story. Bull stated his case, telling Sussman and his listeners he was a long-time coal miner from West Virginia, from a long family line of proud miners who had only ever harvested coal. He told his tale chronologically, saying to the radio star how nobody in West Virginia had even thought it was possible a complete ban on mountaintop removal could be passed. Gary pointed out how his foreman and the bosses above him always assured the laborers there was nothing to worry about. When the news struck that a ban was approved, everyone was shocked. They were even more shocked to hear the company was shutting down its operations while it fought the legislation instead of working through the ban. Dukeman said he and his colleagues were absolutely stunned when they heard they were all being fired.

Sussman was flabbergasted. He offered his condolences to Gary and his buddies for the senseless loss of their jobs, caused by the President and his cohorts. The host asked Dukeman what he had done for a living before working on the mountaintop removal project. Bull explained how he had worked down in the pits and mines before taking the new assignment. He described the mountaintop site as a miner's paradise, which was safer and cleaner by everyone's standards.

"What happened to your old job?" Sussman asked.

"When the tenured miners took the jobs up in the hills, our old jobs were filled by others..."

"Tell me, Gary, were these others Latino, or Mexican?"

'Some of them, yes..."

"So not only has our esteemed President done his best to shut down the coal industry, he's done it in a way so he takes jobs away from good, hardworking Americans while helping his fellow illegals. And tell me Gary, what have you done to take back what is rightfully yours?"

"No... I'm not sure I know what you mean? What is ours to take?"

Bull could hear the sneer on Sussman's lips as he responded. "Your jobs, of course. From the people who took them from you." With that, Fleet thanked Bull for the call, and told him to call again.

Bull hung up, feeling vindicated, yet confused. He'd hoped Sussman would see things his way, and even though he had been pretty sure that was going to be the case, it was still a relief when that ended up happening. He was glad that one of the most intelligent, outspoken and famous people he knew in America felt his pain, and had an easy time understanding it and how it was Rodriguez' fault. Unlike the anti-Fleet pundits, Dukeman didn't believe or didn't care about the notion that Sussman had totally let the mining corporation off the hook, blaming solely the President and the Democratic-controlled Congress for the situation. During Dukeman's call to the show and in his rant afterwards, Sussman also managed to focus solely on the non-Anglo new miners instead of talking about corporate bosses who had made sure they would be able to maintain their cheaper labor force rather than revert back to the tenured miners. It was that "taking the jobs back" notion that Dukeman was unsure of. Bull couldn't figure out what that meant at first. However, some people seemed to understand right away. A few days after his segment on the radio, it became painfully obvious.

On the third night after Bull's broadcast debut, there was a disturbance in town. The municipality's entire small police force was called out to break up what had turned into a mini riot. A couple of recent Latino arrivals to the small hamlet were ambushed by some of the out of work miners. The new, legal citizens were badly beaten, with a number of broken bones among them. When order was restored, the victims were battered but conscious without any life-threatening injuries. The attacking party numbered 12 individuals, and included a couple of Dukeman's cousins. The lot of them were arrested and taken to the local jail. It was one of Bull's relatives who stopped for the camera of the local news as they were hauled in. He yelled out to the small media contingent, "we're taking back our jobs!"

Bull was saddened by the attack. In his complaints about losing his job and his distaste of the newcomers to town, he hadn't wanted anyone to get hurt. He felt slightly responsible for the attack, as his cousin had quoted the interview between him and Sussman. He felt even a twinge of sympathy when he heard they were legal American citizens. They were trying to make a living for themselves and their families, the way all of the laid off miners had. No, Bull's anger didn't lie with them, it lay with Rodriguez as the primary cause of the situation.

As Bull tried to figure out things in West Virginia, Freddy Villanueva was getting angry up in New York. Over Rodriguez' campaign, Villanueva heard the reports of Sussman's racist slights, but they were just words. Freddy had heard about some incident at a Texas school that involved a student wearing a Sussman shirt, but Villanueva hadn't considered the radio host the cause of what happened. The attack in West Virginia though he believed was instigated solely by Sussman's veiled threat. Villanueva had for years heard of attacks against his fellow Mexicans after the news ran a story suggesting his people were responsible for a rise in crime, or drugs or unemployment in the country. He always felt those stories were distorted, or didn't give a full explanation of the situation. He never remembered a major celebrity figure though suggesting violence was the best way to resolve such an issue. He felt that's what Sussman had done in this situation.

Sussman's response to the attack was to say he hadn't provoked the attack. He focused on how he had used the word "rightfully" in his comment. "Rightfully," he said, "could mean by petition, by boycott or by lawsuits." At no time, he pointed out, had he said "go beat their brains out" was a legitimate response. His listeners and his supporters in government all agreed the attack wasn't his fault, but the result of a small set of angered, misguided people. The network did not punish Sussman, agreeing with his devotees.

Up until that point, Freddy hadn't felt even a twinge of raw negativity on the national scene since Rodriguez had been elected. Pride in the new President had caused a wave of euphoria in the Villanueva household, one that both generations of the family was riding. While the President hadn't passed anything yet that would help the family, he was still pushing for an improved government student loan system, as well as for an increase in employee wages and benefits. It was just the fact that a

Latino-American was in the White House that made the Villanuevas the most hopeful. Now though, Freddy was afraid of what was happening in his country. This was the first time the President did something which, in the minds of some people, favored Latinos. If Sussman was going to turn every issue into a racial issue and make innuendos all the time about how not just Hispanics but Mexicans in particular were to blame for everything, Freddy was afraid more troubling times could lie ahead. However, Freddy felt there was little he could do about the situation, except hope and pray his bleak vision of the future would not come true.

In West Virginia though, Bull Dukeman was past the point of hoping and praying. His reality was as grim as Sussman had indicated it would be. It had little to do with his radio spot, which made him a folk hero of sorts to the people around him. It was attention he didn't want, especially from those who suggested he had wanted his friends and comrades to show their strength by intimidating the "outsiders." True, he'd admit he didn't want the Latinos around, but he would say he hadn't meant to intimidate or hurt them.

What was more troubling to him though was the pall unemployment was casting on him and his family. While he applied for unemployment benefits and compensation, they became a one-income family for a while as his wife Joanna continued to work. His only daughter, aged 16, was quickly able to find a weekend job at the local mall to help out. This embarrassed Bull tremendously, but he had little choice. He and his wife decided they'd do their best not to disturb their retirement funds. While they weren't close to cashing them in, they figured they could forge ahead without disturbing their savings. Bull toyed with the idea of applying for openings at the mines, the types of positions he had when he first started his career. However, like many of his former coworkers who were also laid off, it was insulting to them to think they'd have to start low, below even the people they had been laughing at when the tenured miners first moved into the mountaintop operations.

A month after he lost his job, Gary's first unemployment check came in. It made a considerable difference after a rough 30 days for the family. Bull told his daughter to keep her money for herself, and said he was proud of her for her sacrifice. For the next few months, the family lived off Mrs. Dukeman's wages, Bull's unemployment checks and the money he made doing odd jobs in town. Things were tight, but felt considerably normal for a while. Then Bull strained his back while on a job.

He had been working for a local mom and pop convenience store every Tuesday, helping the elderly owners stock shelves and put things into storage when deliveries came in. One morning while taking two boxes of canned vegetables off the back of a truck, a neighborhood kid rushed past Bull. The young boy pushed his way around Gary, apparently oblivious of the weight of the boxes Bull was carrying, or the fact the adult wasn't able to see clearly over the load in his arms. The shock and the heavy load were enough to cause Dukeman to lose his balance. He fell on his back, with one of the boxes falling on his stomach. The impact of the box's landing caused Bull's back to lift up, then crash again onto the concrete of the curb outside the store. The child continued on his merry way to school, still not paying attention to what his actions had caused. The husband store owner rushed out to help Bull up. Dukeman took a minute to stand, then stretched with his hands on his hips. As he twisted his spine to the left, he felt something pop as he'd never heard or felt before. He ignored the pain for a moment, hoping he had just imagined the sound and that the pain was just his being sore. He reached down to pick up one of the boxes he had been carrying and raised it a couple of inches off the ground before dropping it again and recoiling in tremendous pain.

As it was a small town, the store owner walked his part-time employee down the block to the town's long-time doctor. They entered the office and the physician saw Bull right away. It didn't take the doctor too long to diagnose that Bull had strained his back. After he completed his examination, the doctor scolded Bull. "I'm treating this one visit as though you had acceptable insurance because you're a good man Gary, and as a favor to your boss," the doctor's friendly tone during the business part of the visit turned serious, almost angry, "I do not accept government insurance." Although Doctor Jones' participation in the national healthcare system was mandatory, he was able to convince his patients and neighbors that that wasn't the case and he wasn't in the federal system as part of his own personal protest. Doc Jones gave Bull one shot then told his patient he wouldn't prescribe any medication as long as he was on the government plan. Dukeman didn't think to question whether or not the doctor had that authority. Instead, he went back to the store, then painfully managed to get into his car and drive home.

Bull spent the next few days at home trying to limit his time out of bed and on his feet. On the fourth day after the accident, he ventured out of the bedroom and spent time in other parts of the house. He was able to sit on the sofa and in his chair in the den, so long as he took his time sitting down and standing up.

Although his condition was improving, he still felt nowhere near ready to go out and become a manual laborer again. He had few options available to him since he had little in the way of formal education. He still warned against his daughter working to help the family, saying they at least had his unemployment check to help pay for things.

Nine days after the accident, Bull called Fleet Sussman again. It took him just as long to get through to the host as it had for his first call, but when he introduced himself, the producer was quick to welcome him back. She then gave him the hotline number, and said he'd be welcome to use it to get through quicker, provided he used it only once every week or two. After the producer put him on hold, Fleet was again quick to take the call once he saw Bull was on the line. After a brief reminder to the listening Susspicous Minds, Sussman welcomed Bull back to the show and asked him how he was doing.

"Not well, Fleet. In fact, pretty lousy."

"Gary, what's happened? Tell us all about it!"

Bull described his recent life since his last call. He described his take on the attack the call had caused, the humility of having his daughter help support him and his accident and injury. He told Fleet and his audience how the local doctor was not taking any form of government insurance and how he was unable to work for the foreseeable future.

When Bull was finished telling his story, Fleet opened up on a new rant. He congratulated Gary for his part in organizing his friends (which Bull said he played no part in outside of providing unintended motivation), and berated the Obama/Rodriguez healthcare plan (Bull didn't say he wasn't sure if that was in Doc Jones' legal authority, nor did Fleet seem to care about placing blame on anyone except the two most recent American Presidents). Sussman told him he should be angered by all that had happened to him, and his anger should be focused on President Eddie Rodriguez. The radio star then suggested Bull should be scared for his future, especially in his condition. The President had started his push to raise taxes. Sussman left out the fact that the increase would affect only the wealthiest of Americans, and that Dukeman would be unaffected by the change.

The call ended with Sussman again thanking Bull for his time and called the out-of-work miner a true American patriot. Bull hung up, feeling proud, angered and scared emotionally and in pain physically. The negative feelings were having a negative effect on his back. He had to wait a couple of hours for his wife to come home, to help him get off the sofa and to bed. He stayed awake much of the night because of his back, unable to twist around and find a comfortable sleeping position. He was finally able to get to sleep around 2 a.m. and was woken up as his wife started getting ready for work around 6:30.

In the late morning there was a knock at the door. Although still in pain, Bull's short night of rest left him able to once again start walking around. It took him longer than usual to get to the entryway, but he reached it in a fairly acceptable timeframe. When he opened the door, Doctor Jones was standing there. The physician who had helped Bull while admonishing him a week-and-a-half prior stood out on the porch, looking sheepish and apologetic. He asked to come in and Dukeman happily obliged.

"Look, Gary," the doctor started, "I'm sorry about last week. I'm as mad as you are about what the President is doing to us and I shouldn't have taken my anger out on you. I heard you on the radio yesterday and Fleet's right. You are a great American and somebody we can all rally around. Will you let me make it up to you by letting me take a look at your back?"

With a small tear in his eye, Dukeman accepted. The two made their way to the living room, where Dr. Jones helped Bull lie down on his stomach on the sofa. Instead of examining Bull, the doctor asked a few questions about his condition. He then discerned Bull had a herniated disc. He told Bull, so long as the pain wasn't too bad, he should try to keep active and take warm showers every so often. As tactfully as he could, Jones suggested it was a good thing Bull was out of work, so he could treat the injury properly. He then threw a small plastic vial of pills to Bull. "These are a little stronger than anything you can get over the counter. Use them sparingly, since I'm not giving you a prescription."

Bull thanked the doctor and offered to pay him at least something. Dr. Jones refused the offer, saying it was the least he could do for a patriot. He helped Bull up and Dukeman walked the doctor to the door to let him out.

Just the visit made Bull feel better. By the end of the day, and without the assistance of medication, he was walking around the house in near-normal fashion. He turned on the radio and put on the <u>Fleet Sussman Show</u>. Although he was starting to become a regular caller, Dukeman hadn't listened much to the show before he reached out to Fleet. He was touched therefore, when he heard other callers offering their prayers to "the poor miner from West Virginia" as they started their conversations on the radio.

It took another week before Bull left the house again, about 16 days since he had suffered his back injury. June was coming to a quick end. Over the first half of the year, he had gone from being happily employed to being shockingly downsized. He'd started the year as the breadwinner of the family, only to see his wife and daughter start supporting him. After weeks of temporary work, he had been knocked out of commission by some young kid in town. Despite the small population of his hamlet, he still wasn't sure which child had been the -

presumably - unintentional culprit. He had gone from being a likeable person in town to something of a folk hero for Susspicious Minds around the country. It was the latter which made him a sensation when he walked into Maloney's, his favorite bar, that afternoon.

His friends and family had kept a distant eye on Bull throughout his ordeal. Some had indeed taken jobs back in the mines, even at the low, entry-level wages. As with most Mondays when he too was in the shafts, the men had gone to Maloney's for burgers and beers during lunch. The workers and the other still-jobless people who met at the bar looked up when he walked in, then started clapping. They were all happy to see their friend up and about unexpectedly. Some of the people closest to the door went to slap him on the back as he approached the bar, but he stopped them. "Back's still not 100-percent," he said, and his friends instead offered their hands to shake.

Bull told the other patrons he was getting better and how Doc Jones had come over for a free consultation. A couple of Bull's friends mentioned they had spoken to the doctor after his most recent call to Fleet Sussman, suggesting the physician reconsider his treatment of the town's new celebrity. Jones told those who did confront him that he too was moved by Bull's call to the show and he had already decided he'd pay Bull a visit the following day. Everyone in the bar agreed the doctor was a stand-up guy.

The conversation turned to politics, at which point everyone turned to Bull. He tried in vain to tell the other patrons in the bar he wasn't an expert on the subject, but they persisted in asking him questions. They figured anybody who could hang tough with Sussman for two segments must know something about how things should be. Bull was making his third attempt to tell everyone present he wasn't a political genius when the breaking news graphic flashed on the television screen on the wall above the register. Everyone quickly became quiet. The graphic was quickly replaced with an anchor. Above her left shoulder was a picture of Supreme Court Justice Antonin Scalia. Under his picture read the word "STROKE" in capital letters.

The people in the bar listened as the television commentator said Scalia had been rushed to a Washington-area hospital and his condition was unknown. The woman on the screen said the station would have information later in the day. The bartender then turned the TV from the local network to one of the national news stations, which was already fully embedded in its coverage about Justice Scalia. The network had a correspondent outside the hospital where the Justice had been taken. The reporter was waiting for a press briefing by a hospital spokesperson and had no official news to pass on. Anonymous members of the hospital staff and paramedics however suggested it had been a mild stroke and that the Justice was in good condition. Unofficially, there was every reason to think Justice Scalia would be fine. However, the questions started arising about what Scalia's condition would mean for the Supreme Court. Already, the people on the network were wondering whether his health and age would allow him to continue in his position.

Despite his previous denials about being a political think tank, it was Bull who spoke first about the Justice's situation. "This is bad," he said. When the others around him threw him puzzled looks, he explained it was very bad news for the people gathered in the bar. He told his friends that if the balance was shifted in the Supreme Court before the mining case was heard, they could likely kiss their jobs goodbye for good. Somberly, some of the others joked with Bull, telling him this showed he did have a better understanding of politics than anyone else in Maloney's.

Eventually, those people in the bar who had jobs settled their tabs and headed back to work. That left about half the people still in the pub, watching the news. It was maybe twenty minutes after the others left when a hospital spokeswoman addressed the media. She confirmed Scalia was in good and stable condition, and the woman said the prognosis for the Justice was positive. The reporters started to ask if and when Scalia would be able to return to work. The spokesperson said it wasn't up to her and it wasn't her place to speculate about his future outside of relaying the information the doctors gave her about his medical condition. After the spokeswoman excused herself, the network returned its broadcast to its studio, at which point the hosts and a quickly-assembled panel of political and medical experts started to discuss the potential future of Justice Scalia and the Supreme Court.

The other bar patrons turned their attention from the television back to Bull. After some discussion, everyone agreed that his assessment of the situation sounded legitimate. Some people at Maloney's suggested Bull call Sussman the following day. It was a suggestion he acted on.

That Tuesday he used the hotline number for the Fleet Sussman Show for the first time. As the phone rang, he felt a little bit nervous. He was afraid he might already be overstepping his boundary by using the number so quickly after receiving it. His fear subsided when the producer picked up and happily put him on hold.

Unlike his previous calls to the show, this time he had to wait for his turn to speak. When Fleet did pick up, he was as cordial as ever. Fleet asked Bull how he was and the caller responded by simply saying he was scared. After Sussman's prompting, Bull relayed to the host how he saw the situation. He gave the crowd at Maloney's a shout out, saying how his friends had agreed with his view of the recent, tragic news.

Sussman paused for a second before praising Bull. "I'm very proud of you, Gary. How quickly you've figured out how if Antonin isn't able to return to his job, it could have a serious, scary effect on you, and in fact, on all of us."

"Yes, I'm very scared. Some of us were just holding out, hoping our jobs would return. But now, now if Justice Scalia isn't able to return, I'm afraid I'll have no hope of getting my job back."

"No hope is exactly what the President will leave us with. It's what his predecessor left us with, and it is something to fear. We'll all be poor and jobless and without healthcare soon. You're an inspiration Gary, to face everything that President Rodriguez has thrown at you, and to still be on your feet and surviving. This country needs more people like you."

Sussman ended the call soon after that. Dukeman felt proud and vindicated after the conversation. If Sussman felt that way about him, he was sure most of America agreed. At least the people who mattered the most.

Bull had started to feel as though the President had a personal vendetta against him. The way Fleet had described the situation, saying how Bull himself had withstood everything thrown at him, made it seem as though it was a one-on-one competition. And while Bull was still on the losing end, he was staying in the game admirably, against a team of opponents who had every advantage.

The following day, Bull returned to Maloney's. This time the patrons were waiting for him. As soon as he walked in, camera flashes went off amid a boisterous reception. Everyone inside the bar started chanting his nickname. As he walked up to the counter, the other customers made way for him. When he ordered his beer, four men each immediately called for it to be put on his tab. After a heated if friendly exchange, they worked out who would buy which of Bull's rounds so long as he was drinking.

After he had a few swipes at his first pint, people started asking Bull for his own State of the Union. Unlike a couple of days before, he now was confident in himself and his view that it was only a matter of time before President Rodriguez drove the country into ruin. He said everyone at the bar had to stay vigilant in the wake of America's biggest threat.

At the other end of the bar, another customer had been listening to the conversation. Bull knew him as Dick Patton. Patton was one of the few people in town, outside of Doc Jones, who was college educated. He had grown up in the town and returned home after getting his degree. Patton worked at home, with some sort of Internet or telecommunications job. Bull and his friends always thought he was odd, as he didn't often leave his house. He was known as one of the few people in town, and probably the only Caucasian person, who was a staunch Democrat and who had voted for Eduardo Rodriguez.

With just a hint of anger in his voice, Patton yelled across the bar, "how is it all the President's fault?" When Bull and the others became silent and gave him strange glances, Patton continued, "the mine owners are the ones who put that clause in your contracts. The government hasn't issued a moratorium on mountaintop removal yet so you should ask your employers why they locked you out so fast. It wasn't the President who told the company to get rid of the tenured workers in those positions. Also, it's Doc Jones, bless his heart, who decided not to treat people with government healthcare... Except for the elderly people on Medicare, because he and they don't see it as the government insurance it really is."

Bull looked across the bar at Patton. "What's your problem... Dick?" It was a sophomoric joke that Bull and his friends used when Patton wasn't around, emphasizing his first name as innuendo. Some of the others around Bull chuckled at the emphasis.

Patton let the slight pass. "My problem is you're placing blame on the President because you want to. How about looking at the facts. You've probably been listening to Fleet again. He just spouts all types of lies and you just eat his bull... Bull."

"Ha, ha," unlike Patton, Dukeman took exception to the play of words using his name. "All I need to know is the President closed down our operation. And yeah, I'm listening to Fleet, and he's right! He said the President would cost us jobs, and that we'd be screwed on healthcare, and he's right!"

"Gary, have you read the news recently, or looked online about the mountaintop ban? Other companies are still keeping their sites in other towns open until the Supreme Court has a chance to rule on the case. Only your company has shut down, and I'm willing to bet that's only because all their highest-paid people were on that site instead of down underground. That's not the President's doing and that's not the fault of the more recent employees.

"As for Doc Jones, he's made it no secret he's not accepting government health programs by choice. I don't know what he's ever said to you, but during my visits, knowing my political beliefs, he's always sure to point that out. I'm just glad my employers have a good health plan, otherwise, he'd be happy to charge me full-price for my visits.

"And although you haven't mentioned it, I'm sure you think the President's tax proposal will be a further threat to your well-being. It won't be. Even if you still were up in the hills, you weren't making anywhere near enough money to be affected by the tax breaks the President wants to eliminate."

Bull did his best to ignore most of what Patton had said. He responded to just one part, "if Justice Scalia steps down, *I'm* willing to bet there's no way the Supreme Court will restore mountaintop removal operations."

"You're probably right about that," Patton said. Dukeman relaxed slightly, feeling he had won the argument. Dick decided not to press for an answer on his other points. "That's the way the Supreme Court works though. Scalia did his best to hang in there, but after all that time, his age has caught up with him. Let's just all hope he keeps living a normal life no matter what happens to his career."

Dukeman and the others at the bar all raised their drinks to Patton's last words. Dick then settled his tab and walked out with only the slightest acknowledgement to and from the other patrons. After he left, Bull and his friends started making fun of Dick, suggesting he knew nothing about politics or what was truly wrong in the nation. "And it is the fault of the mining rookies that we're in this situation. They are working for cheap and I'm sure all of those Wetbacks voted for Rodriguez." Again, Bull's friends raised their drinks. Soon after that, everybody finished their meals and drinks and left Maloney's.

The next few days were relatively uneventful for Bull. He was at home when he heard Scalia's own statement about his condition, and was happy to hear it sounded like he'd be able to live a pretty normal life. However, he was nervous that Scalia himself was putting his career in doubt. While his back was definitely getting better, he decided to not try and get a job until after Independence Day. Instead, he stayed around the house, with occasional trips to Maloney's.

The Fourth of July came and went, with the whole Dukeman family meeting for a grand picnic at a local park. Bull sat out the family softball game, and said the pain of missing one of his favorite Dukeman traditions was worse than any suffering his back had caused him. Still, he erred on the side of caution and watched from the rickety bleachers down the first base line. The night ended with a small fireworks show.

Bull returned to the store where he first was injured two mornings later. The couple that owned the store were happy to have him back, and were apologetic about what happened, even though he assured them his injury hadn't been their fault. Bull continued to carry packages for the couple, but was careful to not carry too much at once and was sure he could see all around himself whenever he picked something up.

Despite limiting himself in how much he carried and how slowly he moved while loaded down, Bull finished the work the store had for him by mid-morning. The couple paid him better than they had before his accident, then told him to come back in a few days when they expected their next big delivery. With money in his pocket and still on the town's main street, he decided to wait around until Maloney's opened. To kill time, he went down to his church, where he lit a candle for the ailing Justice.

By the time he left the church and made it back to Maloney's the bar was open and half-full. Bull walked in. Instead of the cheer he had gotten used to over his last few visits, the people inside were quiet and subdued. The patrons and barkeeps were all glued once again to the television, where a man was reading off a piece of paper. Bull's heart sank as he listened to the spokesperson on the screen. He was reading a statement from Justice Scalia, one that said its writer would be hanging up his robes and retiring.

Bull first issued a quick, mean thought to the Heavens for letting his prayers go unanswered and for his candle lighting being for naught. He followed that up by sheepishly and silently asking for forgiveness for his previous thoughts. He then focused on everyone else in the bar, who had turned to him as their perceived leader. "Well, that's that," was all Bull said, and he took a swig of his beer.

He spent the next few days either at the shop moving boxes or at home. He didn't want to be the political voice of the town because of his growing angst for the future. He was afraid of letting others see his fear and decided to avoid Maloney's for the rest of the week.

Bull was at home doing some light chores that Sunday afternoon when he heard a report on the radio that a successor for Justice Scalia had been chosen. The anchor played a soundbite taken from one of that morning's national news shows, in which a White House spokesperson said Brian Payton, a federal judge from San Francisco, would be Rodriguez' pick to replace Scalia. Bull didn't know anything about Payton, but hearing he was from San Francisco was enough for him to figure the potential Justice was an ultra-Left wing activist judge. As the day wore on and more reports about Payton were aired, he knew his assessment was correct.

The following day, Bull went back to the store, then made his way to Maloney's. The bar was surprisingly crowded, considering how early it was. The patrons clapped as he walked in, and some of his friends explained how many turned out because they wanted to be at the bar with the town's political celebrity to watch the President's press conference.

The news channel showed the conference in its entirety, after which the barkeep turned Fleet Sussman's show on for all to hear. The radio host went ballistic after the announcement was made. After lashing out at the President for a good ten minutes, he went to break before coming back and taking phone calls. Most of the callers were as livid as Fleet, using such terms as "traitorous," frightening" and "immoral" to describe the nomination. Some callers used his living in San Francisco to question Payton's sexual orientation, even though the man was heterosexual and there were no laws against homosexuals serving in any part of the government. Still they called him evil and a menace to the country.

It was about a half-hour before Fleet's sign-off that a Ronnie from Rochester got on the air. The man from upstate New York claimed to have followed the politics of his state for years, and had never trusted Rodriguez since he was elected to the New York State Senate. Ronnie pointed out how the now-President favored his "low-class ghetto neighborhood" in all he did, and how Rodriguez was the lone reason there was a new, unneeded convention center in the Bronx. The President had always had a history of supporting the riff-raff he grew up around, the dregs of society from which he had arisen. "He's filthy," Ronnie exclaimed, "he's a regular New York City subway rat, the likes of which everybody hates and nobody would miss. He's destroying our great nation, lifting his other rats out of the sewers at the expense of great, hard-working Americans like you and me. It can't go on anymore, we have to protect ourselves. Wouldn't it be something if some patriot shot and killed the President."

"Wouldn't that be something..." Fleet echoed Ronnie's last sentiment, then went into his last commercial break of that day's show. When he returned, he offered a prayer to everyone listening, saying he hoped everyone would make it through the coming tough days. Better times must surely be ahead, Sussman said, times without President Rodriguez. The show's closing music then played, and another commercial break started.

For the first time ever, the political landscape made Dukeman break down. He had been sipping from his mug as Sussman gave his closing monologue, but the listener slammed the mug down and yelled that what the Democrats were doing wasn't fair. After the initial, shocked reaction of those around him to his outburst, they nodded in agreement. "But what can be done?" a number of people responded.

"It sounded like Ronnie had an idea," Bull grumbled in a stern tone, but then went silent. He didn't really mean it, or he didn't think he did. It was his spur-of-the-moment answer, being slightly drunk and very scared. Nobody else around him responded either.

The lunch rush soon came to a close, and the patrons of Maloney's shuffled out the door and on to Main Street. Bull, being one of the few people without a real job, was one of the last to leave. He walked outside and waited a second for his eyes to adjust to the bright, abundant sunshine making its way through the trees. As he stood there with his hand above his eyes, he heard somebody call his name. He didn't need to look up to know who it was. "Hey, Skip," Bull said, as his cousin Pete approached.

Peter Dukeman, known to his friends as Skipper or Skip, walked up to Bull. He too had become a bit of a celebrity since being laid off from the mining company; Skip was the person caught on camera quoting Sussman after the attack on the local Latinos. While the authorities took a dim view of what he had said and what Skip and his friends had done that night, the unofficial response was much more sympathetic. Nobody would admit to actually supporting his actions and Peter himself would act sheepishly whenever the subject came up. It was obvious few were upset by what he had said or done.

"How are you doing?" Pete asked, "I tried to get over to you in the bar, but that crowd around you made it kind of hard."

"I'm doing well. I think I'm ready to find something better. Job-wise, I mean. I think my back's getting better. How are you? How're the kids?"

"Everyone is as they were last week," Pete said, alluding to the annual Independence Day family picnic. "Hey, Bull, you have a second to walk?"

Bull said he did, and the two started walking down Main Street. They continued their small talk as they walked down the block, talking about sports and the family. They laughed about how once again, the Pirates were destined to finish under .500, even though the season was barely half-way over.

Every so often in their short jaunt, Pete would look around to see who was about. Every now and then, they'd walk past a few people and say hello. Main Street always had a few people milling about, even if the town was rather small. Skip led Bull to the parking lot near the local all-in-one store, where Skip's car was parked. Pete had taken a job at the large, national chain store soon after he was fired from the mines. Despite his actions the night of the attack, he managed to keep that job. Skip leaned against his car, which was alone at the back of the lot. After one more glance to see if anyone was near them, Skip started speaking.

"Look, Bull, I heard what you said there at the end of Sussman's show, and I heard what that Ronnie guy said as well. What if I told you something *is* going to be done?"

As Bull gave Skip an awkward, questioning look, Pete continued. "I don't know if you've heard, but Rodriguez is coming to Morgantown. It's been planned for a matter of weeks, actually, and news of the visit has only just been made public. I've known about it for a while because I have a friend who works in security there. A good friend, a smart friend..." Pete paused, as if unsure about what he was going to say next, "and he's become a fan of yours over the last few days."

Bull shot his cousin another questioning look and Skip went on, "He listens to Fleet all the time too, and like me and the others, he was inspired by your words."

"So what does that have to do with me?" Bull asked.

"Well, he's been working on... Something special since he heard the President was coming to the university... Him and some of the other security guys and custodians there. It's... It's big. It's something that will save America, a moment which will stand out as a great moment in history. I can tell you more about it, but you have to promise me that if you don't get involved, you will never talk about this conversation to anyone ever."

Bull laughed for a second, "what are you going to do? Kill the President?"

Skip gave Bull a knowing look, but remained silent.

"Oh, my God, you are! How could you think of that and why are you telling me?"

"SHHH! Calm down!" Skipper looked around to see if anyone had noticed. Once Pete was sure they still were not being watched, he spoke in whisper, "you said it yourself at Maloney's. That guy on the radio had a good suggestion. I went to the bar today hoping you'd be there to see what you thought. When I heard your reaction, I figured I'd just cut to the chase. The guys want you to pull the trigger. They figure you deserve the glory."

Bull's mind was swimming. He was unsure how he was brought into the conversation, "I still don't get it... Why me?"

"Because you have lost as much as anyone because of the 'President,'" Pete emphasized the title to show his disgust in Rodriguez. "And because you've become the symbol of all our problems. Your calls to Fleet have inspired a lot of people around here. You are the resistance, you have motivated us. You weren't with us when we beat on those Wetbacks, but it was your discussion with Fleet that made us decide to take action."

"But I didn't want anyone to get hurt!"

"But you are okay if the President gets hurt, you said."

Bull thought about the phrase he had uttered just a little while before at Maloney's. He realized it was true. While he felt some sympathy for the people Pete and his friends had attacked, he felt nothing similar toward Eduardo Rodriguez. In fact, he wished nothing but ill will on the man who had caused him and a number of friends and loved ones so much pain.

As Bull continued to sort out his feelings, Pete explained more about the plan and why they wanted Gary to be a part of it. Almost as soon as the security staff was told of the visit, some of the personnel immediately started formulating their plan. Not being strangers to the security processes and background checks that the government would use, they knew despite their personal political leanings, they all had spotless records and there would be no reason for the government to suspect any of them would try anything. A few of the campus police were decorated officers from the nation's operations in the Middle East, and none of them had ever uttered a word of discontent in public or posted anything questionable on any sort of website. Some of the more tenured officers at the school also realized security under the current administration was rather lax: an example, they figured, of what was wrong with the party in power. They knew, with their inside knowledge of the President's visit, and with the connections some of them had to disgruntled former intelligence and army leaders from their service days, they could facilitate the murder of the President, planned by professional military minds, to be carried out by someone outside of the school's police staff.

That was when, Skip explained, his friends at the university had come to him. The plan called for somebody not connected to the school's police force to be the triggerman. The military vets planning the assassination figured keeping the security staff updated only on a need-to-know basis would give the secret service less of a chance to figure out an attempt would be made to kill the President. Those orchestrating the event, when they heard of Pete's relationship to Gary, decided he was the perfect assassin. He lived nearby, was a friend of a friend and therefore viewed as unconnected to everyone else who was in on the plan. Plus he had an obvious dislike for the President. Some thought his minor celebrity status might also be a good thing, to show the country and the world how fed up people were with the Liberal agenda. It would demonstrate how serious people were about fighting the Leftist tyranny.

Pete thought Bull looked horrified and yet interested in the plan. It reminded Skip of an occasion when the two helped with the salvage efforts of the body of one of their friends from the mine. There had been a methane explosion in one tunnel and one of their close buddies was caught right by the center of the blast. Their friend's body was horribly burned, and much of his clothing had disintegrated. Chunks of his flesh had been blown away in the blast, and most of his skin was bubbled. Skip watched Bull, who looked ready to vomit at the site, but still seemed unable to take his eyes off the corpse in front of them. The disgust on Gary's face now was just a fraction of what it had been then, but it was unmistakably there. And yet, Pete was sure he could see the slightest curl on Bull's lips, as though his cousin was trying his hardest to suppress a smile.

"Do you realize," Skip started, "how much so many of us look up to you? You've brought our plight into the national spotlight. Fleet knows you, man! You're like a hero to us, and if you go through with this, you'll be like a Savior to us, perhaps to him too!"

Bull thought about everything he had heard. He again realized he had no love or respect for the President, and was more angry at him for

58

all the pain his policies had caused Bull and his family. There was nothing to suggest Rodriguez' evil plotting to hurt the American people would subside on its own. For eight years, Bull watched as President Obama had terrorized the country. When he did have the occasional chance to listen to Fleet over the years, the radio host always pointed out how hard-working people were having their money taken away in taxes in order to help pay for those who weren't willing to take care of themselves. Now, though, President Rodriguez was making his predecessor look like a moderate, and just during the first months of his first term. Bull knew something had to be done, and perhaps drastic measures would be the only way to protect the American way.

"So how will we do this?" Bull asked.

Skip smiled and put his arm around his cousin. He started to explain the little he knew about the plan as the two walked towards the store where Skip was employed.

The Death of Two Kings, Part Two

Bull's heart was racing as he was let into WVU Coliseum. Or at least he was pretty sure it was. He was surprised, after the limited training and extensive briefing he had received, that nobody had noticed his angst as he was admitted to the venue. He had been prepared to be stopped, and to say he was just so excited to see the President in the flesh! He was even wearing an Obama T-shirt to give the impression he was a lifelong Democrat. He was disgusted by what he was wearing, but was told it was best for the image he was trying to convey.

Now that the day was upon him, he was amazed by how little was done to help him prepare for the event. In the course of just over a week, he practiced virtually non-stop with firearms but that had been the only sort of training he really received. The weapons he was given were all modified airguns and he got used to firing them at a small, fixed target from point-blank and short ranges. The organizers weren't sure exactly what kind of gun they would funnel to Bull or from where he would be able to take his killing shot, therefore he prepared for all sorts of probable scenarios. He was told to put an emphasis on point-blank target practice, as that was still the main hope. He was also instructed to aim for targets the size of a quarter, as though he would be a sharpshooter at extremely close range. After hours of practice, he was able to hit his mark with a millisecond's aim with all the firearms he had been given.

Besides Skip, the only other person Bull was able to talk with about the plan was a man who asked to be called "Sarge." The new man obviously came from a military background and helped Bull with his target practice and gun handling. He was also the person who briefed Bull on the plan. Sarge explained exactly what was expected of Bull but

60

said nothing about the planners or anyone else in on the plot. The less Bull knew, the better for everyone involved. Bull was given a code phrase which would signify if he was in the presence of somebody else who was involved with the operation. Meantime, Skip was there mostly for moral support. His only real part in the plot had already been completed: he had recruited Bull to pull the trigger.

Bull and Sarge had made the most of the little time they had together to prepare for the attempt. By the end Bull knew he was as ready as he would ever be. The day of the attack he was given a ride to Morgantown. Then he was in the hall where Rodriguez would soon be speaking. Once he passed the entry security checkpoint, Bull milled about the lobby of the coliseum. He looked - from a distance to try to not talk to anyone or draw attention to himself - around the area. Tables with pro-Rodriguez and pro-Democrat memorabilia lined the outskirts of the room. He saw t-shirts, bumper stickers and Leftist publications all for sale. He saw a couple of tables set up just for collecting donations for "the cause," as he called the Democratic machine in his mind. He went up to one table and bought not only a Rodriguez shirt, but a canvas reusable shopping bag to put it in.

It was nearly a half-hour later when the room started to thin out. The majority of the people were making their way into the auditorium. This included many of the volunteers who had been manning the tables in the lobby. He got onto one of the lines going into the performance area before announcing to nobody in particular that he better go use the facilities before the program started.

Bull walked through the lobby to a restroom near the portal by which he had entered the building. There was an "out of order" sign on the front door but the restroom was still unlocked. There had been bathrooms closer to the auditorium entrance, but he had been specifically told to use the room he was entering. After going in, he checked to make sure nobody else was inside. Once he was sure he was alone, he locked the door of the three-stall public bathroom. He then went into the middle toilet. After opening the stall, he lifted open the toilet's reservoir tank. Inside was a tightly-sealed plastic box. It was a smaller version of the canisters he would carry food in when he went hiking with his family. Such containers were meant to keep their contents from being hurt by the elements, as well as to keep odors from being detected by hungry beasts. Like bears, Bull, thought, or bomb-sniffing dogs.

He opened the brick-sized box and took out its contents. The gun inside was similar to the one he had had his best success with while practicing. He had gotten used to it quickly and had stated he thought he was a very good shot with it. He'd better be, Sarge told him, because he'd only have one chance at this "glorious, historic kill." Sarge had made it seem as if the President were a wild animal, no different than the deer Bull had hunted in the past. In conversations, the other man had even suggested the deer was superior. "Unlike that Spic, the deer isn't out to kill us." A voice in the back of his head rang out to Bull, suggesting not only was the plan morally wrong, but it was more about race to its organizers than about the dangers the President presented. Sarge's words were proof of this. Dukeman thought for a second he could put the gun back and nobody would be any wiser of the plot or his part in it. Nobody had spoken about the consequences of what would happen if he suddenly pulled out. Maybe life would go on as it had since he left the mines. Bull didn't think his cohorts would be that forgiving. He wrapped the gun in the shirt and put it in the bag. He then made use of one of the urinals, washed his hands and left the bathroom.

Bull knew he was intentionally being kept out of the loop, but he'd find eventually that some of his hunches had been correct. The sealed box, inside the water, was supposed to keep any possible gun-detecting dogs off the scent. As an added measure, the gun was a carbon-powered pistol, accounting for the lighter weight while eliminating the possibility of a dog smelling any gunpowder. The weapon was also modified to remove some of the metal pieces, in case of metal detectors, and to have the same kickback as a regular gun of the same caliber and design. He hoped the changes would make the firearm he now possessed act like a regular handgun of similar design, weight and size.

Dukeman walked toward one of the entrances to the theater, where a security officer was standing. The guard gave Bull a strange look. "Don't you know what 'out of order' means?" the other man asked.

"Oh, I was looking down when I went in. I didn't even see the sign," He had been given that line to rehearse in case of a situation just like this.

The other man looked at him oddly for a moment, then broke into a large smile. "Don't worry," the guard said with a wink, "you're among friends here."

Bull tried hard not to smile back. That was the countersign he'd receive if he came across anyone who was also in the plan. He was happy to know he wasn't the only person in on the plot who was in the auditorium, but he was still wrapped in fear. At that point he was certain there was no turning back.

The guard opened the door and Bull was surprised to see how many people turned up to see the President. In his small corner of the world, there was so little support for the man and he was led to believe that it was the same throughout the state. To see the room he was in packed was shocking.

The guard next to him also surveyed the room. "This isn't going to do," he said, nodding at the assembled people. He then grabbed Bull by the arm and told him to follow his lead.

The two men worked their way down one of the side aisles to a section next to the front auditorium wall. Bull's companion told him the section was for VIPs, but as part of the security detail the guard had secured access for both of them to the area.

"You have one of the best seats in the house!" The guard raised his voice over the crowd. A local Democratic representative was speaking, and the crowd was cheering after every few phrases. "The President will pass right by us here when he's done speaking!"

Bull now knew his fate was sealed. Barring some unforeseen obstacle, he would be given the perfect chance to carry out his assigned task. He felt more nervous than relieved by this revelation, still unsure if he would be doing the right thing. Next to him, his colleague looked at him before whispering to him. Bull's apprehension must have been apparent, as the other man spoke into his ear, "you better not mess this up. I'll be right here assisting you. If you leave me out on the line alone, you'll be sorry."

There it was, the confirmation that he would be held responsible if he didn't fulfill his mission. As various speakers came and went from the stage, Bull thought about what would or wouldn't happen to him if he just let Rodriguez walk past him. Would his own life be on the line? The lives of his wife and daughter? Even though he didn't know much about the other people he was allying himself with for the cause, he knew they knew a lot about him. He wondered if even his cousin Skip, who recruited him as the triggerman, would have a part in destroying Bull's side of the family if he didn't try to kill the President.

Dukeman was brought out of his pensive trance by a sudden uproar from the crowd. The final speaker leading up to the President had just wrapped up by saying Rodriguez was just moments away. In an attempt not to look suspicious, Bull also started cheering with incredible, false fervor. In reality he was feeling sick to his stomach, not just for showing his support for the opposition, but because of what he would do in the very near future.

Rodriguez soon came to the stage to an ovation which made the previous one seem like a round of golf claps. Bull continued to cheer with the others in the audience. Soon the President started his speech in earnest. Bull was so preoccupied with his thoughts that he barely heard anything Rodriguez was saying. Instead, Bull clapped when others clapped, screamed when others screamed. The only thing he was able to remember was the President talking about coming to "enemy territory," saying it was appropriate because he would be discussing the coal mining ban and his plans for student loans at universities like the one they were all at. The former stood out because Bull recognized the irony in the comment, that that was why he was there. It felt like salt in the wound to Bull. Had the President kept his hands off mining regulations, Bull wouldn't have been involved in the plot and would have stayed home that day. Bull also heard mention of taxes and Judge Payton, but the mental fog he was in kept him from absorbing what the President was saying.

The President spoke for about 45 minutes. Much of what he said was received with boisterous applause, which Bull didn't agree with even if he too was cheering. Rodriguez ended his speech with the traditional "God bless the United States of America," which was the one thing he said that Bull genuinely cheered for. The President then clasped both his hands above his head before shaking hands with the people who had been flanking him on the stage. He then started his way down a small staircase at the side of the stage opposite Bull. Once he was on the auditorium floor he started walking towards the soon-to-be assassin. Bull's heart was racing faster at that moment than it had been at any other point that day. He reached into his bag and grabbed the gun's handle. He just stood there as Rodriguez approached, clasping any hand that was offered to him. The next 90 seconds felt like a day to Bull as he waited for the President to come within ideal range. Soon though the President was in front of Bull, the politician offering his hand to the spectator as the two men looked one another in the eye. Rodriguez at first smiled at Bull, but his look turned to one of puzzlement as the other man refused to take his hand.

In that instance, the guard who had ushered Bull to the place where he was standing was pushing against the other men with the President. He turned quickly to look at Bull with a manic determination in his gaze. "Now! NOW!!!"

Bull quickly snapped into action, pulled the gun from the bag and leveled it at the President's face. The bag and shirt fell to the floor as the people around Bull started to scream. In the short instant it took for him to take aim, the look on the President's face turned to one of fear. Bull aimed for the President's right eye, and pulled the trigger. The shot found its target dead on. The President stiffened and froze momentarily with pain, giving Bull another shot at the eye. He fired again, another perfect strike. For good measure, he then aimed for Rodriguez' other eye and fired once more. Another direct hit. Bull was able to get off six shots before Rodriguez tumbled over.

Even though there were more rounds in the gun, Bull dropped the weapon after he thought he had completed his task. As he did this, he fell to his knees and put his hands behind his head. He started to weep as the chaos continued around him. The guard who had held the government agents back had also given up once Bull's deed was done. The secret service men forced both attackers to their stomachs and pulled the assailants' arms behind their respective backs. After a few seconds the government security men were forced to let up, instead defending their prisoners from the people around them in the crowd. Through the confusion and turmoil, Rodriguez supporters were realizing the President had been injured, and those close to Dukeman and his accomplice were trying to figure out who had shot Rodriguez. In anger and fear, those nearby started kicking Bull and the other man and the secret service men had to protect the suspects.

The medics reached the President in a matter of seconds while local and university police arrived in the immediate area in about a minute. Bull tried to listen to the medical technicians over the ruckus around him. No sooner had they knelt down by Rodriguez when one of them uttered "My God!" then told her companion to radio for a stretcher and ambulance. He heard terms such as "stabilize," "frontal lobe hemorrhaging" and "traumatic brain injury" mentioned, but wasn't sure what they meant. He'd heard those or similar phrases on the medical shows he'd watched on television, on which they seemed to signify serious conditions. Before he could hear anything else however, he was pulled off the ground and hurried into a police detention vehicle.

Yer Blues (I'm so Lonely I could Die)

Bull guessed it was roughly 20 days after he shot President Rodriguez before he saw sunlight again. He had been kept in solitary confinement and treated as a prisoner of war by soldiers and intelligence people from his own country who kept telling him that it was different dates in an attempt to confuse him. One day they would say it was mid-October, then the next day he'd be told it was still July. During his incarceration, he had no idea what was happening in the world, or even if he had succeeded in killing the President.

The day of the shooting was a blur to Bull. He had had trouble focusing through his nervousness before he shot the President, then was buried under a crush of government agents and various other authorities. He was quickly handcuffed and hauled off. The officers had to protect him from an attacking mob of civilians. He didn't think his then-protectors really wanted to be in that position, but that they'd rather also be taking shots at him.

Instead, while people in the auditorium screamed and cried and yelled for information, the officials pulled Bull and his cohort off the floor and moved them into a waiting armored vehicle where they couldn't be harmed. The two attackers were loaded into the back of the truck, along with four of the security officers.

The truck travelled around for a couple of hours before stopping. It was a nerve-wracking ride for Bull. Everyone in the back of the vehicle remained silent for the duration. He was warned beforehand about saying the wrong thing after the shooting, about intentionally or inadvertently telling his captors too much about the plan. He found this demand from the planners to be funny. Except for Skip and Sarge, all he knew about the plot was where to get the gun. He didn't know Sarge's real name. For that matter, he didn't even know the name of the other man being held in the truck with him.

When the truck stopped and the doors were opened, Bull and his accomplice were forcefully pushed out the door into a large, dark warehouse room. Other government men immediately came from around the vehicle and roughly put heavy canvas sacks over both men's heads. The guards grabbed Bull by his arms and marched him for an unknown time and distance.

Bull was soon stopped and was able to hear a door open. He was shoved forward then told to wait. With the ability to see stolen from him and his hands in heavy cuffs, he scoffed at the idea of his trying to get out of wherever he was. Soon he heard more people come into the room. One man removed his hood while another told him to undress. The three men were in a small, unremarkable room. An orange jumpsuit and sneakers were on the floor in front of him, as well as a plastic rectangular container. He was told to leave all his clothes and possessions on the floor and change into the prison uniform. Once he had complied, the guard took Bull's clothing off the floor and put it all in the tray. The lead officer listed everything which Bull had taken off to his companion, who wrote it down on a page on a clipboard. The guard handling Bull's clothes checked all the pockets and rattled off anything he found in them. He stopped when he found Bull's wallet. "Suspect's name is Gary Dukeman," the guard said after comparing Bull to the picture on his driver's license. He then read Bull's address off, before listing the other cards he was carrying, as well as how much money was in the wallet. When the inventory was completed, Bull was told to confirm the list and sign. Once he did so, the hood was placed over his head again and he was escorted out of the room.

Bull was again marched through the building. All he could tell about his travels was that he had been on at least one elevator. When he was told to stop again, he heard another door being opened. This door was different. It sounded large, heavy and metal. The door to the changing room had been like something he would have imagined to be a classroom door at a school. He was made to walk another few paces before he was stopped again. The hood was taken off his head and the guards left the cell without saying a word. Bull turned and watched as the door was slammed shut behind them. He looked around his new home. There was a metal shelf for a bed with a thin foam mattress hanging from one wall. On the next wall a toilet and sink. One Styrofoam cup was on the sink's upper surface. The room was dimly lit by a fluorescent fixture placed in the high ceiling. The thick plastic light covering let barely enough light in so that he could see his way around. He was able to make out what he thought were holes near the top of the tall walls, which he figured held cameras inside them. There was no mirror over the sink or any type of reflective surface in the room. Everything was metal, painted in a matted grey. The large door was the same color. He could make out two places where somebody outside could open small portals in the door. One was about face-high while the second was at ground level. He had watched enough television to know the higher opening was where somebody could talk to him from and the other allowed food to be passed into the room.

It didn't take long for him to realize there was nothing for him to do in the chamber. The only things he was able to touch were the bed, toilet, sink and cup. The light was way too high for him to reach, even if he stood on any of the objects in the room. The only sounds he heard were the echoes of anything he did, or of anything he said as he began to mumble to himself. His watch had been taken from him when he changed clothes and there was no clock to tell him the time or date. Later, as he started to fall asleep, he realized the light was staying at the same brightness and there was no way to tell even if it was day or night. At last check, when he was in the truck and still had his watch on, it was 2:17 p.m. He hadn't bothered to look when he surrendered the watch, although he knew it would have been little consolation at this point to know the time.

All Bull could tell when he was again in the presence of other people was that he had gone to sleep four or five times. Even when he was given food, it was always pushed through the door while he happened to be sleeping or using the toilet on the other side of the room. This made him feel all but certain he was being viewed with cameras. He also had the suspicion he was being drugged, because he had the uncanny desire to fall asleep after each meal. This sleeping pattern kept him confused and he wasn't even sure if he was sleeping during the night or day.

When other men had finally come into the room, he was immediately hooded again and walked out of his cell. He was taken to an interrogation room. Once again, his surroundings reminded him of what he had seen on television police dramas.

A majority of his interrogations would happen in this room and all of those sessions were pretty much the same. Bull would constantly tell everything he knew about the event, but his interrogators acted as though they thought he was holding out on them. From the moment the first session started, he tried to cooperate. He almost felt obligated to help in the investigation, as he felt guilt for what he had done. He questioned his actions although he believed he had acted in the best interests of the nation. No matter his reasoning though, and no matter what he said to the people interrogating him, they wouldn't believe him when he said he was telling them all that he knew about the plan. They insisted he had to know more.

For all Skip and Sarge talked up how famous Bull would become and how he'd be forever remembered as a hero in the nation's history, they never mentioned what would happen to him personally after the event. He thought he understood why he was being kept on a need-to-know basis and why he was told nothing about the others involved in the plan. He believed it was so he couldn't say anything to investigators. However, he hadn't been warned about how hard his captors would try to pump information out of him. He was feeling as though he was the scapegoat. He understood now the real reason he hadn't been told anything: even if he felt like ratting out his co-conspirators, he couldn't.

While the questions never changed, the tactics did. He was told on one occasion that his accomplice (who his guards told him was named Mark Carter) had put all the blame on Bull. Another time, he was told others connected to the plan had been found, arrested, and had also fingered Bull as the organizer. Then there was the time his handlers said his wife had implicated another family member, who had been picked up, and he *and* Carter had agreed that Bull was the person who organized the shooting and carried it out himself for the glory. All Bull could do was stick to his original story.

One day he was escorted to another room. Even with his hood on he could tell he was being marched in a different direction than he had been previously. When the canvas sack was removed from his head, Bull saw he was standing in the brightest room he'd been in since he was

72

brought to the facility. Instead of the chairs and table he had grown accustomed to, there was a metal medical bed in the room. Leather straps were hanging from the sides of the slab, which were positioned where one's lower chest and ankles would be when someone was laying on it. Five guards were in the room, with four surrounding him. The fifth told him he had one last chance to cooperate before things became "unpleasant." For the first time in his captivity, Bull was frightened about his physical well-being. He tried to scamper back from the table, but was being held in place by the guards. He shrieked "No!" then turned to the guard who had spoken to him, "Where's my lawyer? I'm under arrest, I want a lawyer!!"

The main guard sneered at him. "You're funny," he said, "after all this time, you're just now asking for a lawyer? It's a little late for that, and you're not entitled to one."

"Bullshit I'm not! I'm under arrest, I should have a lawyer present! I want to talk to my family!"

This time the guard reacted with a hearty laugh. "Did anyone read you your rights when you were arrested? No. You know why? You aren't under arrest. You're being held as a prisoner of war, not as a criminal. You don't have many friends out there who care anyway. You're a shitty-maggot-terrorist, so don't expect any help. I don't think even your wife or kid want to hear from you anymore. Your wife wasn't happy when we questioned her. I don't think she cares to know where you are. For that matter, I'll tell you a little secret. Most people think you're being held at a prison camp out of the country. Heck, for all you know, you are. But wherever you are, we'll make you talk."

With that, the lead guard nodded towards the table. The men grasping Bull's arms moved forward as he struggled in futility and screamed. The guards easily picked him up and strapped him to the operating table. Bull could see various instruments and hoses he couldn't recognize. Before he could ask what they were, a cloth was placed over his face and he could feel water being poured over the material covering his mouth. He tried to shake free and scream again, but was unable to accomplish either task. The sensation started again soon after, then again after that. He blacked out between the third and fourth instances of his waterboarding.

He woke up back in his cell. He was unsure how long he had been unconscious. It took him only moments to realize it had been a matter of days, not just hours. First off, his jumpsuit was soiled with a number of bodily discharges. Anything his body could produce was either on him, his clothing or the bed he had been laying on. In disgust, he removed his clothing. If his guards had a problem with his nudity, they could address it when they came in. Once he had taken off the dirty, orange one-piece, he was able to see where his arms and legs had been bound. The marks and wounds weren't fresh, and he could see that scabs had already formed over the few parts where his skin had been broken. At first, he had been surprised at how little the strap burns hurt, but then he came to understand that the injuries had had time to heal. They caused him to feel sore, but he didn't feel achy.

As he continued to wake and come to his senses, he realized he was very hungry. He'd never been unconscious like this before, and wondered if his desire for food was natural considering the situation or if it was because of the time that had passed since he had last eaten. He had last eaten, if his memory was correct, prior to the last time he had slept before he was taken for his waterboarding session. He had no idea how long ago that may have been. He did know that all the factors were making his stomach growl worse than he ever remembered.

Bull got up from the bed where he had been sitting after getting undressed and stood up in his naked splendor and looked into one of the holes where he thought a camera might be. He stretched his arms out to expose his whole body. "Well, I'm naked and hungry!" He yelled up to the hole, hoping if there was a camera in it that it also had a microphone, "are you going to do anything?"

As he expected, nothing happened immediately after his display. He waited what he thought were minutes before he started to count off seconds. According to the clock in his mind, he waited five minutes. Then it was ten. He lost count soon after that. He tried lying down, then got up and started pacing. He had been left alone in the room in the past, but not like this. In those instances, he hadn't been treated as roughly as he had been before he woke up this time, and he had never been left to starve. Nor had he ever been as humiliatingly filthy as he had been when he woke up this time. Despite the fact he'd been in solitary confinement the whole time he had been in captivity, he hadn't felt as though he had been so ignored as he had been at that point.

He tried counting the seconds a number of times again, but kept losing count after two or three minutes. After what he estimated was an hour, he started waving his arms at the perceived camera hole again, and started yelling for help. Here was still no response. He went back to pacing, then back to waving for the camera. This time he screamed he'd tell them everything he knew. If they were so insistent he knew more about the plot, he'd try to make up a story, something they wanted to hear. Maybe he could tell them about Skip, although if they truly had rounded him up too, who knew what he was saying?

Bull was certain his willingness to cooperate would make his captors come running to him, but that wasn't the case. Instead, he still was tormented by silence and loneliness. He started to wonder if something had gone wrong. He couldn't believe this treatment was legal. Maybe the video image had frozen, and his watchers thought he was still napping. He didn't think after those first acts of cruelty that they'd pour it on so hard for so long. He was sure, even as a POW, he was being treated inhumanely.

Another countless amount of minutes or hours passed by without any evidence that the outside world still existed. Bull tried to maintain a strong demeanor. He went over to the sink and took a drink of water from the Styrofoam cup. When he was done with his drink, he tried throwing the cup up at the camera. The flimsy, light container just floated up a couple of feet before drifting pathetically to the cell floor.

Bull went over to the bed and turned the flimsy black mattress over due to the filth on it. He then laid down to try to sleep again. His hunger and anxiety over the situation kept him awake at first. Then he realized he had no idea what the history of the padding had been and that too kept him from sleeping. Eventually though his exhaustion won out and he was able to fall asleep.

When he woke up, Bull couldn't believe the magnitude of the pain in his stomach. He looked over at the door, hoping to see even just a piece of bread on a plastic plate there. He would have been happy even without the plate, but it didn't matter. No food had been pushed into the room. Feeling weak, he was still able to roll out of the bed. He went over to where the cup had landed and picked it up. He hadn't bothered to do that earlier. He took another drink before meekly walking over to the cell door. He started banging on the portal and yelling for attention. He was certain his weakened state and the size of the door made the display seem rather pathetic. His only hope was that someone was watching on camera but he wasn't even certain anyone was paying attention. His yelling gave way to sobs. Bull's body relaxed as he melted against the door into a puddle of weakened human flesh and tears. He crumpled up on the floor and rolled himself into a naked ball, rocking back and forth and begging for forgiveness from anyone or anything watching him. Quickly his lack of energy forced him to be still.

He wasn't sure how long it was before he heard it. At least five minutes had passed since he had broken down yet it didn't seem like a half-hour had gone by. However long it was, he was still scrunched up in the fetal position when he heard the tapping at the door. It started as a muted, steady rapping sound. It was like a woodpecker looking for breakfast, except it had a distinct metal-on-metal sound. The sound went on for a matter of minutes and with each passing moment it was getting louder. Bull started to realize somebody was trying to make his or her way into the cell. This certainly wasn't what he was expecting when he had cried for help, but he would be glad for any human interaction. And some food. Food and clothing. Then he remembered he was naked and lying on the floor.

As quick as he could, he made his way to the bed. It took him a while to stand up and then to stretch. He hadn't realized how weak the lack of food had made him. He looked at the jumpsuit and realized he really didn't want to put the disgusting rag back on, but he also wasn't going to greet his company in the buff. He experimented with the apparel, trying different ways to wrap himself in it. The clothing was too tough for him to rip in his weakened state. In the end, he wrapped it around his waist, with the dirtiest parts not touching his skin and visible only from behind him. He stood and waited a few moments. The knocking soon became nearly unbearable, as the tapping got closer and closer. Soon, he could see dents on the metal of the door, as the pounding continued. Then, with a loud crack, a thick drill bit made its way through the door. Once it had broken the surface of the metal, it stopped. The jackhammer head was retracted back out of the room. Bull could hear muffled voices outside, questioning yells being answered by an authoritative voice.

It was another two minutes before the door started to open. As it slowly moved, Bull's heart began pounding with the same ferocity as the hammer had attacked the door with moments before. Once it had opened a few inches, it stopped. He could hear the commanding voice tell the others outside to take hold of the door and pull at once. After a count of three, the door was slowly hoisted from its steel frame. A man with a semi-automatic rifle looked in, with another person with the jackhammer peering in over the first man's shoulder. The two men were wearing combat fatigues. Bull didn't recognize either man from his time in prison. The front man yelled out of the room that it was "him," and commanded the people to immediately bring clothes and food. He heard a voice outside confirm the order as the leader approached and took off his camouflage top. The lead newcomer introduced himself as Ronald Roberts then said to Bull, "You look like shit!" Roberts then asked Dukeman if he had eaten recently. Bull answered he had no idea, as he had completely lost track of time.

Roberts told Bull it was August 2nd, nearly two weeks since he had shot and killed the President. Bull admitted he hadn't known if his mission had succeeded. He told Ron (as he he'd already been told to call Roberts in the short time they had known each other) he didn't know anything about the outside world since he had been in prison. Roberts whistled, "buddy, you've missed a lot!" He told Bull to sit down, as they had some time before some clothes and food would make it to the cell. Ron proceeded to tell Bull about what had happened in the country during Gary's captivity. By the time Roberts was done, Bull was dressed, fed and in shock.

The Death of Two Kings, Part Three

As Bull went over to the bed, Ron started his story. Roberts was full of pride when he admitted he was one of the key organizers of the assassination attempt. Ron called himself a high-ranking official in the U.S. intelligence community, a Susspicious Mind, a loyal patriot and a very concerned American. Ron said he had been contacted by renown millionaire and fringe politician Thomas Hannigan. Going back over a decade, Hannigan's exploits to sink Democratic candidates were legendary, especially to Fleet Sussman's most devout listeners. Hannigan made outlandish claims about Left-leaning politicians, and with his fortune always backed his claims up with television commercials featuring people who said they were witnesses to their targets' wrongdoings. When writers from some of the country's most respectable newspapers would question the accusations, Hannigan, Sussman and their like would cite a Liberal bias in the press, and say reporters were suppressing the truth to fix elections. Ron called Hannigan a patriot and an example of American success. Bull, while being vaguely familiar with the businessman, felt that if Hannigan had Sussman's seal of approval he must be an upstanding individual.

Roberts wouldn't say much about his actual position in the government or specify which branch of U.S. intelligence he was with. He did say he had almost the highest levels of clearance and the authority (he stopped short of saying responsibility) to oversee all aspects of the President's security. That had included Rodriguez' itinerary for his trip to West Virginia and the security plans for the visit. When Bull asked Ron where exactly they were, Roberts replied that it was the Marine Corps Base in Quantico, Virginia, not too far from the Washington, D.C. area.

Ron continued his story. He said like Hannigan he had been very frustrated with the direction the country had been taking. He had always been afraid of a shift to the Left, knowing it would mean a softening of American pillars such as free enterprise, the military and Capitalism. They had kept quiet during Obama's tenure, hoping American politics would reverse themselves naturally, but that didn't happen. Instead Rodriguez was elected Obama's successor. Their fears were realized, not only when Rodriguez started to put his agenda into action, but by the President's unpublicized plans for a drawback of military and intelligence operations. The attacks around the start of the year were determined by many experts to be the last gasp of the collective enemy terror machine. Rodriguez of course agreed, and was getting ready to announce the unilateral cutbacks of the nation's defensive forces. Ron and others like him who had a personal interest in the matter decided this was the last straw. It was time to take action to protect the nation, not only from the terrorist threats overseas but from the internal threats Rodriguez and his kind posed.

Roberts and Hannigan had been friends for a long time. Between them, they knew many powerful and influential people in American business, entertainment, defense and politics. Many of those people either helped devise or fund the plan to attack and kill Rodriguez. Just about all of them had been told of the plan and those who were aware of it endorsed it. Roberts had all the connections to make the assassination work. By placing some sympathetic officers at the event in West Virginia, quietly reaching out to a vast anti-Rodriguez demographic in the state and university staff and getting a number of people in on the plan who didn't know anyone, they had what they thought was the best chance to kill the President.

According to Ron the day came and went without a hitch. Rodriguez' escort, composed mostly of people Roberts trusted and who he knew had no love for Rodriguez, pulled off a convincing performance of seeming to have conducted their orders perfectly, while in reality they intentionally put the smallest holes in their net to let Dukeman succeed. The secret service men hadn't done a thorough sweep of the bathroom, and their pre-speech debrief cited the weapons-sniffing dogs hadn't identified any indications of something being amiss. The restroom had been locked most of the time until a school custodian unlocked it five minutes before Bull was to get the air gun. Security's diligence in its job seemed absolute on paper. The guards turned a number of "suspicious" people away from the event, and had been quick to react to minor disturbances between Rodriguez fans and detractors outside of the auditorium. As for the attack, they had made it look like Bull and Mark Carter worked in unison, with Carter having been able to separate the guards and giving Bull the chance to take the shot. In reality, the men were already out of formation and responded slowly to the disruption, placing all their feigned urgency into subduing Carter instead of Bull. It was another intentional act to make it look like they had done their best in the line of duty, when in reality, they were carrying out their role in the plot.

Ron told Bull he had carried out his portion of the mission perfectly. He'd shot the President in the eyes multiple times. Hitting him in the vulnerable part of the skull compensated for the weak power of the air pistol. Still the numerous hits hadn't killed the President immediately. Even though Bull had been ushered out of the auditorium before Rodriguez, it was the President who was taken from the building first. He was rushed by ambulance to the trauma center of the university's hospital group where he was pronounced dead hours later. While his situation was critical when he was brought in, he was stable. However, surgery did not go well, and doctors were unable to save the President. Ron said the surgeons were not in on the plot, and their inability to save Rodriguez' life was genuine and fortuitous.

Much of the nation grieved after the assassination. People from both sides of the traditional political aisle were devastated by the news. The GOP as a whole was genuinely upset about what had happened, and by Ron's assessment, surprisingly strong in renouncing Dukeman's actions.

To most of the United States, Bull Dukeman had become public enemy number-one. It was the moderate Republicans who suggested he be sent to one of the offshore facilities where the country held its terrorist suspects. Even after fifteen years, people captured during the early days of the nation's actions in Afghanistan and Iraq after the 9/11 attacks were still being held at the base. Most were prisoners after drawn-out trials, which extreme Liberals still questioned the validity of. Some still, after over a decade of captivity, hadn't been tried. Few people knew for certain what actually happened to the prisoners at these facilities. Questions and rumors about torture and near-torture techniques still abounded when it came to these prisons. When Roberts mentioned this, Bull asked if that had been waterboarding he had been subjected to that last time the guards had handled him. Ron answered in the affirmative. Bull, who initially agreed with Sussman's belief that the technique wasn't torture, immediately reconsidered that thought.

It was decided behind closed doors in Washington that Dukeman would be interrogated to the fullest extent allowed by law, and perhaps beyond legal parameters. The CIA made a big show of transporting their captive out of the country. The event raised the ire of some human rights groups, but few made a big effort to stop the relocation. The move went without a hitch, except for one problem: The person shown in the jumpsuit and under a CIA windbreaker wasn't actually Dukeman. It was a government agent of similar size to Dukeman who was put in the armored van, then on an Air Force transport. The actual "alleged" gunman would stay near the nation's capital, where the government's top officials and interrogators could have access to him.

And yet, while much of the nation was in mourning over the heinous event, others were unphased by the shooting. Ron said he was among those celebrating Rodriguez' death, at least in private. There were some more brazen people though who weren't ashamed to voice their satisfaction at what had happened. Fleet Sussman and his most loyal listeners were in this group. Many of them called Sussman's show the day after the assassination.

For the first hour of the show, Sussman didn't even bother to address what had happened. Instead, he spoke about the substance of Rodriguez' speech, and how the discussed plans would ruin America. It wasn't until the middle of the show's second hour that the President's death was mentioned. When it did come up, it was first brought up by the show's first caller of the day. Fleet claimed mock ignorance when he heard what had happened from the caller. As other listeners got on the phone, Sussman continued to hold back from saying anything except for thanking everyone for their calls. Instead, he let the Susspicious Minds have their say. Not surprisingly, their opinions were hardly flattering or sympathetic towards Rodriguez. Many were calling the as-of-yet unnamed shooter a hero. A handful of callers stated they had some remorse for what had happened but of those few most still believed Rodriguez had brought death upon himself for trying to turn the country into a Communist state. Through it all, Sussman stayed unusually noncommittal, and pointed out such as the day's broadcast came to an end.

The press was unrelenting in its response to Sussman. His detractors called the show one the lowest points in broadcast history and even some of his staunchest middle-of-the-road supporters were aghast. Sussman did receive support from the ultra-far Right, who stated they were sick of the political correctness members of the GOP were showing.

That first show after Rodriguez' death was nothing compared to the following Monday's production. The mainstream media had all weekend to assail Sussman. In the days between the two broadcasts, it was revealed that Dukeman was the killer, and it was also determined that he was the same man who had become an icon to Sussman's followers. After opening Monday's show with soundbites from national news anchors about the death of Rodriguez, Sussman addressed the situation. He pointed out how, once again, the Liberal pundits were putting words in his mouth. He had been accused of saying all sorts of horrendous things about the President's assassination, but he adamantly pointed out he had said absolutely nothing about what had happened. He then went on the offensive, saying it had been his callers who were excited about what had happened, and said it was a sick violation of the First Amendment for his detractors to suggest his listeners should not be allowed to express their obvious, deserved elation. He stated he had no part in Gary's actions, and Dukeman was just an avid, if overzealous, listener. Sussman neither condemned nor condoned Dukeman's actions and did his best to continue ignoring the subject when he spoke.

Everything else on that Monday's show though belied his true feelings. Ron called it a masterpiece of subliminal suggestion. Sussman's listeners continued to call and say how happy they were with what happened and glorified Dukeman. They were gaining more bravado with every call, feeling as if they no longer had to hide their true feelings. Meantime, the production elements demonstrated Sussman was truly giddy about Rodriguez' death. After his anti-Liberal media tirade to start the show, Sussman went into his first break with "Ding Dong, the Witch is Dead" playing in the background. He used songs such as "Nah Nah, Hey Hey Kiss Him Goodbye," "Thanks for the Memories" and "Happy Trails" to lead him into subsequent commercial breaks. To add to his obvious excitement, he would return to the show by playing soundbites which portrayed the former President in a poor light over his rejoiner music.

It wasn't until Tuesday's show when Sussman weighed in on the matter. His critics had continued to grouse about his despicable demeanor since the death of the President. He opened the show by again saying he had not said anything about what he had felt about the death and protested against those who said his downplaying of the tragedy was evident. He claimed he had nothing to do with the "offensive" music selection, but refused to elaborate on who did, and why so many objectionable songs were played. However, he said he did have an opinion on the situation, which he would reveal towards the end of the show.

Bloggers immediately went to town discussing the revelation. Pundits supporting every conceivable viewpoint in American politics promoted Sussman's upcoming announcement on television and social media sites. The major news networks asked for and received permission to carry the final segment of that day's Fleet Sussman show live. The radio star had played the nation like the media expert he was. The whole nation would be tuned in.

The show between the opening and closing segments was much like the two previous broadcasts but without the use of controversial music cues. By Tuesday, callers were strongly defending Fleet. They proclaimed their gratitude towards Gary Dukeman and their relief the Fascist movement in America was stalled, if not derailed permanently. On this third broadcast after Rodriguez' death, many of the Susspicious Minds were making not-so-veiled threats towards the Left, saying the death of an out-of-control madman was warranted, and the same would happen to Democrats who didn't heed the killing as a warning shot. Despite the blatantly illegal threats made against federal lawmakers, Fleet Sussman refused to challenge his listeners.

Sussman went into his last break later than usual to build the excitement and to make sure his last segment timed out perfectly. He had started scripting the moment ever since he heard Rodriguez had been shot. He had written and rewritten and practiced his speech multiple times and knew exactly how long he needed to make his points. When his rejoiner music started, Sussman let it play for a little while before speaking.

"My friends, these have been extraordinary times for the United States. It is a historic time, and yes, even a tragic time. The President of the United States is dead. It is an event which should sadden everybody in this country. The death of our leader is not a thing anyone ever wants. We are the greatest country in the world, where Democracy and Capitalism reign. We are the land of the free and the home of the brave.

"Up until last November, I believed nothing could ever shake those pillars which our country was based on. For those of us who endured President Obama's tenure, we still believed in this nation. Even Obama often tried to maintain a sense of unity and bipartisanship.

"In November though, my faith in the United States was rocked. A man who I still believe wasn't born in this country was elected President. And he was elected by others who don't belong here. Our country was being invaded by our poor neighbors to the south in an attempt to take us over and bring us down to their level. 'President' Rodriguez,'" the sarcasm dripping from the term as he continued, "made it obvious he was part of this conspiracy. In his short time in office, he did his best to weaken American business by looking to raise taxes and ruin a large part of the energy sector. He chose a fellow Socialist for the Supreme Court, obviously with the intent of destroying American liberty. Maybe he was missing his home, where drug cartels run the government and terrorize the public. Surely he was trying to make everyone in this country as poor as the people of Mexico.

"President Rodriguez was a menace to this country. His election was just the latest step in the Socialist drive to take over, a plan started by Obama. But Rodriguez tried to move way too quickly to make us all drones in his sick system. In months, he had proven we, the people meant nothing to him. He was begging for what happened to him. As far as I'm concerned, he committed suicide.

"As such, Gary Dukeman is a hero, a true patriot for all of us to honor. He saved this country from being led down a dark path, being led blindly by the special interests of the President and his supporters. And Rodriguez' followers should be happy. Dukeman gave him just what he was asking for. If Rodriguez' supporters don't like it, they can all leave the country. They probably aren't supposed to be here in the first place."

With that, Fleet wished everyone listening a good day and told them all to tune in for tomorrow's show. While other media outlets exploded over Sussman's now-official pleasure over what had happened,

Fleet went on planning for the rest of the week on how to deflect the obvious barrage that was headed his way. Little did he, or anyone, know there would be no other installments of the <u>Fleet Sussman Show</u>. Instead, Sussman would begin his show normally that Wednesday, but would be pleading for his life by the end of his opening monologue. "A Spic friend of Rodriguez broke into Sussman's studio that day and shot him. In cold blood, that Villanueva bastard killed an American patriot. But the son of a bitch got his that day too!" Ron went on to say that the funerals for both "the man and the maggot" were held that Sunday, and it was that day that the country erupted into war.

The Death of Two Kings, Part Four

Freddy Villanueva began 2017 thinking it would be one of the best years of his life. He had never felt he had so much to live for as he had then. The younger of his two daughters was certain to graduate from high school as her class' valedictorian and both his children would soon be in college. His older daughter was already off to a great start at SUNY Albany, where she was getting excellent grades while making a name for herself in the student government.

He was almost as proud of his country as he was of his offspring. A fellow Latino would soon be the nation's President, winning November's election and surviving a grueling barrage of unfair attacks from his opposition. In parts of the country, the anti-Rodriguez rhetoric had led to violence, but not in New York. In Spanish Harlem, everyone rejoiced as the election results poured in that Tuesday night.

A similar sense of euphoria swept El Barrio on Inauguration Day, as Eduardo Rodriguez was sworn in as the 45th President of the United States. It was an unofficial local holiday all over Harlem as proud people from many races came together. Freddy had heard stores on 125th Street wheeled televisions out to their windows and cranked speakers so passersby could watch and listen to the festivities taking place on the steps of the Capitol. He had seen news reports from Harlem's main drag where people flowed into the street, stopping traffic, chanting "Eddie! Eddie!" Many motorists honked, not for the sake of being delayed, but in celebration.

A few blocks south, Spanish Harlem was also abuzz as Rodriguez was sworn in. Block parties were held to watch the event on Jumbotron trucks rented and paid for by community pots raised to celebrate the historic event. There was chanting as well, calling the incoming President by his last name. Like Roberto Clemente generations before him, Eduardo Rodriguez tried to keep the press from Anglo-izing his name. His didn't face the same amount of resistance as the Pittsburgh Pirates star had, but there were still plenty of people who insisted on calling the President-Elect "Edward." Friends and foes alike seemed to like using Eddie, although the President tried to insist at times on using a more professional name. In El Barrio - and in many Latino communities around the United States - he proudly remained Eduardo.

Freddy and his family watched the ceremony at one such block party. Trailers and food trucks serving fast Mexican and Dominican favorites were set up along the street and a DJ played music kept low enough as to not drown out the Inaugural broadcast. Still the music was quickly muted as Eduardo Rodriguez began to recite the Oath of Office of the President of the United States. After Rodriguez finished, the television flashed the headline "Edward Rodriguez becomes 45th President of the United States." Everyone around Freddy cheered loudly. Villanueva was certain he could hear the yells from the huge party on Martin Luther King Jr. Boulevard mixed in with his own hoots and those of the people immediately near him. The fanfare didn't last too long however. The jubilant viewers hushed each other up to listen to Rodriguez' first speech as the leader of the free world. When the President was done speaking in Washington, there were many teary eyes in Spanish Harlem, and shouts of joy.

The frivolity continued all night in Freddy's neighborhood with friends and strangers alike congratulating one another with handshakes, high-fives and hugs. The Villanuevas watched everything on the mobile big screen, with Meagan skipping school to spend the happy, historic day

91

with her family. Like many of the high school seniors playing hooky in the neighborhood, Meagan was allowed a couple of celebratory drinks as the afternoon went on. Everyone stayed around as the Washington party moved from the Capitol down Pennsylvania Avenue to the White House. As day turned to evening and President Rodriguez started his ball crawl, the street the Villanuevas lived on also turned into a dance hall. Even as the nighttime chill took hold after the sun went down, the parties in the middle of Manhattan continued. It was about 2 a.m. when the festivities came to an end, both in Washington and New York. According to news reports the following week, NYPD's 23rd Precinct reported a staggering drop in crime in the neighborhood all day Friday and into Saturday morning, despite the fact that almost all the apartments in the region were empty as people celebrated.

The cheerful mood continued through the weekend, although many people in El Barrio soon developed colds due to their late-night partying. The overnight low was an unseasonably "warm" 42 degrees that night and many people were underdressed as the day had also been exceptionally warm.

There was still a bit of euphoria come that Monday as the Villanuevas returned to their employment and learning endeavors. Freddy worked full-time at a furniture distribution warehouse on the Bronx side of the East River, not far from where Eduardo Rodriguez had grown up. The building had an unusual but expected buzz about it as the week began. A small handful of Freddy's peers were especially excited, knowing Rodriguez personally from the neighborhood or school. As one such person said, she never dreamed in a million years she would be personal friends with the leader of the United States.

Despite the fervor, the men and women in the building did admirably to conduct business as though it was a normal day. Freddy returned home feeling content. He reflected on his bus ride home he felt more secure than he could ever remember during his lifetime. Meagan was four months away from graduating high school and she and her older sister Maya would both be at SUNY Albany in September. Between their choices of staying at a state school, the scholarships both girls had earned as high school students and the financial borrowing plans Rodriguez was expected to pass early in his presidency, Freddy was hoping the money the family had saved for higher education could become added retirement savings for the parents. In the last year, with Meagan sure to receive financial gifts to attend Albany, Freddy had already limited himself to just one job. Soon, he hoped to tell his wife she didn't have to work anymore, that they had enough to support themselves on his slightly meager but nonetheless decent earnings. Maybe the couple would move up to the state capital as well, where the cost of living was lower and where it would barely cost anything for the children to visit. When he asked at work about possible opportunities upstate, he was told the company had another warehouse in the region and his supervisors would be open to discussing a transfer for him.

Freddy's jubilant mood lasted until dinner. He crossed the threshold to his apartment humming a song which had been stuck in his mind since Friday's celebrations. As usual, he made his way to the kitchen to find his wife preparing dinner, where he gave her his traditional kiss on the cheek and a stronger-than-usual hug from behind. The subtle change to the embrace did not go unnoticed, as Nicole Villanueva chuckled and said she was looking forward to the next four years.

Freddy answered with another quick squeeze before correcting his love. "Eight years," was all he said, and added another kiss. Without turning away from the stove, Nicole blushed, bowed her head and admitted her error. The two were discussing the brave new world when about five minutes later they heard the front door open. Meagan was home at her normal time. She popped into the kitchen quickly to say hello and kiss her parents, before heading to her room to start her homework. It was this devotion to her studies, Freddy thought proudly, which made her an honor student.

Nicole soon called out that dinner was ready, and father and daughter sat at the dining table. Instead of having small dining and living rooms, the two were combined into a nice-sized common area. Most of the food was already out, so Nicole was only a couple of seconds later in joining her family. The Villanuevas swapped stories about their days, and how people where they had been that day were so exuberant about what had happened the previous Friday. Both mother and father had nothing but positive experiences to report. Meagan's day hadn't been as much fun.

For the most part, the youngest Villanueva's day was much like everyone else's at the table. Everyone in school was just as excited as she was, and the inauguration was discussed as part of every class Meagan was in. Even her science teacher Mr. Montera found a way to include it in discussion.

Things took a depressing turn towards the end of the day, when Internet reports cropped up about the <u>Fleet Sussman Show</u> that morning and afternoon. Sussman was a familiar name in the school for his outlandish comments, but until that point, few students could say for certain why they knew of him. While working in the computer lab,

Meagan read about Fleet's comments, in which he alluded to people of Hispanic descent being foreigners. That seemed tame though, compared to the suggestion that it would have been a perfect time for a terrorist attack on the nation's capital.

Meagan immediately turned to her friend Alisha, who was sitting at the station next to her. Meagan read the comments to her friend, but it was another friend, Alexei, who responded first. "Shit," he said, "I was one of those people who went down there!" With a worried look on his face, he pointed out he was as proud an American as Sussman. He looked slightly ashen as he pointed out that the radio star had essentially wished death upon him and his family.

Meagan told her parents as they ate how Alexei's reaction turned out to be how many of the kids at school had felt. A number of their classmates and their families had also gone to Washington. The primarily Latino student body felt as a whole Sussman's stereotypical tirade was a personal, unfair slight about each of them and it was wrong for Sussman to generalize about the lives the radio host believed they lived and were all destined to lead. Meagan pointed out to her parents that Alexei was also headed to college on a scholarship, and was also among the top students in their class. Who was Sussman to suggest Alexei, or anyone, was a bad person just based on where his family came from? Neither Freddy nor Nicole had an answer, but all three of them knew well the biases that festered in some people.

Freddy went to bed with Meagan's revelations fresh in his mind. Like his daughter and her friends, he had a vague familiarity of Sussman and some of his more outlandish comments, but none had bothered him as much as those attributed to him that day. None of them had hit home the way this had. He'd never had to explain racial inequalities or strife to her, not nearly to the extent his parents had to when he was a teen. That wasn't to say they didn't have to have talks when somebody threw racial epithets at Meagan, but her schooling had done better to prepare her for the intolerance of the outside world, and Freddy would say there were less racially-motivated incidents than he remembered. During Obama's time in office, as gay marriage opponents lost more and more ground in their fight, they seemed to get their satisfaction from slights and violence against homosexuals. The physical attacks were few and far between, but were on the rise in some states. With their attention on fighting homosexuality, their anger against other people they tended to dislike subsided. It was as if all the hatred in the country stemmed from one group of people and they only had the power to focus it at one target at a time. It seemed to Freddy it had become the Hispanics' time. There had been some hostility towards Latinos for a number of years as immigration reform was addressed in Washington but nothing as venomous as what Sussman had said that day.

Freddy's mind was still on Sussman's comments when he woke up in the morning. He was glad at least it wasn't something he lost sleep over, but the derogative ideas were still nagging the proud father. Freddy was happy to see when he got to work that many of his coworkers felt the same way, especially his fellow parents who had similar discussions with their children.

For the first time anyone could remember, the radio in the warehouse that Tuesday was not on a music station. Instead, everyone wanted to hear what Sussman would say in response to his own words and his critics. Freddy and his friends and anyone else who tuned in for the same reason, weren't given the satisfaction of listening to what they had hoped was to be the radio host pleading for his job. Instead, the show started with a network spokesperson reading a statement about Sussman being suspended for Monday's rant. Then a clip of an older show, focusing on then-President Obama, started to play.

Sussman's detractors were caught off guard when he returned to his show the following Monday. Again, it was Meagan who alerted her father to the radio host's doings. Sussman's three-week ban was cut down to one. He returned with little publicity from the network, which while happy to have its top star back, didn't want to admit it had caved to the listeners' and advertisers' demands. Freddy surprised himself when he admitted to his daughter that he had been looking forward to hearing Fleet's return. He was curious what Sussman would say, and was hoping to hear him squirm. Instead, Freddy became angry as Meagan read a transcript of the star's monologue off the Internet. Sussman offered a backhanded apology. Freddy thought Sussman's attempt to say he hadn't wished for an attack fell far from its mark. Fleet mentioned he had nothing against Latino-Americans, but he made his remarks about illegal immigrants sound as if they were meant for everyone in the Latino community. Once again, Sussman asserted the President was not a legal citizen, and that made Freddy's stomach turn. He was disgusted when Meagan read to him about Sussman's listeners staunchly supporting the claim they would all suffer under the new, illegitimate President.

This time though, Villanueva's feelings didn't simmer the way they had the week before. By the time he woke up that Tuesday, he was instead thinking of - ironically enough - the upcoming Presidents' Day weekend. This time when he got to work, nobody mentioned what had happened on the radio. If Freddy had taken a moment to think about it, he probably would have figured everyone else had also missed Fleet's return. Sussman instead remained out of Villanueva's mind for weeks. When Sussman reintroduced himself to Freddy, he did so with a bang.

During Fleet's absence from Freddy's life, the latter had turned away from politics. He had never been much of a follower of the political engine, so long as his life remained status quo. He'd been told Rodriguez had been doing a good job, and since there wasn't anything major upsetting his routine, Villanueva accepted the observation as truth. Then came the attack.

Once again, it was Meagan who had brought Sussman to her parents' attention, this time with a yelp of surprise from her bedroom one March evening. Both older Villanuevas rushed to Meagan's door. Nicole knocked and asked if everything was okay. Meagan responded by saying she was fine, and asked her parents to come in.

Both parents entered the room. Meagan found time to keep her small, windowless bedroom clean, despite being a star student. Even the upper bunk, which had been hers until Maya moved out to college, looked welcoming should anyone need a place to sleep. Meagan was lying on the lower bed, with her tablet in hand. Before Nicole could repeat her question, Meagan pressed a button on the tablet. A video started running on the minicomputer as the child held it up to her parents. The digital recording seemed to be from a cellphone, and showed a crowd of people. They were angrily kicking at the ground and yelling. It was half-a-minute into the video that it became obvious this crowd was a mob, stomping on some downed victim or victims. As the attack let up, it became apparent the assailants were Caucasian, while their targets were Latino. The video then turned to a news anchor, who said this incident had happened in West Virginia the previous night. The report pointed out that the region had been hit hard by Rodriguez' decision to curtail a mining procedure known as "mountaintop removal." The video then cut to a film of the alleged attackers being let out of jail. One of them yelled out something about taking back what was theirs. The anchor explained this was a comment similar to one which Fleet Sussman had said recently, to one such miner who called his show, who had mentioned he had lost his job to somebody of Hispanic descent. The report did not reference the caller saying anything about mountaintop removal. The video ended and Meagan turned off the computer. "Why does Sussman hate us so?" the daughter asked. Nobody responded.

It was a question that this time did cause Freddy to lose sleep. In a matter of months, Sussman went from an outlandish radio person who Villanueva knew little about to a dangerous, loose cannon. Freddy couldn't remember any of his comments leading to physical confrontation before that point, not that he'd paid close attention. More to the point, this time the comments were hitting close to home. Never had he seen his family concerned about what the radio star said nor had they ever discussed Sussman until then. Freddy was saddened that his daughter and all Latino children were having to live in fear over what somebody said on the radio.

The following day at work, Freddy tried something he'd never done before: he tried calling the Fleet Sussman Show. For the first time he considered himself fortunate for getting a state-of-the-art, ear piece-only phone which his daughters insisted he needed. His friends had gotten microcomputers which doubled as phones, but his small receiver fit snug around his ear, and worked solely on voice activation. It allowed him to call the show without interfering with his work, and he was able to program it to keep redialing through all the busy signals. It took 40 minutes until the other end of the line started to ring. It took another five minutes for somebody to pick up the line. Freddy gave his name, said he was calling from the Bronx, was of Mexican descent and he and his family were quite upset about the host's comments since Rodriguez took office.

The person who answered told Freddy to hold on to talk to Fleet. Freddy was placed on hold but was able to listen to the show through his earpiece as he continued with his daily routine. Freddy listened to the broadcast, concentrating as much as he could through work. Mostly though it was just background noise. When he was able to digest what was being said, he was far from impressed. Freddy had apparently missed Sussman's denying that he had anything to do with the West Virginia attack. It seemed the host said he couldn't be held responsible for how others interpreted what he said, or how they acted upon his words. Villanueva was able to determine the gist of Sussman's apology by the way the other callers were agreeing with his version of the situation. Some hinted that it was the attackers, having lost their jobs to those they attacked, who were the actual victims. Few seemed anxious to point out that the lead attacker considered himself a Fleet Sussman fan.

Freddy had lost track of time and the show when the broadcast was cut off in his earpiece and someone spoke to him. "Hello, Freddy?" the same person who had answered the phone was back on the line. When Freddy responded, she told him Fleet didn't have time to talk to him and thanked him for the call. Freddy looked at his watch. There was still a half-hour to go before the show ended and it had been over an hour since he had been on hold. When Freddy tried to protest, the producer apologized quickly and hung up.

Freddy was annoyed by the whole situation. He thought back to the time he was on hold and could count at least seven distinct callers he'd heard. Those were only the ones he remembered and he knew there had been others. He was pretty sure Sussman's station didn't have the number of lines needed to keep all the callers on hold that whole time. He came to the conclusion that Sussman just didn't want to talk to him. He had a few guesses as to why, none of which stretched far beyond elitism or racism.

From that point on, Sussman became a regular topic at the Villanueva dinner table. Meagan, having heard about her fathers' futile attempts to call the show, was making an active effort to see what Fleet was up to. It became a project for school as well, where she and her friends wanted to keep other students aware of the misstatements being made by the media about people of different origins. She'd bring her extracurricular work home with her, to parents who were just as concerned and scared for their children. Much of the time there wasn't much racial rhetoric. However, there was plenty of Rodriguez-bashing. Anything the President did, even things which the Villanuevas thought would be liked by his opponents, was wrong to the Sussman fans.

Outside of the sometimes dismal dinner discussion, it was happy times for the Villanuevas. Meagan continued to do well in school, even though it was the second semester of her senior year. Things also went well for her sister upstate. The youngest Villanueva graduated in late June and the family celebrated. There was little concern about college, as her sister and soon-to-be college roommate started to tell her stories of Albany. As a fine student who would room with her sister, there was little fretting compared to what many freshmen went through. Instead the summer started quietly, with Meagan taking a job tutoring younger kids in the neighborhood and her parents silently planning to move upstate with their children.

Meagan's attention to the <u>Fleet Sussman Show</u> dwindled, as it wasn't a project she wanted to continue over the summer. News of Justice Scalia's stroke, Rodriguez' replacement pick and his taxes rhetoric passed without much speculation in the Villanueva apartment. So did the response of Fleet and the Susspicious Minds. All that changed on July 26th, when the President was assassinated in West Virginia.

The Death of Two Kings, Part Five

July 20th, 2017 started off as a normal summer morning in the Bronx and all over the country. Freddy, Nicole and Meagan had all left their apartment together for their various jobs that Wednesday morning. Nicole quickly said her goodbyes as she turned the other way down the block to get to work, leaving father and daughter to walk to the corner bus stop together. The remaining Villanuevas boarded the same city bus headed uptown and to the Bronx. Meagan got off first, while the transport was still on Manhattan Island. She attempted to hug her father, but the bus was already packed with commuters. Instead, she blew him a kiss as she jumped from the back ramp and onto the curb. She was off to help a young teen with his mathematics. The boy had barely avoided summer school, but was lagging behind his classmates in algebra. Meagan, not worried about saving too much for college because of her scholarship, offered to help the child for a modest price just for some summer spending cash. She was highly trusted by the faculty at her now alma mater, and the teachers were always quick to point out good students to her She therefore was willing to take a lower fee from this family. She liked working with kids who wanted to do better in school, and whose parents didn't shirk away from their responsibilities when it came to their children's education.

Freddy got off the bus and walked the last two blocks to work. As always, he was early and some of his coworkers were already in the staff room. Freddy grabbed a bagel from the small shop in the warehouse and finished it moments before he was scheduled to be on the floor.

He was loading a truck for delivery when his earphone signaled he had an incoming text message from his daughter. He told the phone to read him the message. The automated female voice lacked the emotion for the message it relayed, but Freddy could hear Meagan sobbing through her message as though she was the one saying the four words the phone's processor recited: "The President's been shot!"

Freddy exclaimed "Holy shit!" but was able to hold onto the antique hardwood desk he had been helping to schlep into the truck, The cry caught the attention of everyone around him, but it wasn't until he put the desk down that he explained his outburst. "Meagan says someone fuckin' shot the President!" he explained, fighting back tears.

Freddy and everyone who had been on the floor around him finished their immediate tasks and ran to the staff room. Other loaders and drivers were already in there, huddled around the television. Those who were already in the room said the shooting had happened about an hour before. The station replayed the graphic instant countless times and it didn't take long for Freddy and the newcomers to see the footage. A look of horror crossed the President's face before his eye burst into a pool of crimson. One of the people in the room remarked how television stations wouldn't have allowed such a scene to be shown over and over again years before.

The shift manager then burst into the room, livid. "What the fuck's going on in here?!" he yelled. Everyone just looked at him, with one of the truck drivers pointing to the television. The boss then appealed to God in Spanish and his anger immediately dissipated. Even if he had been able to remain mad and pretended to not care about the situation, he wouldn't have been able to do anything. Many of the men and women in the room had personal ties to the President, a local product, hero and near-savior. The manager watched with everyone for nearly fifteen minutes before pointing out they still had guaranteed deliveries which needed to ship. Most of those orders were already on the trucks, so despite sympathizing with the involved drivers, he ordered them back to work. They complied without complaint, but the manager allowed everyone else to remain in the room for some time.

Slowly Freddy's coworkers started returning to work even though there had been no update on the President's condition. It was only minutes after Freddy left the room when somebody turned the building's PA to one of the local radio news stations. The regular anchors on the station had given way to a national network feed, and commercials and regularly-scheduled traffic reports had disappeared. At the warehouse in the Bronx, the day went by slowly and work slowed to a near-stop. Everyone kept an ear to the nearest speaker. The reports and speculation were not promising. Experts who were interviewed watched the video and listened to what they could hear from the paramedics on the scene. They said there was a possibility the President would survive, but even if he did, he likely would have severe brain damage. Government officials and the police in West Virginia were staying silent.

The speculation became much more sinister within an hour. Without any news still on the President's condition, there were confirmed reports that Vice President Sydney Armitage had been sworn in as President. Nobody on the broadcast seemed to know what to make of the news, but they already had the audio recording of the moment. Arguments erupted on the radio. Some figured that meant Rodriguez was dead, as no VP had ever been sworn for emergency reasons for anything short of the President's death. Even if Rodriguez was still alive, everyone on the other end of the airwaves was saying with certainty that he must've been injured so badly that he wasn't going to be able to resume his term for an extended time, if ever.

A while after Armitage had been sworn in the White House announced a press conference to take place within the next half-hour. Freddy, like everyone else around him, finished what he was doing and went back to the staff room. Everybody was somber and hushed. After a short eternity, the television image faded to Vice President Armitage. He was sitting at the President's desk in the oval office. Armitage seemed stunned as he looked directly into the camera and started speaking:

"My fellow Americans. It is with tremendous sadness that I address you today as the President of the United States. Eduardo Rodriguez was shot and killed this morning, after giving a speech in West Virginia. Details about the heinous event will be announced later today, but I will confirm now the gunman is in federal custody and there is an ongoing investigation. It would not be appropriate for me to say much more at this time, without knowing much about the situation or the killer. Instead, it is time for the nation to mourn this tragic loss. The death of the President of the United States is something which hurts us all.

"I want to take this time to offer my condolences and prayers to the Rodriguez family, especially his wife Stephanie, his son Antonio and his daughter Michelle. I became close to the Rodriguezes during the campaign, and my family and theirs became close friends. We grieve with them as though we lost a family member ourselves.

"I was sworn in shortly before the President's death, when it was apparent he would not be able to continue in his office. It was with a heavy heart that I accepted the responsibility, as I knew at that moment how truly grave the condition of my friend was. I will miss Eddie, who was more than just a close confidant and running mate. He was indeed a true friend, and the charisma and care for others he displayed during our campaign was genuine. In the short time that he was President, he already had passed a number of items to promote equality and to help protect our environment. He had planned to continue fighting for these ideals which he too believed in, to make the world a better place for everybody. I will do my best to keep his dreams alive and see his goals come to fruition. I will continue to fight for his most recent ideas, such as closing the gaps in the tax code, and I will keep supporting Brian Payton's bid to become a Supreme Court Justice. I will also keep to President Rodriguez' schedule to bring our troops home from the Middle East.

"While we aren't sure who the shooter is or how or why he committed this despicable act, one thing remains clear: this is a time when our great nation must pull together and 'we the people' must have love and compassion for one another. The death of the President is a tragic loss for us all, but we will remain strong and find our way out of this dark hour.

"Thank you. God bless the Rodriguez family, God bless us all and God bless the United States of America."

There was a pause on the station, and a graphic of the President, with his name and the years he was born and died, printed under his smiling face. In the break room in the Bronx warehouse, people were hugging and consoling one another. Tears were flowing freely. Freddy was sobbing while embracing one of his co-workers when Meagan called. He answered the call by just saying, "I'm sorry." All he could hear from his daughter was uncontrolled wails of sadness and grief. He let her cry for a minute before offering to come meet her where she had been tutoring. He could be there within a half hour. Freddy wasn't positive Meagan had given her approval to the idea, but decided to leave just to be safe. Before he could ask his boss for permission to leave, the manager announced the warehouse was closing for the day. Somberly, people filed out of the room and left the building.

Freddy arrived at the apartment building Meagan had been working in in 20 minutes. As he walked down the street, he could see her sitting on the staircase outside with the boy she had been tutoring. Even from a distance, Freddy could tell both children had wet, red eyes. Some people who passed them before Freddy reached the stoop nodded to the boy and girl, greeting them with sad smiles. When the father reached them, his daughter sobbed again. Instead of the lunge and grab Freddy had expected, Meagan put her arms out, and hoisted herself up on her father when he reached to hug her. The young woman's usual energy had been drained. As she took to standing on her own, Freddy offered his condolences to the boy as well, then asked if he would be okay and if anyone else was home. He said he would be fine as his grandmother also lived in the building. He would go to her once they left. With that, Meagan grabbed her book bag from the step, kissed the boy on the forehead, and grabbed her father's hand to lead him down the street.

When they got to the bus stop, Meagan protested. "Do we have to go straight home? I want to go somewhere with you." The father agreed. It was still early afternoon, and he would have had another couple of hours of work ahead of him if he hadn't been dismissed.

Meagan led her father across the street. They got on the bus they would normally take in the morning. Meagan put her still-active student pass into the fare-collecting machine. The city had started allowing students in summer school, as well as recent graduates whose schools reported the former students were working in ways which benefited the education system, free bus service over summers. However, the machine beeped in disapproval, as Meagan was traveling the wrong direction for the time of day. The driver was about to protest, but took a look at Meagan's dirtied, sadden face and pointed with her head for the teenager to get on board. Freddy thanked the driver for both of them.

The bus made its way over the Third Avenue Bridge and into the Bronx. They quickly rode back past the warehouse where Freddy worked as the bus continued up Third Ave. Meagan pressed the "stop requested" tape as they approached 163rd Street. The dad was surprised when the transport all but emptied at the same stop they disembarked at. He would have expected it if the Yankees were playing at home, as the Stadium was about a mile away, however the team was on a West Coast road trip (Freddy hadn't heard at the time that the commissioner of Major League Baseball had already postponed all games that evening). He was even more perplexed when he realized everyone was going in the same direction, away from the Stadium and the way his daughter was leading him.

After walking a couple of blocks, Freddy realized what was happening. Ahead of them was a stream of people, all turning into the same apartment complex. Some people carried American flags while many had flowers and candles in their hands. This was where Eduardo Rodriguez had grown up and where his parents still lived. There was a strong police presence in front of one building which must've been the one in the development in which he grew up. The elder Villanueva also saw men in dark suits around the entryway, which he figured were federal secret service officers.

Despite being early afternoon visitors started lighting the candles they had brought with them. The sullen crowd was singing songs, alternating between songs of patriotism, religion and solidarity, in English and Spanish, famous in both the U.S. and Puerto Rico. Even though there were hundreds - if not thousands - of people now in the courtyard of the complex, Meagan and Freddy were both able to find friends among the mourners. The father and daughter were able to talk with their friends but remained within eyesight of each other. An hour had passed when Freddy called his wife. He could tell by the tone and wavering of Nicole's voice that she already knew. It wasn't surprising in this age of instant communication. "Don't worry about us for dinner," Freddy said to Nicole on the phone, "I'm in the Bronx with Meagan. We'll grab a couple of slices whenever we leave here."

That departure wasn't until after 9 p.m., six hours after they had arrived outside the building. They had already eaten by the time they left, as the mother of one of Meagan's friends who lived in the complex had brought them out tamales and soda. Friends of Freddy had brought down candles, and father and daughter were part of the candlelight vigil which the local media estimated was over two-thousand-people strong. It was 10:30 when the two walked through the front door of their apartment. Nicole was in the dining/living room, watching the television. When Freddy and Meagan came into the room, the mother walked over to her child and put one arm around her upper back while cradling Meagan's head between her left arm and right shoulder. Meagan started crying again and said she was scared. Nicole told her it was okay and that just because a madman had killed someone they respected and loved tremendously, that didn't mean the girl had anything to worry about.

Over the next few days though, it became apparent that the words of consolation may not have been true. The video of the incident itself showed two people were involved in the attack. The day after the event, it was announced that while the names of the alleged attackers were still being withheld, the two men were unlikely to have had any connection to each other. Many media analysts were quick to wonder how many people were truly involved and who those others might be. While security experts were able to pick out anomalies here and there in describing what went wrong, the notion of a conspiracy was limited.

Freddy, his family and many of his friends were among the people who did believe there had been some sort of larger plot against Rodriguez. The irony that their one-time local politician had been killed in the same state where weeks before there had been a biased attack against Latino people was not lost on them. The identity of the killer furthered that belief. It was announced on Saturday that the killer had been one Gary Dukeman, and the man was quickly connected to Fleet Sussman and the attacks in West Virginia.

The funeral for Rodriguez was that Sunday. In the tradition of John F. Kennedy's assassination, the President's body was brought to the White House that afternoon, and was scheduled to be brought to the Capitol to lie in state a couple of days later. Meagan asked her parents about going to Washington for the ceremonies, but they both had safety concerns. The child put up a small protest, pointing out how her mother had said they had nothing to worry about. The parents changed their argument to one of overnight safety and finances, and Meagan took the amended defense for what it was worth. Instead, she stayed home that weekend, spending a large amount of time reading political posts online and following what Fleet and his listeners were up to.

What she read frightened her. From what she could tell of the show the day after the assassination, Fleet was barely interested in discussing the incident and downplayed its significance. The anti-Sussman crowd considered this to be a disgrace, considering how he would often pick up on the smallest little piece of minutia on his show to make a never-ending point around it. Detractors said to intentionally play down the travesty of the century was a mockery of the worst degree. What made Meagan nervous though was amongst Sussman and his listeners, it was the host who seemed to be the voice of reason. The Susspicious Minds were not as concerned about political correctness. On Friday's show, they started suggesting the triggerman be released from prison and given the Congressional Medal of Honor. On the Internet, there were suggestions to make July 20th a national holiday and that Rodriguez had it coming to him.

The notion that the shooter was a hero was appalling to the child. To Meagan and all the people she knew personally, he was not so much a murderer as he was a man guilty of treason and worthy of the ultimate punishment such a charge carried. That was her feeling even before finding out it was the same man who had incited the previous West Virginia incident, and that he was a regular on Sussman's show.

Sunday came and went and the family watched the funeral on television. Maya came down from Albany, feeling the need to have the people she loved most around her at that time. The Villanuevas sat silently during the ceremonies on TV as the President's casket was moved from Washington Cathedral to the White House.

After the procession arrived at the White House, Meagan left her family in the living room and went to check on the Internet again for the latest from the Susspicious Minds. It wasn't long before she cried out to the living room, and ran back to be with her family. She then handed her tablet around the room, starting with Nicole, who was the closest to where Meagan was standing. On the official Fleet Sussman posting boards, his fans were having a field day. The most recent items were mocking the ceremony and those who they figured were moved by it. There was an undeniable racial undertone to the writings. It was suggested that all Mexicans should go back south of the border or they would be sent "south" just as Rodriguez had been. Now that it was known that fellow listener Gary Dukeman was the killer, the praise for him grew. A number of posters said they wished they could have had the honor of being there to pull the trigger. Some said they had admired Dukeman since his first call and all demanded his release and safety.

The Villanuevas were all crestfallen as they read the posts appearing on the tablet's screen. Meagan looked at her mother, who returned the gaze with knowing eyes. The mother looked at her daughter apologetically, with Nicole silently saying she was sorry. The posts displayed unabashed hatred, from their cheering for the death of Rodriguez to an unending display of ignorance by posters who considered anyone of Latino ancestry to be "Mexican." Freddy watched the wordless exchange with fear and anger. His own growing hatred for Sussman would double the following night, when the family had dinner and Meagan relayed through her tears what Sussman had done during Monday's show. The music selection for the show made it obvious to the child that while Sussman still wasn't vocalizing his feelings, he was obviously giddy about what had happened the previous week.

After Monday's dinner, Freddy told his family he was going for a walk to clear his mind. He said he wanted some privacy, but still left the apartment with his microphone.

Freddy went downstairs and knocked on the door of one of his neighbors. Charles Rosales was not one of Freddy's favorite people in the world. Rosales made no attempt to hide the fact that he had a sketchy background and still led a questionable lifestyle. However, Rosales did try to be a model neighbor, and if he had anything illicit going on in his life (Freddy admittedly wasn't certain), he didn't bring it to the building with him. Charles was also very friendly and seemed to take a genuine interest in caring for and protecting all the children in the building. This included the Villanueva offspring. While Freddy wouldn't want Rosales babysitting his children, he didn't mind that his children seemed to have an amiable rapport with the neighbor. We could have worse neighbors, Freddy would think at times, then he'd remind himself he undoubtedly did have worse neighbors.

Charles opened the door to his unit and voiced his surprise to see Freddy standing there.

"Hey, Charles, may I come in?"

Rosales let his visitor into the apartment. Freddy noted a video security monitor focused on the entryway to Charles' apartment. Charles' system allowed him to see who was at the door while most people in the building, including the Villanuevas, still only had peepholes. Freddy also noted how nice Charles' apartment looked and thought the furniture and the state-of-the-art 3D-TV were a little too new and too high-priced for the average person who lived in the building.

"So what brings you down here?" The out-of-the-ordinary house call apparently made Charles as uneasy as Freddy had been knocking on the door. "How are the kids?"

"They're both home, and they are both are... Concerned. That's why I'm here."

Charles became a little defensive, "I didn't do anything..."

Freddy chuckled nervously, knowing what he said had come out of his mouth wrong. "No, you didn't. I'm sorry, I didn't mean to seem to be accusing you of something, but... Well, you do have a certain reputation."

"Are you accusing me of something or not?" Charles looked both agitated and amused, and unsure which state he would be in after Freddy finished his statement.

The visitor decided to change his tact. "The girls are scared, but it has nothing to do with anything around them physically. The President's murder is really frightening them, especially Meagan. It's not just the shooting though. Do you know who Fleet Sussman is?"

The mention of the talk show host launched Rosales into a Spanish tirade of anti-Caucasian epithets. All Freddy could do was laugh and say "si." Charles then asked what that had to do with anything.

"I know somebody who works in the building where Sussman's studio is. I think I could get into the studio to see that bastard."

"That's nice," Charles responded, "what does that have to do with me?"

"I... I want a gun."

Rosales looked at Freddy with an odd sneer. "You sure about that? Do you think you can do it? Do you want to do that to your girls?"

Freddy had been hoping for a protest, but one that was earnestly trying to talk him out of what he was suggesting. "I want to do it for the girls," he responded, "I don't want them living in fear."

"You do this, and they will have to live in more fear all their lives! Those gringos are loco," Charles played up his natural accent, which had been missing for most of the conversation, "Look at what they did. Do you think they'll be afraid of you? They keep fighting to keep their guns, say it's for protection. They will use them against you, against your family, Heck, even perhaps against me, even if they have no reason to think I'm connected to this. Look at the last ten years. They talk like anyone who is not like them is an animal. They mocked Obama during both his campaigns, as they did Eddie. Each time, getting more serious."

"And that's why we have to stop them now. We have to show them we're not going to take it anymore!"

"Dude, take it from me, they are waiting for something to happen. They funnel their stupidity through Sussman. If he's gone... If he's gone, they will take it to the next level."

Freddy was getting angry again, "then how do we stop this?"

Charles hunched his shoulders and shook his head, "I don't know," he said, "but I know enough to tell your idea will only make things worse."

Freddy stewed for a second. He looked down and ran his tongue over his teeth. He looked back up and responded as though he hadn't heard the objection, "will you get me a gun? Tell me yes or no and how much I'll owe you."

Charles told him to return the following evening and gave him a price. He then unceremoniously asked Freddy to leave the apartment. Freddy left the flat and the building. He walked down the street, thinking about the exchange. His frustration seeped into his thoughts. He figured Rosales, with his spotty history and without kids of his own, couldn't understand. If he was such a good judge of people and smart enough to think he knew the situation so well, why was he a two-bit criminal?

Freddy walked over by the Metro North elevated tracks and walked along the large stone structure. The manmade ramp supported the tracks which bolted out of the ground from Grand Central Terminal downtown and towards the north. With little curb space and no real sidewalk against the wall, few people walked on that side of the street. Once he was satisfied he had enough privacy, he called his cousin Nick.

Nick was a custodian in the building where Sussman worked. It was something Nick used to mention with both pride and disdain in years past even if Freddy hadn't cared much before that moment. Freddy knew Nick had no love for Sussman as Nick sometimes spoke about the insults he had to endure from the star and his staff. Fleet's disregard for non-Judeo-Christian, non-Caucasian people was genuine. Sussman had once accused Nick of stealing something from the studio. Even though the item was found pretty quickly and there was no evidence of any wrongdoing, Nick received no apology but instead was barred from doing any work in Sussman's studio or offices. That suited Nick fine.

Nick's dislike of the star didn't end there. Like Freddy's immediate family, he too was disgusted by what Sussman said on-air. Nick had to endure the show daily, because as a courtesy to their most famous tenant, the building's owners wanted it to be heard in all public areas within the structure. On a couple of occasions since Meagan had started giving her father updates on the program, the cousins had discussed Sussman's show. In their talks, Nick said more than once he would be extremely happy the day somebody put Sussman in his place.

Freddy told Nick what he was thinking of and wasn't surprised when Nick immediately agreed to help. Despite increased security he could easily get Freddy access to Fleet's studio. He was very familiar with the portion of the building Fleet rented and how it was situated. In recent days Sussman had increased his private security, however Nick told Freddy he'd heard the added rent-a-cops were overconfident and continually overlooked a utility entrance near the studio door. Building staff paid extra attention to these matters and often spoke about them, as though they all hoped someday somebody might act on the information. After discussing the basic frame of the plan, the cousins said they'd each work on certain aspects of the plan and talk again soon. Freddy disconnected the line and started back home. When he arrived he found Nicole in bed waiting for him. His attempts to hide his anxiety were unsuccessful, but his wife didn't press him to know why. It had been a sad, stressful day for all.

That Tuesday was a normal day until Freddy returned home. He told his bosses he wouldn't be at work the next day due to a fictitious doctor's appointment. When he stepped through the door to his apartment, he found his family glued to the television, watching the news. Sussman had gone on record on his show, earnestly addressing the death of the President for the first time. Sussman confirmed what many had already figured his view of the assassination was. Nobody seemed to feel like talking at dinner that night. Discussing Sussman's hatred had become too much of a norm. Instead the Villanuevas ate silently.

After dinner, Freddy excused himself and went downstairs. He entered Charles' apartment and Freddy briskly exchanged two-hundred dollars with Charles for an automatic pistol. Rosales was virtually silent the whole time, letting his disapproval of the idea permeate the air. He did say he was able to get a better-than-expected price and the gun would be untraceable, at least where he was involved. Charles commented that mentioning what the weapon might be used for made it cheaper: many of his business associates apparently were as misguided as Freddy. After the transaction Freddy went back upstairs and hid the weapon in his underwear draw before snuggling up to his wife. He was surprised at how easily he went to sleep that night.

The Death of Two Kings, Part Six

Freddy walked into the lobby of the midtown modern high-rise mid-morning. He had ridden with Meagan to her tutoring job again, so as not to bring any suspicion upon himself. He wasn't as successful as he had hoped he would be. His hugs to his wife and children were just too long and too strong to be normal. Luckily, "just because" was an acceptable answer when they asked why.

When he entered the building, Nick was there to greet him. Nick ushered his cousin to the maintenance and security office instead of the main desk. Nick spoke to the receptionist in hushed words which Freddy couldn't hear. The receptionist called somebody on the phone, then told Nick and Freddy to proceed down a small corridor.

They approached an office door and Nick told his cousin to wait outside while he went in. Nick was in the office only a minute. When he came out he threw an envelope to Freddy and said, "put it on."

Freddy ripped open the envelope and pulled out a lanyard and ID card. The card matched Nick's and had an old picture of Freddy on it, taken during a party the cousins had attended years ago. "It was the only picture I had available in time," Nick said apologetically. He explained getting the card made during off hours and without Freddy was the best way to proceed without being detected. Whoever had made the card was able to create it as a replacement, without any meaningful paperwork or security checks. The explanation kept Freddy from asking how he'd become Mel Torres.

Nick led Freddy further down the corridor to a freight elevator. As they boarded the car Nick explained by coming through the maintenance entrance they avoided the cleverly disguised metal detectors and any unwanted scrutiny. Getting an ID card and building clearance was easy since many of the building's employees loathed Sussman. The people at the front desk however were wildcards and it was better not to pique their attention.

The two had a half an hour before Fleet's show was scheduled to begin and the two walked around the building talking. While still guarding their speech, the two alluded to what Freddy was about to do. Nick joked that he hoped they would become cellmates and that they would enjoy prison life. The men were fairly certain Sussman was not a favorite of those incarcerated in the New York penal system. Nick was a bachelor and had no children and wasn't afraid of what would happen to him if they connected him to his cousin. Both of them took that outcome as a given, but Nick said it was worth it for the future of Freddy's kids and children all over the country no matter their ethnicity or religion.

With five minutes left before the moment Freddy was planning to strike, Nick offered to take the gun and the responsibility. He reminded his cousin that he had no ties to worry about, nobody who was counting on him. Freddy immediately dismissed the offer. Perhaps it was that Freddy felt an obligation to Rodriguez to avenge his death. The President had brought his family so much joy and excitement in such a short time, since before they had even met the then-candidate at a campaign stop. Maybe it was that Freddy felt he had to do it for his family, to prove Nicole's words of the previous week that they didn't have to worry. Even if that meant taking matters into one's own hands to show others they wouldn't accept racial persecution. It may have been about pride, the pride Freddy felt for his family and people, which angered him about

Sussman's attacks on Latinos. Freddy grew up at a time when he had had to live with racial epithets thrown his way on a regular basis, but he noticed less of those attacks as he got older. It seemed to him, until Sussman's recent tirades, that his daughters hadn't had to deal with the same anti-Latino mentality he had had to deal with. If the host was eliminated, hopefully they wouldn't have to deal with such biases again. There may have even been a bit of glory in his motivation, wanting to be the person who silenced a man who instilled hatred in his fans and fear in his foes. It was motivation to do something with his life which would be recorded in history.

Whatever his reasoning was, he felt it was his burden to carry. He would not allow Nick to take the responsibility or to suffer the consequences.

Nick quickly reminded Freddy about the facility, pointing out that he'd have to rush into the studio itself because the control room glass was bullet-proof. From the maintenance door Freddy would emerge from to the studio itself was a short distance and only Sussman's staff of three was usually in the area for the show. The security detail always stayed in the studio's lobby, down the other end of a corridor, behind a closed door. The studio door was never locked, as Sussman's producer and intern often brought in papers for their boss to read. There was little chance anything could stop Freddy.

The two men hugged, and said they would see each other at their arraignment. After that, Nick walked back down the service corridor to the elevator, leaving Freddy alone. It was ten minutes after ten when Villanueva burst through the service door and ran for the studio door. The producer, intern and technician were all caught by surprise as Villanueva rushed passed them. Sussman had just started his show, having allowed affiliates a five-minute window for a top-of-the-hour news update and commercials. The host was reading his monologue and only looked up when he heard the studio door slam open. His first notion was to give a menacing look to whoever had caused the disruption. His crew knew better than to upset broadcast etiquette by not opening the door slowly and quietly. Instead, the balding, pudgy man looked up and saw a dark-skinned stranger standing there. His eyes widened and his pupils shrunk. 'Oh, my God!" he gasped. The gunshot was the last sound he heard, followed quickly by a pain in his forehead. They were the last sensations felt in Fleet Sussman's life.

Freddy fired four shots in total. The first, to the head, was enough to kill him but Freddy didn't want to take chances. He discharged three more shots, all to the heart. When he was done, Freddy was surprised how easy the physical action of shooting the pistol had been. He wasn't prepared for the emotions he felt upon committing the deed and seeing the blood ooze out of the dead body in front of him. Suddenly, Freddy was sickened with himself, disgusted with what he had done. He thought he had been prepared for this moment. Up until then he was sure he was doing the right thing for everyone in the country. In that brief instant after the shooting he looked down on a man he hated - a man he had just murdered - and realized he was dead wrong. Still, it was done. He turned to look towards the studio door. He dropped the gun and put his hands on his head, his mission complete. He was ready for a life in prison.

It was only seconds before Sussman's guards burst into the control room and then into the studio. Angry eyes met Freddy's submissive gaze. The security men didn't even look at their boss to see what condition he was in. For two seconds, their cold stares were focused on Freddy. Then the first guard who had entered the room raised his own gun and cocked the weapon.

Freddy's heart, which was already beating faster than he could ever remember, kicked up another notch. Now it was his eyes which widened. "I'm unarmed!" he yelled.

"So what, cocksucker?" the guard said dryly, then fired six shots of his own at his target.

As Freddy dropped to the floor dying, he realized it was another miscalculation. He'd figured his surrender would be taken without question, and he'd be immediately arrested, just like Gary Dukeman had been in West Virginia a week ago. In his dying moment, he realized he was wrong again.

He died unaware how badly his poor judgment would affect his family and country.

There's Battle Lines Being Drawn

A majority of Americans in the summer of 2017 hadn't been alive during the Cuban Missile Crisis some 55 years prior. Many of those who were likened the national level of anxiety and tension of that fall in 1962 to a five-day span starting July 26th, 2017. Two famous men, both well-liked and deeply respected by people with similar political beliefs had been murdered for their ideologies. One was the President of the United States, the other had been the unquestioned pacesetter in political radio.

Unlike the Cuban Missile Crisis though, this wasn't an international affair. This was solely an American event. There were strong emotions on both sides, with people feeling they had been pushed too far one time too many. The American public was torn in a way it hadn't been for about a century-and-a-half.

That was the most dangerous difference between the 1960's incident and the one brewing in the 2010's. When the U.S. found itself at the brink of war over Cuba, it was a political game with the Soviet Union, but a confrontation mainly fought between world leaders in the media and on the phone. The events of the early 21st century were a conflict blossoming between regular people. Despite what people said about politicians, those leaders often managed to keep things safely in check in the end. The masses of the country were more volatile, more unpredictable and harder to reign in than political leaders. It wasn't surprising therefore when hostilities broke out.

Millions of people listened live or watched the simulcast as Fleet Sussman was shot during the opening minute of his show on July 26th, 2017. The webcast and television broadcast showed the event live, as well as the shooting of the murderer. The incident polarized anyone who cared about politics in the country. The Susspicious Minds were shocked and outraged and in mourning. They would have been calling for the shooter's head, had he not been killed during his assault.

The Sussman detractors were split. Those who stayed true to their political beliefs said the shooting was unfortunate. Others were not so virtuous in their beliefs. They shed their so-called political correctness and voiced their satisfaction that Sussman was dead. To back up their stance, they suggested Sussman himself would have shown little remorse if the tables had been turned.

Whether in support of Fleet's murder or against it, the Sussman foes all agreed on one thing: the guard who had shot Villanueva was himself a murderer. The video of Fleet's and Freddy's deaths, which the media showed as often they had the shooting of President Rodriguez, proved without question that Villanueva had been killed while unarmed and in a state of surrender. The anti-Sussman crowd therefore believed the hired gun who had shot Villanueva was rightfully being held on murder charges of his own. The Susspicious Minds however felt the guard was justified in his actions, and were infuriated the man wasn't free.

Among politicians, everyone was condemning the death of Sussman. Those who had benefited the most from his show were naturally the ones who spoke the most about losing their friend and voicing their sadness and anger. The politicians who were not fans weren't as fervent in their comments, but all voiced their condolences. Sussman, the biggest detractors said, was wrongfully gunned down for exercising his right to free speech. Although he didn't hold a national address the way he had after Rodriguez' death, President Armitage had gone on record calling Sussman's death a travesty while issuing appeals to the public for peace.

Despite the pleas from Armitage and most politicians, the ripples were starting to spread. The radio airwaves were flooded with people on both sides calling their respective outlets, spouting venom at either Sussman or Rodriguez and Villanueva. The network on which Fleet had aired turned to John Rodgers in Chicago as an immediate replacement. Rodgers was one of the hosts who would fill in during the times Sussman was on vacation in instances when the network decided to forego the standard "Best of Fleet" shows. Rodgers was perhaps even more radical than Sussman had been, and had been suspended more times for racial and violent suggestions than the illustrious Fleet. However, with his lack of national exposure, his punishments often weren't newsworthy on a national level. Despite a lack of recognition, his style made him the perfect replacement for the week.

The day after the shooting, he opened the show with a minute of silence in respect of Sussman, followed by a eulogy for the fallen icon. He called Fleet a friend and mentor, a voice of reason and a leader for all those who cared for the truth and America. The country and the world were worse-off without Sussman, who was the "last, best hope" to convince politicians to turn away from Communism and corruption. He went into his first commercial break audibly broken up and weepy as he said one final goodbye to Fleet.

When he returned, he was nothing but venom, leveled at the country's Hispanic communities. It was difficult to tell whether he hated the former President or the murderer of his friend more. Instead, he blamed Latinos overall. It didn't matter if they were from Mexico, South America, or the Caribbean. He said they were all evil and were going to

127

destroy the country. The Susspicious Minds called and agreed and threatened to take matters into their own hands.

It was the following day when the situation escalated. At that point, nobody had been surprised with Rodgers' tirade. Considering what had happened to Sussman, it was almost expected, as was an immediate suspension. However no such ban was issued, and Rodgers was back on the air Friday. This outraged Liberal show hosts, who returned the verbal fire. It was time for Rodgers to shut up. If Sussman had been able to speak with any amount of civility, Rodriguez, Sussman and Villanueva would all still be alive. Callers to the Liberal-based shows suggested both Rodriguez and Villanueva were heroes, and wondered where the outrage was from the Susspicious Minds that Sussman's guard was also a cold-blooded murderer. They started to say enough was enough. If their opponents wouldn't be held responsible, why should they care about civility? On one show, there were suggestions from fans that people head down to West Virginia and give the people there a taste of their own medicine. On another program, one caller said it was time to send the White people back to Europe. When the host objected that it wasn't all Caucasian people who sided with Sussman or Rodgers, the caller responded with anger: "So? We aren't all Mexicans either." He was cut off before suggesting all White people deserved to die.

The rhetoric continued on all the political shows that Friday, with calls for violence and the words of hate growing more vicious each hour. By early afternoon, the FCC took unprecedented action, warning of the harshest punishment if media companies didn't reel in their stars immediately. Never in the nearly 100 years of commercial radio had the seven-second dump button been used so many times to censor content. Rodgers' own staff used it a couple of times on their own boss, although the host wouldn't know about it until he read the papers on Saturday.

Callers and listeners on both sides found something to agree on, as both were angered by the government censorship of what they called free speech. The crackdown was meant to calm everyone, but both sides instead called the crackdown Fascist. Listeners turned to the Internet, where they wrote about how the government was watching them all, getting ready to silence everyone. Paranoia grew, with the fringes of both sides threatening each other and the abusive government which wanted to control them all. This mentality remained through Saturday and into Sunday, when the funerals for both Fleet Sussman and Freddy Villanueva were scheduled to take place on the island of Manhattan.

War

The weather in New York on Sunday, July 30th was normal for that time of year: mostly sunny skies and hazy, hot and humid. Crowds began gathering at St. Patrick's Cathedral by 8:00 a.m. for the memorial service for Fleet Sussman. The famed church filled up early, leaving thousands outside for the 10 a.m. service. Many of the people inside the cathedral were regulars for Sunday mass, who had the front of the pews reserved for them. The rows in the back filled up early with Sussman fans, with a decent-sized overflow listening on speakers outside.

As the service began for Sussman, friends, family and new-found admirers of Freddy Villanueva started to gather two miles uptown at another Catholic church in El Barrio. Freddy's immediate family had not come to grips with what he had done. He hadn't left a note, and the only idea of a motive came from Nick's mother, who had seen her son in prison. The cousin had been questioned and arrested the day of the shooting. His mother passed on to Nicole and her children that Freddy had done what he had for their future, and mentioned he had intended to tell them afterwards. Neither Nick nor Freddy had expected the latter to die during his attack and Freddy had planned to tell his loved ones about his thought process from prison.

The Villanuevas couldn't fathom what had happened. Freddy had never given any indication he could be capable of such violence. Nicole doubted her husband had ever fired a gun before and wouldn't have believed him capable of shooting somebody had she not seen the footage. But he was the killer, and she had to identify the body in the morgue. All the family could figure was that he took Sussman's hatred personally and his fear had driven Freddy to drastic measures.

As the Villanuevas entered the church, the service downtown for Fleet Sussman was entering its final moments. The memorial at St. Patrick's had been very touching and moving. The governor from Florida, Sussman's home state, performed the eulogy. The governor would all but certainly have lost numerous elections without Sussman's support. Afterwards, as Sussman's casket was carried out to a hearse parked on Fifth Avenue, those who were waiting outside started chanting the host's first name. The New York Police Department estimated about three-thousand people were outside the cathedral. Sussman's body was loaded into the vehicle and the hearse led a procession of limousines south down Fifth Ave. As the cars drove slowly downtown, many of the people who had been outside for the ceremony started to disperse.

It was a helicopter reporter from WNBC-4 who first observed something strange was happening. He noted that instead of people breaking away to reach the various nearby transportation options, a good-sized portion of the crowd was walking uptown. Grand Central Terminal, one of Manhattan's two major train hubs was the other direction, but only a few people were walking that way. Fewer people seemed to be waiting at the numerous bus stops that were within two blocks of the cathedral. The reporter instead said it was odd when those walking reached the south side of Central Park and continued north instead of turning east towards the Columbus Circle subway station. They kept marching through the 60s and 70s of Manhattan's East Side. It also seemed as if the crowd actually grew larger as it marched. People who had been in the park were now walking too, many of them toting bags, as though they had just left the Great Lawn after a morning of sunbathing. As they reached the 80s, the people in the helicopter reported that only then there seemed to be a police presence gathering ahead of the walkers. It was also about that time that the reporter noticed a change in dress among the marchers. Many of them were suddenly wearing some strange sort of headgear.

The reporter told the camera operator on board the helicopter with him to zoom in on some of the oddly-dressed marchers. They were wearing odd hats, made of cotton or linen. Some seemed round from above, while others were pointed. Soon it became more apparent that all of the headwear was shaped like cones. The cloth draped all around the heads and faces of their wearers.

"My God, it's the Klan!" The reporter exclaimed, and quickly added to his report, "and they're headed towards Harlem!"

As they approached 90th Street, the police blocked off Fifth Avenue. Other cars had also reached similar positions on Madison, Park and Lexington Avenues, down which the small army had splintered off. The Channel 4 reporter and people in his and other nearby helicopters watched in horror from above as the marchers stopped briefly for the police, then started sprinting up the street. Police reports would later say the leaders of the assembled people first told their troops to stop, then told the officers they had no issues with them. After that, they yelled "charge" as if they were playing cavalry officers in some Wild West film. The people on Park broke through first, as most of the crowd had made their way to the widest of the north-south-running streets. They ran over the median, where the already thinly-spread police had been unable to set up barricades. The police were soon overwhelmed on the other avenues as well. Despite the hysteria, no shots had yet been fired.

It was midway through their sprint when the invading horde started drawing their weapons out of concealment. Everyone had at least one pistol in hand, with most of the men and women brandishing two handguns or a single, larger weapon. From its high vantage point, the news reporter in the helicopter could discern some people had automatic weapons and rifles which looked like they belonged in a military armory.

The mob reached a perimeter about a block from where Freddy Villanueva's funeral was being held when police in riot gear stopped them. The NYPD had been prepared just in case there was some form of disruption, but had grossly misjudged how big an anti-Villanueva group might have been. They also weren't prepared for an armed force, larger than an army battalion, or the notion that the people paying respects to the Villanuevas might also be well armed. Much like in the case of Sussman's funeral, there were many paying their respects outside the packed church. As the Klanspeople, Susspicious Minds and members of various other groups represented arrived, the people who had been listening to Freddy's eulogy turned to see they were surrounded by police and the Klan. Those attending the Villanueva memorial had been estimated to be a thousand in number. The police urged - pleaded may have been a better term - with both sides to remain calm. New York's finest were suddenly in between two factions ready for war, and were vastly outnumbered by both sides. Their plea went unheard. Nobody was certain who fired the first shot or who the first casualty was, but once the initial discharge was heard by each side, Hell came to Saint Francis de Sales Roman Catholic Church on East 96th Street. A large firefight erupted. At first, it was the friends and family of Villanueva encircled by the Sussman supporters, with the police becoming more the victims than anyone. Shots rang out from both sides, catching the police as their numbers broke apart. Some pushed their way out of the fracas, knowing they had no chance, but a number of the brave officers stayed, unsure who they were supposed to protect, but knowing it was their duty to try and preserve life and order.

The combatants saw the police as just obstacles and were willing to shoot their way through them. Nobody in the years that followed held the officers who retreated in poor light, as those who tried to stay between the armies were brutally slaughtered. The pro-Sussman group continued to smother the church and the Villanueva supporters inside, laying siege on the holy building.

The greater numbers and better-armed Sussman crowd were quick in their push and it seemed as they would win this battle. Within minutes, they were at the doors of the church. They kept chanting, sometimes calling for the Villanueva family to come out, other times saying "Spics go home!" A cheer of victory was raised as the forward assault group was able to break down the doors of the church. If it truly was a victory, it was short-lived. Just as they were set to storm the church, a second skirmish started outside. Nearby residents of Harlem who had been watching on television or heard the ruckus came to support those holed up in the church.

Suddenly the attackers were trapped much like the police had been. Whether because of gross miscalculation or just tremendous oversight, they were pinned between a staggering amount of armed locals of various races and the people in the church who were energized by the arrival of reinforcements. The former invaders started pushing their way out of the battle zone. While severely depleted, their numbers were still strong. They pushed their way back south, firing at anyone who pursued and at the occasional person in the street of non-Caucasian ancestry.

Unbeknownst to the people fighting in New York, similar scenes were taking place around the country. In big cities, these attacks began at the same time as the "March on Harlem" had, obviously coordinated by a bigger group. In Chicago, where John Rodgers had stayed to hold his own vigil for Sussman, the crowd he had drawn out had made its way towards the city's South Side and started to pick fights with minority residents of the area. Rodgers was one of the first to die during the fighting in Chicago. Similar incidents happened in Los Angeles and all over Texas and Arizona, especially in the larger towns closer to the border with Mexico. The major news networks, which had people live at both of the funerals in New York, had shown the escalation in the Big Apple, and soon had split screens showing the fighting there and in the other major American cities. It wasn't long before the regular networks had stopped their normal Sunday afternoon broadcasts for the reign of violence. As people in smaller areas realized what was happening, some people took up arms on their own from both sides. Soon there were battles all over the country. America's Second Civil War had begun.

Part Two:

After the War

Must've Got Lost

It wasn't supposed to be this way, "Bull" Dukeman thought as he tried for the umpteenth time to properly knot the tie he wanted to wear that day. After President Rodriguez had been killed, America was supposed to enter a new Golden Era. Many people he trusted told him that it truly was the best of times for the United States, but it hardly seemed that way to Bull.

Dukeman was preparing for his annual July 20th appearance on the National Mall for "Freedom Day," which had been declared a national holiday within the first year of Rodriguez' assassination. This was the third anniversary of the day Dukeman had become an American hero. There was supposed to be a presidential election that November, but no candidates besides President Norman Dukeman - who shared no relation to Bull - were running. No other party was able to fulfill the necessary requirements to field a candidate so Dukeman, who had been the Speaker of the House of Representatives when Rodriguez was shot, was a shoe-in for his first complete term. The only debate was whether there would be an Election Day or if the process would just be eliminated. Only a small handful of congressional seats actually would see competition. Few petitions stood up to the scrutiny that was needed to allow somebody to run for office. There weren't many voters left in the country registered as anything other than Republican. In most regions where there was some political diversity the districts had been gerrymandered to keep Tea Party-sympathetic candidates in power. Only regions which had always been unquestionably Liberal had survived the redrawing of political boundaries. These areas kept the Right from complete control, but the Tea Party still had an unstoppable super majority. It was supposed to be everything Bull and other followers of the Tea Party could have dreamed of.

And yet, things were not perfect, the way the public had been told they should have been. Sure, Gary and his family were doing well for themselves, but he was hardly as prosperous as he expected he would have been. He certainly didn't feel like he was in the Land of the Free. All these years later and many things actually seemed worse to him than when Eddie Rodriguez had been President.

Gary would readily admit he wasn't the most politically-savvy person in the world, so he liked to tell himself he just didn't understand. After all, the party in power was the one he always believed held his best interests in mind. He often tried to put it all together in his own mind but it was a confusing mess. First off, the war hadn't been anything like he had expected a war would be. It was quick and the country suffered extremely little damage. Outside of the first two weeks after the fighting began there had been barely any violence or death. He had watched the sanctioned records plenty of times and the war seemed like ancient history. In the years which had followed, many of Bull's admirers complained about how anticlimactic the war was. Most would tell Gary how disappointed they had been that they hadn't had a chance to kill a Spic, or a Coon, or a Towel Head, or somebody from one ethnicity or another. Bull heard - or learned - every racial and religious epithet from his adoring fans.

Instead of a glorious war, those who supported the Susspicious Minds were treated to what they jokingly compared to target practice. On the heels of the new Bloody Sunday, there were occasional eruptions of violence around the country. There were gunfights daily in all the southern states and again along the Mexican border. The rest of the country was rather subdued that first Monday after the major riots, fearful of what was to come and hoping it wouldn't involve much violence. In the big cities where most of the action occurred authorities tried to piece together what had happened. It was hard to trace the hundreds of outside invaders to the city, who had done well when it came to seeping into the cracks and remaining unseen. NYPD officers staked out numerous hotels and rooms, reserved by people who were suspected of having a part in the siege or who were from regions where they thought a suspect might come from. Most of those rooms remained empty Sunday night and their occupants hadn't returned by checkout time that morning.

Airport security was tightened drastically that day and passengers on flights to certain parts of the country were closely scrutinized, yet the dragnet ensnared few people of interest. Many a car with license plates from distant states were stopped on the New Jersey Turnpike, but only a few drivers and their passengers were detained. Even sweeps of the Port Authority bus terminal on 42nd Street produced slim results. If the authorities had acted quicker, they would have had apprehended many suspects. Likewise, if more people in law enforcement were paying attention to the morning rush hour traffic patterns in Philadelphia, they could have prevented the true start of the war.

The attack in New York was planned better than anyone would have ever given the assailing group credit for. Many had left the city as quickly as they could, immediately jumping aboard New Jersey Transit trains and buses. Many had hotel rooms booked for them by sympathetic friends from the New York Tri-State area and by organizers who were orchestrating their major campaign for freedom. The hotels in Cherry Hill and Camden New Jersey quietly filled up. Those who took their chances hiding in New York that night also grabbed trains and buses to the outskirts of the metropolitan Philadelphia area, where their gun-laden cars waited in the parking lots of the commuter rail stops. Nobody thought twice about how many extra people were headed to these stations that morning and no one noticed how many people departed the lots not by train or by bus but by car. The traffic reports made mention about the higher-than-usual congestion on the bridges from the Garden State into the City of Brotherly Love. Perhaps because there had been no major traffic on I-95 from the New York City area, nobody had put the pieces together to see a correlation between the non-exodus of the New York Massacre and the then-upcoming onslaught in Philly.

The fight in Philadelphia was ugly. At first, the vehicles driven by the Susspicious Minds paraded past Independence Hall, honking their horns in recognition of all that had happened on those hallowed grounds. A couple of patrolman radioed in this unusual activity, marking the first proactive steps to try and avoid an incident. The Philadelphia police started to mobilize, agreeing this was a worrisome event. However, the cars just rolled by, dispersing in different directions after their initial tribute. Still, small pockets from the local law enforcement agencies gathered at the historic site. Federal officers were notified and extra officers from all agencies were called in on their days off.

A half-hour after the horn-blowing incident, other than the gathering of officers at Independence National Historical Park, things were normal throughout the city. The federal park rangers and local officials started patrolling the area with moderate urgency. Another fifteen minutes went by and nothing unusual happened. It took another half-hour before the first cries for help were received by emergency dispatchers. Then the calls started rolling in fast and furious from different parts of the city. Each caller stated he or she had witnessed a drive-by shooting. These calls came in from all over Philly, spread out through many neighborhoods. These incidents were mostly in the suburbs, near the sports complex and near the campuses of the universities in the city. Hundreds of elementary school-aged campers witnessed killings near tourist sites such as the Franklin Museum and along the waterfront. In all cases, the first person shot was a non-Caucasian, but some people in close proximity to the initial targets were shot down indiscriminately regardless of race.

The numerous law enforcement organizations were thrown into confusion. With officials holding a perimeter around the national historic site, many other beats were left thin and the officers covering those patrols had to oversee larger areas than usual. What was happening that morning was totally unexpected. Where the assault in New York was one giant push on a single target, the strategy in Philadelphia was to attack people of non-Caucasian ethnicities all over the city. The masterful organization of the attack was just as successful as it had been in New York, achieving total surprise quickly and leading to a fair amount of confusion and bloodshed.

The various government agencies were soon forced to react as best they could. A handful of those gathered at Independence Hall were immediately dispatched to nearby Penn's Landing. Others waited for orders on whether to stand their collective ground or disperse. With calls coming in at a steady pace, all the Philadelphia police and many federal officers who weren't specifically national park rangers were sent to look into the other calls. After a fair amount of time had passed and when the defending forces seemed adequately depleted, the attacking generals called for their forces to move back in on what had been their primary target all along.

Within minutes, cars started returning to the vicinity around Independence Hall. The vehicles' drivers left them haphazardly parked and all the occupants jumped out. They ran towards the shelter housing the Liberty Bell, telling the few park rangers they met to run or be shot and calling the government agents traitors. A number of the lightly armored guards were shot and a few were killed, but most had seen what they were up against and took the attackers' advice to flee.

Moments later, the Susspicious Minds' forces had a solid perimeter around the Liberty Bell Center. As the defensive wall was set up, a posse of men made its way from the Omni Hotel a block east of the Center and Independence Hall towards the waiting army. Among those walking from the hotel was oil magnate Thomas Hannigan, a number of well-armed and well-armored guards and a hand-picked television crew from the nation's Right-leaning news network. The latecomers walked through the first line of tense defenders.

Hannigan and his party passed through the ranks and entered the Liberty Bell Center. He took a position next to the national symbol of freedom as the television crew quickly set up for the broadcast. In just a few short seconds they were ready. The network had been prepared for Hannigan's announcement and were just waiting for the crew's go-ahead. When it came the network went live to Philly. Hannigan looked into the camera, his visage, stern, steady and confident as he addressed the nation.

"My fellow patriotic Americans. For too long our great country has been in the clutches of evil outside influences. After eight years of having to smile pretty under the rule of Sheik Barack Hussein Obama, anti-American influences tried to sway us into electing a Mexican national to serve in our highest, most revered office. He undoubtedly was given to us with the mission of making us subservient to Mexico. After trying to corrupt us for eight years spiritually, our global enemies were trying to break us financially and to bring us down to third world status.

"My friends, I've had enough of this. I've gathered a number of friends - a vast number of great patriots - to defend against this threat. It's time this country returned to Anglo, Christian values. It's time we once again become a state elected by and for the people, and we regain our position as the unquestioned dominant world power. It's time America was controlled by Americans once more!

"As you've seen these last two days, our numbers are many and we're well-armed. The President's desire to weaken our military and intelligence gathering made it so we were able to organize with ease. That was his goal for America. Fortunately my band of patriots were able to expose this goal before enemy forces could. When those terrorist bastards killed Fleet in his own studio, they proved they were an obscene threat, willing to come into our own homes and offices to spread their fear and kill us all. We won't stand for it anymore! If you feel like the rest of us patriots, it's time to defend the Constitution! Bear your arms, organize your militias, because if we don't act now, they will win and take away our right to defend ourselves. If you're an American, if you're a patriot, now is the time to fight for your country!

"And if you're not, if you're an agent from vile places like Islam or Mexico, you'd best start packing before we pack you up in a coffin." A cool sneer came to Hannigan's lips as he finished his speech and walked out of camera view.

The Jester Stole His Thorny Crown

Hannigan's declaration of war was panned by most in the media. He was dubbed psychotic, a paranoid schizophrenic, a rich and dangerous threat. The mainstream media was quick to bury him, pointing out so many inconsistencies in his speech. From the fact that he made Islam out to be a place instead of a religion to the point that Barack Obama had repeatedly proven he had been born in Hawaii, they proclaimed Hannigan was speaking gibberish. In a similar fashion, they stressed that he was totally ignoring all the "Melting Pot" ideals of the United States by saying the country should adhere solely to Christian Caucasian rule. Liberal pundits were quick to point out his rage was aimed at a seemingly non-existent threat and that as he claimed this danger had caused the death of Fleet Sussman, he totally glossed over the fact that President Rodriguez had also been shot in an act of treason. Liberal critics were just as quick to note Hannigan hadn't even mentioned the assassination of the President. Hannigan's performance and demeanor were considered calm yet rushed, leading observers to all sorts of questions about his seriousness and his preparedness. His message was rejected by most news outlets. He was vilified and labeled a vessel of hate and anger. His speech was generally considered a delusional rant of a madman and few thought it contained any substantial information. He stated his anger and his goals but hadn't really set an agenda. Most of the people on the airwaves were confused and admittedly frightened by what Hannigan said and claimed to have orchestrated.

The station which had broadcast Hannigan's speech exclusively live was the major exception. It quickly started calling itself the home of Thomas Hannigan and the one network where patriotic Americans could turn to get a non-biased look at what had happened to the country and what was yet to come. The network became Hannigan's top defender, making him out as the champion of the Constitution and the victim of the evil Liberal spinsters.

The network downplayed many items other news outlets were pointing out. Where other channels complained about Islam not being a physical place, the pro-Hannigan station's experts said other pundits were nitpicking and accused the mainstream Liberal media of using sensationalism to make Hannigan look bad.

One large bit of grey matter a majority of media outlets treaded lightly around was whether Hannigan was actually guilty of any crime. He took credit for the violence which had erupted around the country and he was there in the thick of things in Philadelphia, but there was no physical evidence he was truly involved in orchestrating the fighting. It wasn't anything anyone would've expected of him until that point. It was common knowledge he was a huge contributor to many Conservatives and their Super PACs in recent elections and his surrogates were vocal and vicious when it came to attacking Liberals. He was known for bankrolling major smear campaigns during elections. However he'd never done anything which suggested he condoned violence. Despite the video of him by the Liberty Bell, the media was universally careful to say Hannigan's connection to the battles was alleged. Only a few ultra-Conservative websites suggested all Hannigan claimed was true, calling him the American savior and trivializing the bloodshed.

Over the next few days, as the media tried to dissect the events of two days of fighting and Hannigan's part in them, the country found itself in various depths of violence. Many of the major cities which had seen skirmishes already remained in an uneasy calm. In many of the more Liberal metropolises, that one day of fighting had been it. Police forces like those in New York vowed to not let something like what had just occurred happen again. In cases like the Big Apple, the initial strike was all that had been planned, and the relative harmony which existed in the city returned once the invaders disappeared. Just about every city, town and village which had lived for years in decent racial and political peace still did the same and in most cases became even more unified, afraid that what had happened elsewhere could also happen there. Meanwhile, after the attacks and declaration in Philadelphia, the City of Brotherly Love returned to a semblance of reserved normalcy. Few arrests were actually made following the events of that day. The Philadelphia police were too busy cleaning up the carnage in their city to go chasing after the shooters, many of whom were believed to have already left town. The multitude of perpetrators faded into the woodwork, just as they had in New York.

In regions which hadn't had such a peaceful status quo, random acts of violence popped up regularly. In much of the South there were continuing attacks on African-American churches and communities. Local authorities reacted timely and with a good amount of competency and care to incidents in Black neighborhoods and the residents were courteous and thankful when the culprits were apprehended. Many of those perpetrating violence in these regions did so with unbridled brazenness, thinking their acts would be championed by all and ignored by authorities. This turned out not to be the case in African-American communities. Police responses were slower though in cases when the attacks focused on Hispanic neighborhoods. In many towns along the Mexican border there was usually no police reaction. The stated reason was the authorities were too busy keeping an eye on the border and the federal officials who were supposed to secure it. For the growing multitude of Hannigan supporters, the belief was anything federal was probably corrupt.

Although there was little fighting up to that point, the turning point in the war, if any of those terms were applicable, came a week later. America had waited in limbo for some major news or response, but there was little federal action to curb the violence. A response from the government didn't come until that Thursday, when President Sydney Armitage addressed the nation, offering his deepest condolences for what had happened and saying there would be no military action in response to the heinous attacks of a few rebels. Armitage said nothing about bringing those responsible to justice.

Armitage's incredibly feeble response was all he could offer. Behind closed doors, Washington was undergoing a coup. The Joint Chiefs of Staff took the bleak situation seriously as it mulled its options. Their reason for not taking action came from a strong belief that a military response would do more harm than good. The notion of American troops attacking the country's citizens was likely to frighten the U.S. population even more and send more people running for their weapons. There was speculation among America's top military leaders below the President that mobilizing the Armed Forces could lead to the troops fighting among themselves as some were undoubtedly more sympathetic to Hannigan's pro-military, pro-Second Amendment message than the drawback plan Armitage had inherited from his predecessor. Most of America's soldiers, Marines, seamen and airmen waited to see what would be asked of them. Observers noted many were afraid of being asked to fire on those they had pledged to protect. A few had made viral statements through the social media saying they felt isolated and scared, saying they weren't sure how to react. Those few, and in reality most of their peers, breathed a sigh of relief when they heard they wouldn't have to fire on American citizens.

Armitage's announcement was panned by everyone and was considered by most of America to be a panicked, frightened response. In later years, those who sympathized with the Liberal agenda would realize this call for inaction was indeed the right choice, one which would deter more fighting which likely would have left a disproportionate amount of Left-leaning Americans dead. The Conservatives backing Hannigan and his followers were livid, many having hoped for that same bloody result.

While the military was staying impartial and inactive, America's intelligence wing was anything but. Soon after the fighting began, an angry Armitage called for his cabinet and various additional military and intelligence leaders to meet. He acted with incredible determination for somebody who had unexpectedly been elevated to the Office of the President of the United States. Armitage sat in that meeting and listened to the opinions and options of all attending. Despite the hesitation of his military advisors, Armitage had told all present he was going to call the armed National Guard and other reserve units into duty as federal protectors of the peace. With that, he dismissed everyone. Just about everyone left as ordered except those present from the CIA and FBI. Armitage, who was already disgruntled and thrust into an overly emotional state by recent events, became even more irritated by the show of disrespect.

"Get the Hell out of here!" Armitage barked.

Most of those present remained where they had been, except the President's guards had closed ranks with the unwanted visitors. At the center of the group was the most senior official present, Ronald Roberts. It was Roberts who responded to the President, saying they remained to address a number of serious security issues. The President gave Roberts an incredulous look, wondering what the intelligence man could say that wasn't appropriate for the whole group which had just dispersed.

Roberts began by talking about the lapse in security which had led to Eduardo Rodriguez' assassination, suggesting that the President's disregard for security and the military was what ended up causing his death. Armitage was about to protest angrily but Roberts raised his voice even higher than the President.

"Furthermore, Mister President," Roberts said loudly but even-toned, "we believe by maintaining your predecessor's stance you've weakened this country and made it nearly impossible for us to do our jobs."

The intelligence chief went on to describe how Armitage's continuation of Rodriguez' security and military policies allowed for violent cells to fester unnoticed and strike seemingly out of nowhere. Roberts told Armitage the President himself was the cause of the bloodshed that had occurred. Had his people been prepared, Roberts insisted, they would have detected the threat with ease and would have been able to detain the assailants before their attacks. Roberts assured the President a military response now would be best. It would show the country's vigilance and that the President had confidence in Roberts and those present.

Otherwise, Roberts hinted at having to investigate the President and his heavily-Democratic cabinet for subversive, anti-American activities should things get out of hand. Roberts asserted that he and those present had no confidence in the President or his ability to lead the military, then offered Armitage the option of having the CIA take over the U.S. Armed Forces.

"Get out," the President said. This time those who were assembled complied, including the President's guards. Armitage hadn't expected his escort to leave, but wasn't surprised or necessarily upset that it had.

As soon as the room had emptied out, Armitage cupped his face in his hands. It took all he had to keep from sobbing. If he had control to turn off all the cameras - known and hidden - in the room, he would have shut them and cried like a baby. Life as the Vice President of the United States had been surprisingly stress-free. He had served as a spokesperson for Edward Rodriguez at some press and public functions and had made a few diplomatic trips around the globe. When he had been campaigning for the Democratic nomination, he had shared many of the same platform items as Rodriguez, so Armitage was an easy choice for the Vice President spot.

Armitage had been very happy with how 2017 panned out from mid-late January through July 20th. That day a good friend and the only person he could truly confide in was murdered, and as a result Armitage suddenly and unexpectedly became President. While he knew perhaps better than most what Rodriguez had planned for the nation, he had little guidance in how to execute that agenda. There wasn't a transitional panel in place as there had been when he and Eduardo had ascended into the top governmental positions in the world, and there had actually been some hesitation from some people in Washington to help Armitage get acclimated to his new job. In two weeks he had to try and learn how to be President while dealing with the most hostile national environment since 1860, all while still coping with the wild emotions which stemmed from the death of Rodriguez, not to mention a fear for his own life.

The threat from Ronald Roberts didn't help. Roberts and many of those who had just left the room were among those who had tried to hinder Armitage when he took over as President. Now Roberts was saying it was the President's fault that America was turning into a warzone. What was of more concern was that Roberts unabashedly bullied Armitage, the President, in the White House, with the President's guards not only present but demonstrating their solidarity with Roberts. The President was already overwhelmed before the confrontation which had just taken place. Afterwards, realizing that even his personal guards were seemingly plotting against him, Armitage felt more fearful for his life and his self-confidence melted away. Roberts essentially stated he was ready to remove the President from office by force, and that he had the backing to do so. Armitage had nowhere to turn for help, and thought he could wind up dead himself if he mentioned what had happened to anyone. He was also certain, having watched the Far Right media machine, that Roberts could find a way to justify his treasonous actions to enough of America to exacerbate the violent situation.

Unbeknownst to the President, Roberts didn't think Armitage was at fault for the violence across the nation at all. Roberts' assault on the President was an act with two purposes. The first was for the intelligence leader to feign his anger and the second was to try and wrest control of the military away from Armitage without having to resort to more violence. In reality, despite his claims, there was no failure to detect the surge in chatter about the attacks. Roberts himself was the mastermind behind what had happened that Sunday. Not only did he plan the basics for the attacks but he assigned his most-trusted confidants to keep an eye out for a rise in communications from groups on the nation's watch list from the time the plan was distributed to his field generals until it was put into action. Posts on hate group websites and emails from various sleeper cell leaders to their troops weren't missed by those who were supposed to monitor them: they were simply ignored.

Roberts and Hannigan were friends and allies with similar philosophies about how the country should be run. The United States deserved strong leadership with a stronger military and little government regulation in business. Both would profit tremendously under such a system. In such a case Roberts would have one of the highest-ranking jobs in the country and would be one of the most powerful people in the world even if few would know it. Hannigan would benefit from a lack of government control over oil and by supplying fuel for Roberts' weapons, which would see more utilization under a good President. Such a President would obviously be a hawk who was pro-business and preferably White.

The men had been introduced at a political soirée in the middle of 2001, after George W. Bush had been sworn into office but before the September 11th terrorist attacks. Mutual friends brought the two together because they all had much to gain under the new administration. They had worked well together trying to sway politics in their favor. Hannigan had the money to fund huge ad campaigns while Roberts funneled information to the ad writers, pundits and political reporters who featured their mutual opponents in a poor light. It worked well during the Bush years and for part of Obama's tenure but soon they found various unsavory groups in America were too numerous to overcome. Even trying to change the electorate itself didn't work as voter ID laws seldom made their way out of the courts.

Hannigan and many business magnates like him suffered through eight years of Obama, watching as regulations grew in most corners of industry and economics. Voter demographics continued to shift and people in the Hannigan-Roberts camp believed the President and the Democrats caused this by making it easy for unregistered voters to illegally have their say. They scoffed at the Liberal notion that the Republicans themselves were at fault for alienating women and minorities through the laws they tried to pass at all levels of government. They had also ostracized homosexuals before giving up that fight to focus on others.

By the time the 2016 election ended, the Conservative powerhouse was furious. None of their tactics had worked. Other than the most loyal members of the GOP and the Tea Party, a majority of the nation faulted the Right's refusal to compromise and continued stonewalling for why they had little faith in Washington. No matter how much money Hannigan et al pumped into campaigns, despite how much they tried to put their spin on the issues and through their failed attempts to keep minorities from getting to the polls, they couldn't achieve their goals. Not only that, but they continued to see Washington fall further from their grasp.

With every passing month, they watched as more and more regulations cut into their profits all for the benefit of lowlifes living in the country. Republican efforts to fight the administration in court were failing on a regular basis and many new consumer-friendly laws survived: alternate energy measures and subsidized pricing for fuel; stricter emission and fuel consumption standards for automobiles; tough environmental rules for fossil fuel providers; cheaper healthcare and regulated drug prices; compensation for airline passengers and penalties for air carriers when travelers had to endure extended time on the tarmac; the contraction of gun rights in direct contradiction to the Second Amendment. These were some of the biggest items Hannigan's crowd complained about. As the Left continued to pick up momentum in questionable ways, many of America's business leaders feared only more regulation was coming. As the people in Hannigan's circle figured the Left was fixing the elections by opening voter registration up to anyone in the country, they started devising a plan to forcibly turn the focus of lawmakers towards backing their own ideals where business, politics and the military were concerned. It was well within their Constitutional right to form militias to combat the illegal government that was in place. The announcement that Brian Payton was being nominated for the Supreme Court and the unspoken belief the Democratic majority in the Senate would approve Payton with little resistance was the breaking point. Hannigan's business conglomerate leaned on Roberts to accelerate his plans. Roberts was well ahead of them and had various militia cells ready to mobilize within a week's notice. The only thing he needed was the right catalyst to push things into motion. He turned to Fleet Sussman for that.

It wasn't a hard sell to get the radio host on board. Months before the Payton nomination Roberts had Fleet in on the plan. Sussman loved to stir the pot. He was guaranteed by Roberts' backers such strong financial support that if they couldn't keep Fleet from being suspended they'd make it very much worth his while should he be kicked off the air. With that, Sussman went trolling with his most venomous attacks, looking for the people who were most likely to start an event. When Dukeman called and his former coworkers went into action soon afterwards, they knew they had their opening. On Roberts' insistence, Dukeman was given the hotline number to the show with the hopes Gary and his acquaintances could be manipulated into striking the opening blow in the war.

Roberts' unseen influence on the national stage was tremendous. As he was ultimately responsible for the President's safety, he had the power to shape portions of the Commander-in-Chief's schedule. Roberts was able to manipulate the two main pieces of the plan's puzzle very easily. He had no trouble promoting the President's visit to West Virginia. The state was close to Washington and while it had voted heavily for the Republican candidate in the most recent presidential elections, Monongalia County - which was home to Morgantown and West Virginia University - tended to be closer to the middle of the road among the traditionally Right-leaning counties in the state. It was somewhat friendly footing in a less friendly state, and a place where Rodriguez should feel comfortable talking about the local impact of some of his initiatives.

Even before the President's staff approved the West Virginia visit, Roberts was already paving the way for making it the President's final public appearance. With all of the nation's records on its citizens at his disposal, he and his staff quickly identified Gary and Peter Dukeman as the key pieces in the game as well as which people at the school would likely be willing to help carry out the assassination attempt. Using the contacts at the local militia cells he'd been working with, Roberts' people identified which other cogs would fit into the plan. Had Roberts' crew been looking for potential threats to the President's safety, the people they were contacting would have been quickly flagged for investigation and apprehension. In this case those same questionable items made them perfect for the plot. As Roberts controlled the gathered information and the people who had put the personnel reports together, he had no trouble hiding the plot from the President's staff.

Originally it was Roberts plan to fan the flames of discontent after Dukeman assassinated Rodriguez over the course of a couple of months to a point where those militia cells would be able to start committing random attacks around the country. This would lead to a massive, semi-coordinated attack from the various groups. He hadn't expected his friend Fleet Sussman would be killed in retaliation for Rodriguez' death. Roberts did however recognize a perfect opportunity to speed up his war. Asking for one last favor from the Sussman family, he was able to convince them to schedule Fleet's funeral on the same day as Freddy Villanueva's. At the same time he told the leaders of the militia cells he was in touch with to assemble in the closest major cities and be ready to fight that same day.

It would have been easy to track Roberts' troops as they advanced on their targets. Emails, phone and ATM records all pointed to the migration of various hate groups to where the first offensives would take place. Had the people receiving this information been truly trying to avoid an incident the signs of danger would have been brought to the attention of the local law enforcement organizations in the cities in question. Instead the warning signs were ignored and the police in cities such as New York, Los Angeles, Chicago and Philadelphia were forced to fend for themselves against unexpected onslaughts.

And so the Second American Civil War began, organized within the same government which the attacking forces were trying to overthrow.

Run (run, run, run)

The day after Ronald Roberts' confrontation with President Armitage, the Commander-in-Chief reversed his decision to activate the military. He wasn't sure if Roberts had corrupted the armed forces, but he was certain that the intelligence man was looking to capitalize on the opportunity. And so, after telling the Joint Chiefs of Staff of his reversal and saying he was thankful for their initial, best assessment, the President addressed the nation and told the public of his disgust at what had happened and how there would be no military response.

The President wasn't surprised when the media suggested he had been personally responsible for the violence. Security leaks hinted Armitage had neglected reports of swelling militia and hate group activity. The media reports falsely claimed the information made it to his desk and he ignored it because he was too anti-military to authorize force. His announcement was further proof of his weak stance. Armitage was positive Roberts was behind the leaks and the President wondered how big a part his chief intelligence officer played in planning the attacks. Despite his growing suspicions, the President didn't dare mention them to anyone. His paranoia about who he could trust was growing to include even his most trusted cabinet members. Even if he had faith in them, he still wasn't sure that he could speak freely in the White House without tipping his hand.

As the President sat huddled in his White House bunker, the media swell against him was rampant. Calls for Armitage to step aside and surrender all control of the country to Speaker of the House Norman Dukeman were growing, especially on the self-proclaimed lone source for unfiltered American news. All Republican legislators and a number of bulldog Democrats started to speak about impeachment. Thomas Hannigan released multiple statements saying the only thing the President could do to preserve American pride was to give his powers to Speaker Dukeman.

In the meantime, the two sides were quickly making their strategies well-known. The isolated violence continued around the country, mostly in rural southern and border regions and between different ethnic and religious groups. Leaders of the militant forces causing most of the violence started to feel a surge in bravado and were giving interviews just to the one news network they trusted. Some wore bandanas over their faces but most unabashedly showed their full faces. They stated their support for Hannigan and how they would stop at nothing to make sure America remained free for everyone while at the same time making it abundantly clear people from certain demographics were not welcome.

While these militia leaders spoke freely to the one network, violent incidents against other news organizations started to take place. The attackers warned the people of other news outlets they were considered enemies, liars and propaganda machines for foreign opportunists and terrorist organizations.

As the Conservative warriors swelled in strength, confidence and numbers, their presumed enemies took action as well. Their actions though were far from what the Far Right expected: they retreated. Many felt even before Eduardo Rodriguez' victory that their political opponents had reached a point where they preferred toxic screaming over civil discussion. The fringe Right started to consider verbal threats and showing up for demonstrations with unconcealed automatic weapons acceptable discourse. People on the Left were concerned about how Tea

Party darlings could be so popular slamming a perceived broken system without offering any solutions. "I'll share my plan when elected" was fine for the Tea Party, demonstrating to its opponents that their concerns had nothing to do with policy. Some Liberal citizens promised during recent presidential elections to move out of the country should the Republican candidate win on their "save the rich, damned be the poor" platforms. The notion of moving away started to gain momentum as the Tea Party's "by any means necessary" rhetoric grew louder.

The Tea Party saw its candidate lose another presidential election and soon after the victor was dead: killed by a man they called a hero and praised without shame. After the fighting began and President Armitage announced there wouldn't be any military action, many Liberals started to follow through on what they once considered their half-hearted threat. The border crossings to Canada were flooded and the U.S.'s northern neighbor was quickly forced to limit how many U.S. citizens were allowed to enter the country. To the South, Mexico was all too happy to welcome anyone who wanted to enter the country. Border towns which had very recently been compared to warzones due to drug-related violence suddenly seemed safer to non-Caucasian people and others looking to escape the fighting in the U.S. Somewhat surprisingly, cities like Ciudad Juarez saw dramatic drops in violence. Speculation among international observers was that the drug cartels didn't understand the situation in the U.S. With so many people on the move there wasn't a stable market for illicit drugs, plus anybody of Mexican heritage crossing the border legally or otherwise faced the real possibility of being shot for no reason. There was also a belief that some government officials within Mexico who had some under-the-table dealings with the syndicates were able to convince the drug lords that a temporary truce was in everybody's best interest. There was an astronomical amount of U.S. currency trying to make its way into Mexico. Even though the value of the U.S. dollar was dropping rapidly on international markets, it remained incredibly strong compared to the peso.

Others started to make plans to take flight to different continents. Those with strong ties to Asia, Europe, Africa and other parts of the world who could afford it started to run from the U.S. as well. A large portion of Democrats found their way out of the country. Many refused to fight and those who considered the aggression option felt it really wasn't worth it.

Roberts and Hannigan watched the migration with amusement. Roberts ordered the "troops" to remain at ease and let their opponents flee. The militias mostly responded as ordered and few violent episodes took place. The greatest show of aggression was forcing Hispanic people to march to Mexico. Those pushed into the other country included Mexican families which had made good, honest lives for themselves as well as illegal immigrants. It included anyone who looked like he or she had Hispanic ancestry, even if they weren't Mexican. Only in Florida were Hispanics left alone for the most part, for fear of accidentally displacing sympathetic, financially-sound and freedom-loving Cubans.

Soon after Bull Dukeman's liberation many of the Liberal-leaning cities on the coasts became ghost towns. While they were far from empty, the void left by those who had departed was impossible to ignore. Around the world, countries warned their citizens about traveling to the United States, calling the situation a civil war.

The beginning of the end of the war came at the end of August. Polls from those networks which still tried to carry out their missions showed the demographics of the country had turned sharply Republican. Most of the news outlets showed people claiming to be Republican outweighing those who said they were Democrats 71 to 21-percent. Less than five-percent of those polled claimed to be Independent or unaffiliated. The drastic shift in the numbers was enough for many of the Democrats in Washington to throw in the towel. Their reasons for stepping down varied. Some feared sooner or later they would be targeted for physical retribution. Others said they would not be part of a government in which they had no constituents to represent. Slowly at first and then with increasing speed, Democrats left their positions in the Capitol. Meanwhile in the White House, it was becoming more and more obvious to Sydney Armitage that he was running out of allies. While his cabinet remained firm, there were few people in Congress who he could trust to bring his issues to the floor of the House or the Senate. Even more disconcerting was that his security detail was becoming amazingly disrespectful of him. Gone was the time-honored and traditional stoic poses which the secret service was famous for. Instead, when Armitage walked through the halls of the White House, he'd see security agents loafing around, leaning on walls and smiling and joking with each other, visually rubbing in the fact that they didn't consider Armitage their Commander-in-Chief any longer.

And so it came as no surprise to the President on August 23rd when Ronald Roberts stormed into the Oval Office unannounced with his top lieutenants and Armitage's own guards to demand Armitage surrender the Presidency. Roberts listed the charges, all either exaggerated or totally fictitious, and pointed out that Armitage would face impeachment should he take the unwise route of ignoring Roberts. The security man then told Armitage he could make the violence subside and he could guarantee safety for the President and his family if Armitage took the offer. The President saw no other alternative. He agreed to Roberts' terms. And so, at 4 p.m. on August 23rd, 2017, Sydney Armitage vacated the Presidency of the United States, advancing Norman Dukeman into the position and ending America's Second Civil War.

Picking Up the Pieces

As Roberts had promised, the organized violence around the country came to an end by August 24th. Armitage was given a security detail and no restrictions as he returned to civilian life. His new guards started showing their respect for the former President again. His life during his short time as President had been more hectic than he would have ever thought possible, and after giving up the position he suddenly found amazing serenity. He felt safer than ever. Not only was his security detail the best he could ask for but the new government did all it could to keep Armitage happy, out of the limelight and inaccessible to anyone with any questions.

After the swearing in of Norman Dukeman as the 47th President of the United States, he immediately signed an incredible amount of bills into law. He would have been quick to issue many executive orders, but the suddenly heavily-Conservative Congress was equally speedy in sending bills to the White House for his signature. Taking initiatives which were sometimes barely legal and others often not, both houses of Congress and the President drafted, voted on and signed off on 87 bills in the first two days of the Dukeman presidency. A third of the new laws dealt with immigration, deportation and the handling of illegal aliens. Most of the others dealt with abortion, reproductive and homosexual rights.

The new laws concerning citizenship served as an ultimatum to many. It gave illegal immigrants a deadline by which they had to leave the country. This included overturning laws and executive orders from the previous Democratic administrations which had given people in certain situations temporary legal status. Even though the laws didn't do anything to overturn the status of people who had legally become U.S. citizens, many naturalized Americans joined their illegal friends and family members in a quick exodus from the country. Even though the war was over, they feared they would be victims of violence if they remained in the country even a minute past the deadline.

Although the flow of people of Hispanic - not just Mexican - descent out of the United Sates had never stopped, it picked up at a tremendous pace. While the government had given a three-month window in which illegal aliens could safely depart the country, most were gone within the first six weeks. Many had already been planning to leave prior to the passing of the laws.

Not only did Mexico open its border to its returning sons and daughters, but Canada admitted people who were able to produce a Mexican passport or could prove they had family origins from the country on the other side of the United States. The northern neighbor of the United States did this while maintaining its quota of how many U.S. citizens of non-Hispanic origin came into the country. Canada refused to be a haven for deserters and self-proclaimed political refugees from the States as it had been in the past. While Canadian politicians agreed America's problems in the early 21st century equaled a humanitarian emergency compared to the other times the country had welcomed U.S. dissidents, the Canadians were more concerned about the repercussions. The new government in the States was unstable and the way it came to power was cause for even more fear. Canada was concerned that the new cowboy politicians in the U.S. might take armed exception in response to any sympathy it showed towards their bewildered opponents. The northern country was also afraid that sympathizers towards the new U.S. leadership might try to come across the border to sow the seeds of discord.

Like Mexico, much of world was happy to take in those fleeing the United States. For years the southern neighbor lived in the shadows of the U.S. Even before the venom spewed towards the country during the election run of Eduardo Rodriguez, Mexico was scorned for the country's lack of security and its economic situation. After the change of power in the U.S., many people went to Mexico feeling both their lives and money were safer in the southern country. Few who had bought tickets for flights to other countries were turned away from their destinations. The fear of proximity that the Canadian government was so concerned about was a moot point in Europe, Asia and Africa.

By the time the U.S. government's deadline passed, a vast majority of Latino-Americans, whether legal U.S. citizens or not, had left. There were a handful of violent incidents against those who had stayed. President Dukeman offered a month's grace before a crackdown. Driven perhaps by the rise in violence, many of those who had stayed reconsidered their decisions. It was estimated by the time Dukeman's second deadline passed that less than 750,000 people of Hispanic descent remained in the U.S. About two-thirds of those remaining were legal citizens, but that didn't keep them from scrutiny and being forced to show documentation on a daily basis to the new, critical government. People who said they were law-abiding citizens and claimed they were defending the nation's sovereignty were quick to request law enforcement officials to demand papers from anyone who looked Hispanic.

Illegal residents who had stayed were rounded up from their homes and forcibly transported to the nearest international border. This action was taken by proud militia members, unofficially sanctioned by the new national leadership. Those being removed from their homes inland were delivered to transfer camps, then the self-appointed guards took pleasure in an Americanized version of the Bataan Death March.

Families were passed off from one group of guards to another from the stations created up to 200 miles from the borders. The prisoners were forced to walk an average of 20 miles a day while the escorts took turns riding in vehicles and marching on the perimeter of their captive herds. Occasionally a detainee would try to break from the group and would be shot in the back while running. No attempt was made to try and bring the escapees back. A handful of those rounded up died from exhaustion. Most of the fatalities were elderly or children.

When those who survived the marches arrived in Mexico or Canada, they told the waiting international media of the atrocities they had witnessed. There hadn't been any news coverage of the marches since the new government had tightened regulations on the press. Only those media outlets which had been on the friendliest terms with people like Roberts and Hannigan had complete, unquestioned access to every sanctioned American issue and location. An item such as the alleged abuse of illegal individuals wasn't considered newsworthy by these outlets. Individuals who tried to cover events that the government didn't support were subject to arrest and harassment from both the government and from individuals who hounded the reporters. People from non-sanctioned media outlets were forced to work for underground organizations which funneled their reports to newscasters out of the country. When these journalists tried to lodge complaints about physical attacks, law enforcement officials shrugged them off. The same officers snapped into action though when a civilian alleged even the smallest, formerly unremarkable misdeed had been committed by the unsanctioned media. As such, the situation didn't receive proper coverage until the marchers were forced across the U.S. border. When charges of war crimes and crimes against humanity were leveled against the United States, officials in the country laughed them off. They first pointed out there was no war in the country, despite its leaders having used the term of their own volition when hostilities first started. Top U.S. spokespeople called these accusations unjustified, switching between defenses that those who may have died were criminals or pointing out that those deaths, if they had truly happened, were so few compared to people who died at the hands of true tyrants around the globe who never were brought to justice.

The U.S. weathered all the claims and criticism from its Second Civil War and the mass exodus which came afterwards. Soon after the dust had settled, an unprecedented Census poll was conducted. Well over 75-percent of those who responded classified themselves as White, from a Christian denomination and some form of Conservative. The same ratio of American citizens also reported having finished high school as his or her highest level of education, living in households of six people with a combined income of under 90-thousand dollars. The sanctioned media only acknowledged the race, religion and political affiliation results from the Census and nothing more.

The one organization which had any leverage against Roberts was the military. Much to the ire of Roberts, the Joint Chiefs of Staff informed him they and the top officers in their various branches of the military didn't consider Norman Dukeman their Commander-in-Chief any more than Roberts himself was willing to follow orders from Sydney Armitage. Even while many top military people were politically more in line with the Conservative's views, their pride and honor still held them true to the belief the new government was illegal. They would not step down and they would not order their forces into action against their fellow Americans. Dukeman could ask for everyone's resignation but everyone begrudgingly agreed that would result in a schism in the military at best. Nobody wanted to guess how that might play out or what worse consequences there could be if the military's chain of command was removed and replaced. Roberts soon realized he wouldn't gain control of the military as he'd hoped. Instead he capitulated and agreed to the military's plan. They would not revolt against the new regime so long as they remained in their positions. To deter as many active service people from taking action one way or another, an inordinate amount of U.S. forces were sent to reinforce the campaigns against terror in other parts of the world. The U.S. issued its sternest warning in history: the world's greatest country remained as vigilant as ever. Any attempt to attack the U.S. would be met with the strongest retaliation. The nuclear option was brought to the table, bringing a chill across the global theater. The rest of the world was on alert: all that was happening in the United States was strictly an internal matter and the world as a whole faced annihilation if the country's unilateral privacy wasn't respected.

We Walked Off to Look for America

Bull settled into his favorite recliner and turned on his television set after his security detail had brought him home. His part in the Freedom Day ceremony had diminished over the few years the event existed. The first year he had been given an air gun similar to the one he had used to shoot President Rodriguez and was told to fire the full load of blanks into the air. After that, he was asked to wave emphatically to the crowd, then to say some words about how happy he was to be living in the Land of the Truly Free.

The following year Bull waved and spoke, his enthusiasm still strong despite the gun restrictions placed on him. The removal of the gun from the ceremony was because he was no longer allowed to handle firearms. The event which made him a hero also made him dangerous in the eyes of the court. The new government was able to keep him from more jail time than he had already served at the hands of the previous administration, but it stood by the court's ruling that Bull was guilty of murder. As a pseudo-felon, he was forever denied the right to own any firearms. Occasionally some political leaders would take him hunting as a way of showing their gratitude to him and they allowed him to carry and fire the various weapons they took. Each time the politicians would remind Bull of their illegal gifts to him.

As Bull sat in his chair, he contemplated the difference between past Freedom Days and that year's. He had been discouraged from speaking at the most recent festival. "Discouraged" was Roberts' word for it. Bull would say he was forced from his speaking role. He had arrived at the National Mall extremely excited about his part in the festivities, but was quickly told by Ron about a change in the program.

Roberts asked first about a perceived lack of enthusiasm on Bull's part, bringing up concerns brought to him by Bull's security detail. According to Roberts, Bull had made comments about how he believed the Norman Dukeman administration was slow in living up to some of its promises made after its takeover. Before Bull could react to the accusation, Roberts firmly suggested it wouldn't be in Bull's interest to speak at the event. "Just in case you have a slip of the tongue," Ron said.

And so, without being given much of a chance to defend himself, the decision was made. Bull went up on the stage and waved and was kept far away from the microphones.

Bull had indeed suggested what Roberts accused him of saying to his house guards. Bull was starting to feel his presidential namesake was as big a disappointment as Eduardo Rodriguez had been and that the new administration hadn't delivered a higher quality of American life. Norman Dukeman was actually more of a letdown than Rodriguez because Bull had no expectations from the latter and total faith in the former. The Freedom Day function that morning was another one of those disappointments. The intimidation and the suppression of free speech he experienced that day was an example of the removal of Bull's rights and he felt powerless to do anything about it.

He thought about years and campaigns past. Bull had often heard the question during election cycles about whether people were "better off now than four years ago." In 2020, the question was not being asked. There was no talk of anyone who could be a serious challenge to Norman Dukeman, therefore there was no reason to wonder if the American Way could be improved.

When he asked the question to himself, Bull realized he couldn't answer with a definitive response. He lived in a great house in a Virginia suburb of Washington, D.C. It wasn't anything he had ever dreamed of or planned for, but Ron insisted on the move so the government could properly protect Dukeman. Roberts adamantly claimed that there were plenty of Liberal militants still out there who wanted to kill Bull in retaliation for his assassination. The guerrilla forces had killed Mark Carter, as Roberts had often pointed out while defending his motives for keeping Dukeman where the government could easily keep an eye on him. This also accounted for the live-in guards that Dukeman had.

Along with his new mansion, Bull and his family received a nice stipend from the government. They compared it to a retainer fee and told Dukeman it was payment for appearances he made and speeches he gave on behalf of the President and his new regime. This was for events such as Freedom Day or at gun shows in the District of Columbia or for sanctioned interviews with sanctioned news outlets, when he spoke about sanctioned topics. The irony of his speaking at gun shows wasn't lost on Bull, even if most of the nation was unaware of his weapons ban. As for the interviews, an intelligence staffer always gave Gary notes about the proper talking points and the media was very good about taking multiple shots should he flub a line or say something which wasn't in total agreement with the government's stance.

Another perk was the complete health care package he received. After the fighting was over, the legislature and President quickly rolled back the Affordable Care Act and privatized many other government health care programs. Only coverage for government employees remained fully as it had been. Dukeman and his family were granted this coverage. This was validated by the notion that through his spokesman role he was considered a government employee. It took a year of chiropractic visits for Gary's back to feel like it had before his accident. There had been times when he thought he'd never return to such a level of physical comfort.

Yet despite having some of the best benefits the nation had to offer, Bull still couldn't say he lived the charmed life he expected to after a change of national leadership. Gary and his wife were required to have an armed escort wherever they went and the number of places he was allowed to go were severely limited. Because of the security restrictions, he was all but constrained to the District of Columbia. He had to admit the government line about not needing to leave the region was pretty much true. The nation's capital still was home to the Smithsonian and its great museums. There were amazing stores and decent malls all over the region. Even though he was a meat and potatoes type of guy, he was still impressed with the selection of restaurants D.C. offered. He knew he would never try the Ethiopian or Indian cuisine, but it was still exciting when he thought of the options. Joanna, who was a bit more worldly than Bull, had tried some of the food offerings. She was seldom impressed and noted that the people who worked in the ethnic restaurants she went to didn't look like they represented ethnicities matching the cuisine.

Bull wasn't sure how much his confinement was connected to the issue, but he was saddened by how much his avenues of communication had shrunk. This was both at a personal and an entertainment level. As the government tightened its grasp on the news networks, it also brought new restrictions for the broadcast networks. The result was a multitude of stations that steered clear of anything which could in any way be deemed inappropriate, for fear of receiving outrageous fines or suspensions. Public broadcasting stations disappeared across the U.S. within a year of Norman Dukeman being sworn in. Government funding for PBS was cut during the second big round of new laws passed by Washington. The government also took new aim at cable and premium stations, some of which had been able to broadcast whatever they had wanted. Many of them shut down, unable to attract the viewers with their new, watered down programming. It didn't help that many of the top American stars had been among the first to leave the country when the fighting began. There were few high-profile television shows or movies being produced in the United States and the government was making it tough for stations and movie studios to import product from other countries.

The declining communications possibilities went much further than that. The Internet had received even harsher new laws and rules. Every site and server had to register with the new Department of Electronic Media Regulation (DoEMR, or "doe-mer"). Only those which could prove beyond a reasonable doubt that they were not-for-profit were spared high fees. Email was no longer free and there were charges by the kilobyte to both send and receive. These fees were ironically done in the name of free enterprise. Despite new rates for the Internet and email, it was still the cheapest reliable option. The United States Postal Service had been further privatized within the second month of the Dukeman presidency and the prices to send letters and packages were astronomical. Landline phones were completely phased out of existence after a rapid three-year decline. DoEMR took control of cellular and satellite phones and in the name of security deemed it necessary to be able to record all conversations and text messages. DoEMR then turned its new costs over to the service providers, who added the lofty costs to their monthly charges. While Bull enjoyed many benefits from the government, he wasn't given any sort of allowance towards travel or communications. As a result, Bull had lost contact with his family and everyone he knew in West Virginia. He felt isolated. He and Joanna had few people they considered good friends in the area. Gary's daughter had made a few friends, but they and their parents had no desire to associate with the elder Dukemans.

Bull hadn't driven since he shot the President and Roberts had strongly insinuated that he shouldn't consider it ever again. Ron made it abundantly clear that if he ever wanted to go anywhere, Bull was to ask his guards to take him there. They were happy to take him anywhere he wanted go within the extended Washington-Baltimore area. On occasional trips with one politician or another, Bull would be treated to a ride in a new hover-car. These rides were exhilarating, as all of these low-altitude airborne vehicles were open-top. Most people rode in these machines with just a pair of goggles but some wore facemasks as well. As a passenger, these flights made Dukeman understand why dogs loved to ride with their heads out of car windows.

Another thing which upset Bull was his daughter's education. While he was thankful to the government for providing her with a grant for school - the amount of available educational funding had been severely cut back by the government - she was forced to go into a business-related field. The Dukeman administration forced all monetary recipients to declare for only certain degrees. Bull's daughter had been thinking about going into writing, journalism or education. However the government didn't fund writing or journalism because they were considered too artistic and out of fear that students might start spewing subversive jargon in their work. Much the same was said about teachers, and anyone applying for federal aid for school was subject to review. Bull's daughter's unique perspective on history where her father was concerned caused a government review board to classify her as a potential subversive.

Bull wasn't only discouraged by the way the President failed to live up to his expectations, he was concerned how there were items the government passed which contradicted their pledges. Washington had done an admirable job eliminating many offices responsible for regulating business and industry as promised, however there seemed to still be much more government regulation for the commoner. DoMER and the way government regulated what college students studied were just two items he constantly thought about. In his special case he had to tell at least one government official about anything he wanted to do outside his own house.

That was the quandary of his new life. While he undoubtedly was living very comfortably, his personal liberties had been taken away. His opinion on whether or not he was better off than before the Norman Dukeman years changed almost daily. On those days when he was distracted from his loss of freedom, he would easily admit his life was better. On the days when he was given a moment to reflect on the basic things he was no longer allowed to do, he was extremely disgruntled with how his life was going. He hated to admit it, but the days of despair outnumbered those of elation.

Skid Row

It was soon after Election Day when Bull was summoned to downtown Washington D.C. His guards had delivered the invitation that morning, telling Gary he had an unexpected and unavoidable meeting with Ron Roberts at the J. Edgar Hoover Building, the home of the Federal Bureau of Investigation. Roberts was now the Secretary of Defense, but spent an inordinate amount of time within the buildings of the FBI and CIA compared to the Pentagon or other military-oriented outposts. When Bull was told about Roberts' request to see him, Dukeman was told there was some flexibility in the time, but it was imperative that the meeting take place that day.

Bull didn't try to delay the meeting. Even if he had had something to do that day, his curiosity was too great for him to push the event back any farther than necessary. Within an hour of being summoned, he and his guards were on the road.

Gary felt excited during the drive, taking in what he hoped was the dawn of a new era. As expected, Norman Dukeman had won a full term as President. In the end, there was a second candidate in the running, a former Democratic representative who was pushed into the contest for the sake of giving people the illusion that there was indeed a choice other than Norman Dukeman. The incumbent won with 87-percent of the popular vote and all of the nation's Electoral College behind him.

To refer to the "other" candidate as a former Democrat was the norm in the post-Rodriguez era. While the party hadn't officially disbanded, the term held a distinctively negative connotation in the

United States. A handful of politicians who had been Democrats prior to the war had changed parties, at least in name. Their new peers took a dim view of them, and in the tradition of labeling some Bulldog Democrats disdainfully called these few Poodle Democrats. There were a few who still proudly or stupidly called themselves Democrats, who were subject to verbal and rare physical assaults because of their undying affiliation of the party which they believed in. The continued gerrymandering of counties and representative districts around the country also limited the number of political miscreants left in the federal government. In total, there were 73 Poodles and six true Democrats in the House of Representatives. In the Senate there were four and two respectively. Most who had held office before the revolt hadn't even tried to run in the following elections. Many had fled the country with their party mates soon after the fighting had stopped. Those who were sympathetic to the old Democratic plight were from regions where the party had always maintained strong control. There was a wave of support for a new Constitutional amendment which would allow these states to cede from the Union. The sanctioned media claimed there was a strong likelihood this could become law very soon. It was suggested the whole of New England plus New York and perhaps New Jersey might be pushed out of the United States, which would leave only the West Coast as anything resembling a Democratic stronghold in the nation.

With things going so incredibly well for the Dukeman administration, Gary's mind raced around the possible topics of the upcoming meeting. Perhaps they were planning a victory rally and they wanted him to be part of it. Maybe there would be a special event for Thanksgiving, since the nation had so much to be thankful for now that the country had finally achieved a one-party ideology. Bull wondered if it was too early for the administration to start planning for Inauguration Day, and they were about to discuss his part in the festivities.

With all these hopeful thoughts running through his head, he was totally blindsided when Ron Roberts told Bull that the Dukemans were being returned to West Virginia, sans any of the benefits they had enjoyed over the last few years.

Bull only paid partial attention as the news was broken to him. He remembered something about Roberts saying that with there no longer being a threat against Dukeman's life, the cost to protect his family was too great. They had been living off government entitlements for too long. Roberts also brought up again various comments Bull had made to his guards. Ron said Gary's words were of the greatest concern, showing he had lost faith in the government and that Norman Dukeman couldn't afford to keep a potential enemy of the state so close to the government. Bull thought he'd heard something about having nobody to blame but himself and mention of being treated very well and more than fairly. Ron thanked Bull for his contributions to American history and told Gary he and his wife would have a few days to collect their belongings. They would then be driven to Reagan National Airport and flown back home to West Virginia where their old house had sat vacant for the past four years. The only benefit they would be allowed to keep was for their daughter. She would be allowed to stay at Georgetown on full scholarship.

Bull rode back to his soon-to-be-ex-home in stunned silence. Joanna eagerly welcomed him home, having expected to hear whatever happy news Gary thought he would receive from Ron. Instead she too was deflated when she heard the privileged life they had been living was about to end.

Over the next two days the Dukemans packed their clothing and the few decorative items they had brought with them or had bought over the last few years into duffle bags and boxes. They hadn't brought much with them since the house they had been awarded remained furnished with the previous owners' discards. Their daughter came over early in the packing process to wish them well and say she hoped to see them soon. They hadn't even thought about the history of the house until that point, and wouldn't have seen any irony in the fact that the house had belonged to one of the Senate's former Democratic leaders before she had moved to Europe during the exodus. Joanna thought about taking some items they didn't really own, but Bull thought anything they commandeered would be noticeably missed and dissuaded her from such actions.

After those few days and a weepy departure, the Dukemans were driven to the airport. Their guards wished them well as they got out of their limo but the couple said nothing. The Dukemans were sure each of the guards had betrayed Bull with their reports to Ron. A different security entourage then rushed the Dukemans unceremoniously through all the checkpoints in a way which kept the couple out of contact from other people using the airport. They were loaded onto a waiting private jet and flown to Morgantown Municipal Airport. From there, they were taken by a rare, enclosed hover-car back to their home.

When they walked into their house, they were happy to see everything was left as it had been and that somebody had done a respectable job cleaning and maintaining the home. The pantry was well-stocked, the towels and sheets were clean and neatly gathered in the linen closet. After a whirlwind three-plus years and a violent rollercoaster of a week, it felt good to the Dukemans to be truly home. They found their bed freshly made and after a light dinner the couple retired early. It turned out to be a very restful night.

The Dukemans slept in late and then ate a big breakfast. It was 10 a.m. on a Friday morning when they went to sit on their porch for a little while. They had decided to wait for the following week before going to look for jobs. If nothing else, Bull decided he'd try to take a job in the mines just to get his foot back in the door. They planned to make it a three-day weekend to relax and get used to being back home. It took the couple a few minutes after settling into their old wicker loveseat on the front patio to realize things weren't as they remembered. Usually on a weekday, especially in the non-summer months, the block tended to be quiet because most people were at work. While there wasn't much activity, there definitely was evidence that there were more people home than the Dukemans expected. The couple watched as some people went about work on their houses or lawns. Upon further examination, they noticed how many vehicles were still in driveways and they were surprised that many of them were dirty. It wasn't just that the trucks were muddy. That was normal since people in the neighborhood often went off-roading regularly. In this case, the SUVs and such were simply dusty.

Bull had spent about a half-hour on the porch, watching his neighbor from across the street Arthur Sheppard working in his own yard. At first Sheppard helped his wife hang the laundry on the lines he had running across the lawn. After that, he started working on the dirt patches around the base of his house. He had long been the envy of the neighborhood when it came to his garden. Every year, his flower bed put all others to shame with the most radiant array of tulips and rose bushes. Art insisted it was his own special mix of fertilizer which made the difference. Considering Sheppard's unquestionable position as the best gardener in the neighborhood, everyone agreed with his self-assessment.

It took Bull minutes to realize what was wrong with the scene playing out in front of him: Art wasn't planting his usual prize-worthy seasonal flowers where he used to. While Bull couldn't tell exactly what Sheppard was putting in the ground, he knew the various seeds were different from the flower bulbs Art so lovingly planting each season.

After watching Art for a few more moments, Bull decided to investigate. He walked across the street. "Hi, Art," he said when he was practically standing over his neighbor.

"Hi, Gary," Art responded, looking up at Bull for the first time. He quickly turned back to what he was doing.

"How's it going? We just got back from Washington. I've been watching you planting here for a while."

"I know."

"Well, uh," Bull was at a bit of a loss of words. Before Dukeman's odyssey started, Art seemed like one of Bull's biggest supporters. He used terms like "inspiring" and "thoughtful" and "unselfish" to describe Gary and his willingness to bring his struggles to the national scene through Fleet Sussman. Dukeman had heard how Sheppard proudly ranted to others in town about being neighbors with Bull, as though that made him closer to Dukeman personally than anyone else in town. In Bull's mind the two had had a regular friendship, nothing any more special than Dukeman's relationship with any of the regulars at Mahoney's. Bull snapped out of his moment of recollection and continued talking to Art, "what are you doing?"

"I'm planting tomatoes and beans."

"Really? What happened to your flowerbed?"

Art looked up again, with a slight display of aggravation in his motions. "I couldn't afford it anymore." When Art saw the lack of understanding on Bull's face, he started to explain, "look, I lost my job a couple of years ago and I had to give up the tulips for something edible to save money."

Bull let what he'd just heard sink in before responding. "You lost your job? When? I'm sorry…"

"Two years ago, I just told you!" Art snapped, "and are you *really* sorry? Most people around here have lost their jobs, but you wouldn't know that. You were too busy living off taxpayer dollars in Washington!"

Bull didn't like Art's tone and allusions. "Are you suggesting I wanted to leave here?"

"All I know is what they showed on television. And it looked like you were living high on the hog, going to all the Washington parties and living in a nice house while your friends here were all struggling to survive." Sheppard put a sarcastic emphasis on the word 'friends.'

Art continued, "Heck, they sent soldiers to guard your empty house once you guys settled in Washington. They left yesterday, leaving you with everything you could need and warning us not to try to take or touch anything. They were so trusting of us, they left only five minutes before you arrived. They even said as much, calling us leeches."

Now it was Bull's turn to snap, "Hey! It wasn't my idea to leave and despite what you seem to think, I went through Hell too! Did the government leave you to rot in a cell? Did you have to live in confinement for the last four years? It may have looked nice to you, but it was still a prison for us. We never were able to leave unless we had somebody to guard us and even then they only allowed us to go certain places."

"You had no worries about food, about losing your house. You took welfare abuse to a new level while we here were left to fend for ourselves with no jobs, no assistance. We all are in a state of limbo right now because our houses, our town isn't worth shit."

"Wasn't that what we wanted? The government to stop giving out benefits, to stop supporting deadbeats?" As soon as that last phrase left his mouth, he knew it was a mistake. He hoped Art wouldn't notice.

Sheppard however did take offense, "are you calling me a deadbeat? Worthless? Screw you! Why don't you go see your friends in town? I'm sure they'd like to talk to you. Just get outta my yard and don't come back on my property again!"

Bull was set to tell Art to screw himself as well, but decided it would be better to listen to his neighbor instead. Dukeman went back to his place, stormed passed his wife who had been watching from the porch and went inside. Joanna followed him in and Bull told her the parts of the conversation she hadn't been able to hear. She asked what he planned to do and Gary said going to Maloney's sounded like a good idea. He looked in the drawer where he had kept the keys to his car and was happy to see they were still there. He was equally pleased to find his old Ford Taurus still in the garage and filled with gas. To complete his good fortune, the car turned over right away, despite being ten years old and possibly not driven for four years. Once the car was warmed up, Bull backed out of the garage and headed to town.

The Times They Are A-Changin'

The sun had just started to set when Gary Dukeman returned home from his adventure on Main Street. As soon as his wife saw him walk through the door, she could tell how shaken he was by the ordeal. Knowing the answer already, she obligatorily asked if everything was okay.

At first, all Gary could do was stutter, then he said, "no, I don't think so." After that he grabbed his wife in a strong embrace before he started sobbing. He then amended his statement, saying, "no, things are not alright."

Joanna led her spouse to the kitchen where she had been preparing dinner from the food supply which had been left for them. The aroma of steaks was strong in the room. She started to brew some coffee for her husband. When the coffee was ready, she gave a cup to Bull, the way she always had when he came home a little out of sorts from the bar. Bull took the drink and thanked her. After a long first sip he told her he hadn't had a single drop to drink at Maloney's. This concerned Joanna to think her husband was sober and still so bent out of shape. After Gary had his second sip of coffee she asked what had happened. Bull, having gained much of his composure back, looked at his wife and started to recall his afternoon.

It started with the unusual ride into town. Bull immediately noticed the horrid condition of the roads. The primary streets were full of potholes and the smaller roads were tremendously cracked by the incredible amount of weeds and plants which had broken through the asphalt. In one place, he saw a large dimple in the asphalt, next to which a medium-sized tree stump laid on its side. Pieces of the cut up trunk were on the shoulder of the road and partially in the driving lane itself. There was another point where what had once been a paved road was more like a dirt drive, with few remaining pieces of blacktop embedded in the soil.

Main Street was in better condition in the center of town, but the improvement wasn't great. Bull noticed there was a lack of cars parked on the street. He also noted that while the streets were okay in town, the storefronts were in dire condition. Most of the shops were closed and a number of the old shops were boarded up. The shoe store, the small appliance repair shop, the corner deli and the real estate office were no more. Also gone was the general store in which Bull had injured his back years prior. The windows of this particular store were still uncovered on the outside. On the inside however, a good number of posters were taped up, advertising the nearby national chain one-stop shopping location. Bull had ambivalent memories of that superstore. It was in its parking lot where Skip first spoke to Gary about killing President Rodriguez. As for Main Street, just a couple of businesses remained open. Among them was Maloney's. With a small amount of adrenaline pumping through his veins, Bull opened the door to the bar and walked in.

Bull told his wife how surprised he was to see the bar as quiet as it was. Maloney's was virtually empty compared to what he remembered, with only four people there, all sulking in their libations. Nobody bothered to lock up when he walked in. They all remained staring at their beers, seemingly unaware of anyone around them. The one barkeep was turned away from the door, playing solitaire or some other solo card game. Bull had to clear his throat to get anyone to notice he had just come through the door. At that point, only the bartender turned to look.

It was a kid Bull didn't recognize, but the barkeep sure seemed to know Bull.

"Well, look who just came in. It's our 'hero,'" the other man's voice full of disdain. It was then everybody looked up. Nobody else said a word.

He told his wife he had to ask the kid if they had met before. "No," the bartender had told him, "but I certainly know you. Sure, thanks to you, I have my job!"

Bull started to feel a bit of pride in himself, a pride he hadn't felt in a long while. The sensation was short-lived. The bartender went on to say how he had been a chemistry student at West Virginia on a scholarship before the President was killed. Once the new regime was in place though, they liquidated all but a handful of federal scholarships for education and appropriated them for athletes, saying that that would help the schools gain money from fans. The young man said he was left without the money to finish school, but that didn't matter because the science department was drastically slashed at the uiversity. The nearby energy-producing companies, such as the one which owned the mines Bull had worked at, threatened to pull funding if the school continued to pursue alternate energy studies. When it became obvious he had no reason to stay in Morgantown, he decided to try to get home. The kid used what money he had to survive as he hitchhiked southeast. His funds quickly ran out and he was stranded in what the kid called "this Podunk town." He pointed out it was a mix of compassion and pity which led to him becoming the daytime bartender at Maloney's. He then thanked Bull again for opening that door and as he said "for closing any other doors I had for a real future."

He spoke up for himself, saying he had been a prisoner in his own house in Virginia, but the barkeep was having none of it. "You got to live comfortably in a plush house and not have a job," the kid responded, "excuse me if I don't feel sorry for you."

Dukeman was getting ready to defend himself again when one of the other bar patrons interrupted, suggesting that Gary give up the argument. Bull looked up to see that the other man was a regular he knew as J.R. The aging patron added that the bartender was the lucky one, having a job, let alone one everyone in the town had wanted. The kid was fortunate that he had tended bar in college and actually had the skills which nobody in town outside of the few already at the pub already had. J.R. pointed out that many would have sold their families for the opportunity and the kid had faced threats of violence not unlike those the Mexican workers had been subject to all those years ago when Bull made his first call to Fleet Sussman. Bull told his wife J.R. seemed completely serious about the possibility of people giving up their families for what was considered such a cushy job.

Bull considered J.R. less of a friend than Art had been, meaning they hadn't gotten to know each other well. They were just part of the same crowd at Maloney's and there wasn't much else to their relationship. J.R. had been more even-keeled than Sheppard, and as far as Bull knew the man at the bar hadn't ever been a braggart about knowing Dukeman.

He was still set to go on the offensive but then curiosity got the better of him. He asked J.R. where everybody else was. Dukeman considered the other three customers at the bar to be similar acquaintances as he viewed J.R. In reality Bull knew the others even less.

Gary told his wife how, according to J.R., the core regulars at Maloney's had been peeled away over the years. A number of the patrons who had been elderly way back in the day had passed away. Dick Patton and Doc had left town when they could. Patton had made a big deal about getting out soon after the War began, saying bad times were on the way. He said he was running to Canada. At the time people scoffed at him, called him a traitor for preferring to be with the illegals than with the honest people of West Virginia. It soon became obvious though that Patton had a better read on the situation than the others at the bar. Doc bolted when Obamacare was officially killed and it became obvious nobody would be able to pay for medical care. Mrs. Dukeman said she couldn't believe that and Bull said he'd explain more about what he heard in a second. Then he finished his rundown on the other regulars. Most of them flatly had run out of money even for the casual afternoon beer. Only the few who were there with J.R. could afford to remain regulars at Maloney's. They were the widowers who didn't have children but had plenty in savings to keep drinking.

In J.R.'s case, he didn't have much in savings, but he was dying, presumably with terminal lung cancer. He couldn't be too sure without a doctor in town and no way to get to a half-way decent medical facility, but he was pretty sure that was the diagnosis. It didn't really matter if he could make it to a specialist. Without insurance, he had no way to pay for any treatments. Instead, he decided he'd die drunk but happy.

What really concerned Bull about the fate of the regulars was that of Skip. J.R. told Bull his cousin had been picked up by some government men shortly after the President had been shot. Nobody had heard from him since.

J.R. went on to describe the little of Skip they'd seen before his presumed arrest. He had ran in the morning of Rodriguez' speech at the university and made sure the television was showing coverage of the event. At first the other regulars thought Skip had lost his mind. They threw rolled up cocktail napkins at him and booed, but Skip insisted they'd see something special that day. The other patrons relented, warning Skip he better be right. As the President finished speaking, the bar crowd started to get boisterous again, turning their half-serious anger back at Skip. He just told them to wait a moment. They watched as Rodriguez walked from the podium, then saw some sort of commotion as the President fell to the ground. It took a few moments for the people at Maloney's –and for that matter the commentators – to comprehend what had just happened. As everyone at the bar started to understand, a few people applauded. Most of those present then turned to Skip, ready to ask him how he knew. He just told them to keep watching. As the television station analyzed what had happened, Skip suddenly yelled out "there!" and pointed to the screen. There, in a freeze frame, was Bull, gun in hand. More people cheered, but not everyone. Dick Patton looked as pale as possible and a few others as well. J.R. looked Bull square in the eye as he explained he was probably as white as Patton. J.R. said he wasn't impressed with Bull for what he had done. While J.R. reminded Dukeman that he wasn't a fan of Rodriguez either, he still was repulsed that somebody he knew could fathom killing the President of the United States.

J.R. remained even toned though as he resumed his story. In the following days, federal authorities released Dukeman's identification to the country. The evening after the revelation it felt like the entire population of the nation descended on the town as scores of satellite vans and reporters drove into the usually sleepy hamlet. Helicopters began buzzing around, filming everything and especially Bull's house. Bull had heard that part of the story from his wife when they were reunited after his liberation. Bull told Joanna that J.R.'s account of the situation wasn't much different from her own. It was two days after the reporters arrived that Skip was picked up and rushed out of town. The rest of the townsfolk seldom mentioned him after that, everyone wondering if it was one of their other neighbors who had told the media or officials about how Skip had known what was going to happen. In the subsequent weeks, the belief around the circle of friends was that Patton was the culprit, although nobody had any proof.

J.R. explained how while there was ambivalence about Gary killing the President, everyone in town was shocked and saddened by the murder of Fleet Sussman. Even Patton, who stated it was going to be the start of something big. It was possibly the first time everyone at the bar agreed with one of his assessments. Nobody was surprised therefore when the war began. Maloney's was usually quiet on Sundays as the regulars always spent the day in church and with their families. Some had been watching the Hall of Fame inductions from Cooperstown when the news broke. The news of the fighting around the country and especially in New York filtered around the town, and everyone converged on the bar to discuss what was happening. Those gathered were in awe and disbelief. J.R. said nobody would ever admit it but everyone was scared out of his or her wits. J.R. said watching the news from Philadelphia later in the week was even worse. As a veteran of both Gulf Wars, he said seeing a national monument like the Liberty Bell taken under siege sent chills up his spine. Something like that was not supposed to ever happen in the U.S. He expected to see something like that back in Iraq: religious fighting among Kurds, Shiites and Sunnis. War between Americans, because of nothing but race, not even ideological differences, was something J.R. had thought he'd never see in his adult life. The attackers didn't care that their targets could even be allies but just figured their racial background was enough to assume they were welfare-loving Liberal cheats. "Between your shooting the President and the Philly Massacre, it made me actually think about leaving the country as well," J.R. said.

As the story went, most people were happy the way the war unfolded. J.R. was as well, although for different reasons. There was a vast majority of people in town who were happy with what was going on nationally. Once Hannigan gave his proclamation, the locals were comforted knowing the country wasn't under attack from an outside power. Just about all the regulars at Maloney's idolized Hannigan and the way he threw countless dollars behind candidates who had their priorities straight. To find out he was taking matters into his own hands and would do his best to clear the country of the unsavory even gave comfort to many. There had long been speculation as to what sort of ties the businessman had to people in government, the military and national security. This left little question in anyone's mind that Hannigan was indeed connected to important officials.

And while the crowd at Maloney's celebrated what they expected would soon be the start of a Golden Era, J.R. felt great sadness. The state of the States was not why he had signed up to defend the country. He was also glad that the opposition realized Paradise had been lost and that many fled. Many people in town considered those who ran chickens, even the Hispanic people who the regulars wanted to see leave. J.R. however saw them as the smart ones, knowing more fighting wasn't worth it.

J.R. hadn't said anything about his disappointment to the regulars at Maloney's and said telling Bull then and there might have been the first time he admitted his frustration to anyone. Mentioning his discontent before would have led to ostracism similar to what Dick Patton received. J.R. expected others would have questioned his patriotism despite being the only regular at the bar to have served in the military. What he could have said no longer mattered. Besides, there was no longer any love in town for the new regime.

When the dust settled after what little fighting there had been and the new government took over, optimism was higher among those who remained than anyone could remember. Only in cities such as New York, Boston and San Francisco - the remaining strongholds of the Liberals - was there skepticism. Those cities remained true to their political roots, but with the upheaval in Washington, they had little say in the national dialogue. Many dissuaded Americans who couldn't afford to leave the country or who were too stubborn to leave migrated to these cities. J.R. described the situation as a tense compromise. The new regime would have loved to let everything northeast of Philadelphia cede from the Union if so much global capital hadn't been vested in New York and Wall Street. Instead, the government made many concessions for the region to keep its residents placated while not threatening to rip apart the Union. They were awkward concessions which J.R. didn't understand. For instance, while taxes were abolished in most of the country, the northeast was granted the right to raise taxes locally. The locals apparently were happy with this, which J.R. chalked up to the incomprehensible Liberal mind. Washington also allowed the northeast to keep using solar power and other forms of renewable energy, despite the dangers politicians insisted these power sources generated. Then there was the fact that all Conservative authorities and reporters stressed how the taxed-out, power-starved region was turning into a wasteland but international tourists still flocked to New York and Boston.

Bull had heard all the same contradictions. He did after all get his news from the same trusted sources as J.R. Conservatives and their media supporters loved to scoff at these items, but never spoke in depth about the various topics. The reasons and discrepancies were avoided as if they were just facts of life and not worthy of explanation. The oddities of Liberal thinking were well-publicized and had been turned into a point of much humor by the main news network and weren't treated as anything newsworthy.

J.R. then turned the conversation to the local situation, saying things in the region made just as little sense. "Mainly," J.R. said, "where the solar power was concerned." For all the dangers that were connected to the capture and use of solar energy, the government had done its best to keep it from being used. And yet, the mining operations nearby were all heavily reliant on solar to fuel their operations. The companies colluded together to say they needed to use the sun to power their massive drills and vehicles, claiming that to use their own coal-based fossil fuels would cut into their output and therefore their profits. They were willing to risk the danger of solar posed to their employees, claiming the industry couldn't afford to stay in business otherwise. The government moved surprisingly quickly on approving this use of alternative energy, considering how hard members of the new regime had fought to suppress all non-fossil fuels. But then, the safety concerns were not in play. The companies were willing to risk damage to their equipment and there was no longer any protection for workers.

That was what baffled and infuriated J.R. the most. When the Conservative leadership gained complete and unchallenged control of the nation, they quickly repealed and removed many workers' rights and protections such as safety boards and other regulatory departments. So when it was announced the lawmakers capitulated so willingly on solar, it

195

left everyone in the mining communities feeling dejected, deflated and defeated. Their lives were worth less than the equipment they ran.

And yet, as dangerous as they had been told the solar-powered equipment was, none of the accidents in any of the regional mining operations were caused by the alternative energy engines. There had been a dramatic increase in accidents, injuries and fatalities on company land, but none of them stemmed from the overheated ground or scorched earth the media had told them to expect. The air at the mining sites was noticeably cleaner. Only the really heavy equipment which needed more power than solar could generate discharged fumes and smog.

The rise in accidents was instead caused by the older equipment. The mine workers would tell stories about how the increase was caused by the dinosaurs which no longer were maintained to the standards they had been in previous years, or about how the companies were no longer constrained by rules regulating how long or at what speed mining machines could be operated. Those safety regulations and the government departments which had enforced them had long been disposed of. Likewise enforcement of the 40-hour work week and the end of overtime pay rates allowed the mining companies to force their employees to work 50 or 60 hours with minimal compensation. This caused many miners to push themselves to the point of fatigue and beyond. The workers were making less money and were afraid to turn down hours when they were offered. J.R. scoffed at the term. "Offered," he said, "it's more like they're ordered to work long weeks. If you refuse the offer, you lose your job to someone willing to work the whole week. The boys learned that very quickly. After the first couple of refusals and firings, they stopped turning down the 'opportunity' to work overtime. They had to take it. It's not like the union is there to protect them anymore."

According to the mining companies however, there was only one cause for any accident: operator error. Every report was written to explain how the workers were at fault for everything. If something blew up, it was because the operator had misused the equipment. If there was an explosion in the mine, it was because a miner drilled in the wrong place. If he (J.R. pointed out no women worked in the mines anymore), dozed off momentarily at the end of a 60-hour week, it was his fault for trying to work too much. When the guy at the controls was at fault, the company didn't have to pay the injured parties. There was no way to dispute the company's findings: the owners wouldn't allow any other party to examine the equipment, not that the employees had a union or any qualified investigators to challenge the official results. The new regulations or lack thereof allowed the mining corporations to get away with not insuring their employees. Those unfortunate enough to be in the area would also not receive compensation. Company policy mandated that the responsible party be financially responsible to the injured parties. The owners went to great lengths to tell the families of those found at fault that it was only out of the owners' collective hearts that they were being compassionate and not holding the survivors responsible for the damage to equipment or the loss in profits the accidents caused.

Needless to say, the families of the dead never received any compensation. They had no representation to try and get a settlement, nor did the families of the so-called responsible parties have money to spare. Nothing was the way J.R. or most people in town had expected things to be. If things were bad under President Rodriguez, they were completely horrid under President Dukeman.

The townsfolk, presumably like most of the Susspicious Minds and Tea Partiers, had long been told deregulation and smaller government would lead to more jobs and better pay. The opposite proved true, as J.R.

demonstrated. Companies – not just the mines but other major local operations - were saving money by not having to live up to the old, oppressive standards. However, the heavily-anticipated trickle down never happened. Instead, things got worse. The lax safety regulations were bad enough for hazardous professions, but the notion that compensation for serious injuries and death would go away had never been brought up by the politicians or the media. Workman's compensation was quietly abandoned. Most states approved right-to-work status, allowing the country to completely dissolve unions and lower wages. Overtime and limits on hours worked, as J.R. had described, were among the regulations which saw a quick demise. It got worse, especially in that region.

With the Affordable Care Act quickly repealed under President Dukeman and companies free from regulations regarding their workers, the miners and their families had no physical protections. What J.R. had mentioned about families not receiving compensation in accidents was just one aspect of the problem. There was no health care available for the blue collar workers or their spouses or children. Most had been forced to abandon their life insurance policies because those prices, like private health plans, were too expensive. It didn't matter much because in both the health and life insurance systems, anything paid in was never returned. The life insurance providers always came up with similar findings about accidents in the mines and while nobody could remember it or find it in the original copies of their policies, apparently there were stipulations that the loss of life or limb due to human error was to be paid out by the party at fault, and that person was also denied payment as having been the cause of some unnatural phenomenon. The discrepancy was in the revised insurance regulations, and the providers insisted they had notified their policyholders of the change though nobody could remember such an advisement. After the first few disillusioned families had been relocated, others just gave up their coverage.

Bull asked J.R. what he had meant about "relocation." J.R. gave a small whistle and chuckled. With total control of literally everything and everyone on its property, the prominent mining companies built barracks on their land. The enterprise then issued orders that all employees and their families had to live in these buildings for safety reasons and for conservation purposes. There were shops and restaurants and bars set up and even a multiplex and some other entertainment options, but what it boiled down to was the workers were restricted to staying on property all the time. Any money they made went right back to the companies. The families with children sent their kids to company-run schools - for a fee of course - as there were no longer any taxes to pay for education. There was no reason, and in reality, little way for anyone who worked in the mines to leave the land they were situated on.

Or, as J.R. further explained, there was no way to escape if one wanted to remain employed. Miners who were discharged and their families were given 48 hours to pack their belongings. They and their property were then loaded into a vehicle and shipped off to God knows where. That was what J.R. had been referring to when he spoke about "relocation." The belief was that the transported parties ended up somewhere in the Mahoning-Mercer area along the Ohio-Pennsylvania border. Nobody knew for sure as none of the so-called "deported" had ever been heard from again. That wasn't surprising, considering those who were transported had no money and there was little in the way of personal communication anymore. That was another sidebar brought about by the new regime, one which Bull already suspected: the disappearance of the Postal Service, phone landlines and the creation of DoMER to regulate the Internet destroyed avenues for people to communicate over long distances. He also hadn't realized how astronomical cellphone costs in the region had become. National prices were a thing of the past. Localized pricing became the norm based on an area's population and economy and how much people traveled to the region. With the locals having little money and with no major travel arteries, cellular providers couldn't justify the cost of maintaining service in the region.

J.R. went on to explain how the town was truly cut off from the rest of the world. Besides having no phones, no Internet and no snail mail, physically getting out of the region was a near impossibility. Again, the promises of the new era turned out to be a curse. With municipalities banned from collecting taxes and the nation also refusing to, everything became a private endeavor. That included some of the basic infrastructure necessities, like roads. The cost of maintaining roads though, something which the residents of the town had never put much thought into, turned out to be incredibly high. That didn't include related costs, such as trimming the vegetation along the roads which grew over and peeked up from under the concrete. With the incredible rate of unemployment and the extremely low wages for those who were employed, it became impossible for the town to maintain all but the most vital of streets, and at that point even those seemed unimportant. Without cheap or easily-accessible gas, there was little reason to make sure the roads were drivable. The only roads in the region which were truly serviceable were the ones the mining corporations used to transport their product. Much of commerce moved through the air now, but large amounts of heavy coal still traveled better over land. The small thoroughfares and the main highways were therefore kept in pristine condition, and the people in town physically had access to what was the best parts of the Interstate system. That was in theory only. The problem for the locals was that the roads were owned by the coal operations, which charged high tolls for any non-company vehicle making non-company trips. The price to use the roads, combined with the inexplicably high gas costs, made driving oppressive, only to be done in the case of extreme emergencies.

The high price of fuel didn't make sense at all. The gas companies had gotten everything they wanted which was supposed to lower costs. The government eased every single regulation possible for the gas companies, from lifting bans in environmentally-sensitive areas, to allowing major pipelines to run wherever the companies wanted, to eliminating the mandates on the quality of fuel, to eradicating all taxes on gasoline. Washington, it had been rumored, had even given the gas companies the right to claim land via eminent domain without even petitioning the government. The oil industry was authorized to govern itself, which was supposed to decrease prices drastically. Instead, the cost for fuel was higher than ever, and gas became a luxury.

Bull was astounded, saddened and scared by what J.R. told him. Gary told the older man he didn't know what had been going on, that there had never been any mention of such things on the news. Bull said all he had ever heard was about how great things were in Washington and in some of the other major cities across the nation. Even New York was depicted as thriving, despite its "backwards ways." The only sign of negativity on the news was about the constant threat of terrorism and the danger of subversive Liberals still at large in the country. J.R. replied he had seen all the same stories because they watched the same news station. He pointed out they didn't have any other choice. The other outlets, any which dared to report anything contrary to the official national dialogue, had been ridiculed and shunned at first, then run out of business or forcibly taken off the air with new regulations which criminalized subversive or defaming programing. It was another example of how, despite the rhetoric against all regulations, the government acted swiftly and sternly to enforce new rules. "Because we here have seen the same stories Bull," J.R. jabbed, "I almost believe you when you say you had no idea."

Dukeman let the slight pass over and made one final attempt to defend the new order, "well, it isn't all bad, right? They let everyone here keep their houses despite their difficulties making payments, right?" It was something one of Hannigan's friends had told Bull a year or two ago when Dukeman had been wondering out loud how things were going back home.

For the first time in their long talk, J.R. looked at Gary directly, the drunk patron's eyes bloodshot and watery. J.R. made a gesture with his head to indicate what was really beyond the bar's front door. J.R then whispered in a weak, almost tear-driven voice, "that's just because there's nothing of value out there anymore. If the banks had decided to foreclose on us, it would have cost them more money than to allow us to stay. They would have actually had to pay for roads and schools and libraries and anything to make this town seem livable for potential buyers. Instead they wrote us off and received huge grants from the government for their bold, charitable actions. Meanwhile we were abandoned here to fend for ourselves in our new jungle wilderness, with a giant general store nobody can afford to shop in anymore and no way to escape. This is a ghost town, just waiting for us all to pass away."

Flustered to a point near numbness, all Bull could do was mutter about his disbelief. He bid J.R. good-bye before leaving Maloney's and heading home. His drive home was uneventful, which made sense now that he had the only car on the road. It was the only operational car in town. With that he finished describing his day to his wife, at times telling his tale through tears. His wife was equally shaken. After Bull was done, he started weeping and she held him as she used to hold their daughter when the child needed comfort. Unlike those times though, she didn't offer words of encouragement, like saying everything would be alright. Instead Bull rhetorically asked, "what have I done?" and she answered by saying it wasn't his fault.

The two were standing in the kitchen, Gary in his wife's arms, when there was a disturbance from the living room. It was the sound of glass breaking and the crash of two hard objects colliding. The Dukemans ran into the main room to find a softball-sized rock sitting on the floor. Glass from the front window was scattered all over. A piece of paper was secured to the stone by a rubber band.

Bull carefully walked through the room, doing his best to avoid the glass, and picked up the rock. After making his way back to the clean floor in the entry hallway, he pulled the note away from the rock. In block capital letters in handwriting he didn't recognize was written, "WE'RE SORRY WE MISSED YOU AT MALONEY'S. HOPE TO SEE YOU TOMORROW."

Gary looked beleaguered as he showed the note to Joanna. He didn't bother looking outside for the culprits, nor did he try calling the authorities. He knew there was nobody to respond, and even if there was, they weren't likely to care.

Judgment Day

The Dukemans didn't sleep well that night. Bull was lucky if he got two hours' rest, battling through his guilt for helping to bring his hometown – and possibly the country – to the brink of disaster and the fear he felt for his well-being, his wife and the U.S. in general. Joanna would have slept nearly the whole night through if her spouse had been able to at least remain still in bed next to her. Alas, that wasn't the case as he kicked and turned through his semiconscious nightmares.

Bull woke up– not that the word truly applied to his case that night – early and walked down the hall to the main room to get a better look at the damage. It really wasn't so bad: the window luckily had stayed mostly intact and all the rock had done upon entry was scratch the finishing on the floor. Despite any major damage, he continued to stare at the scene. He was so focused on what was before him that he didn't realize his wife had also woken up until she reached out and brushed his arm. The two embraced in an awkward cuddle. Instead of the usual affectionate hug they had shared almost every morning for many years, his grasp was rigid and he was shivering slightly while she remained distant, moved mostly by pity.

Joanna continued onto the kitchen while her spouse went to the hall closet to grab the vacuum, broom and dustpan. It took Bull roughly twenty minutes to thoroughly clean up the glass scattered across the floor and on the furniture. When he was done, he joined his wife in the kitchen. Breakfast was already on the table. Much to the relief of the Dukemans, it quickly became apparent Bull's appetite wasn't ruined by his nerves or sleep pattern.

While Gary scarfed down his breakfast, the couple remained unusually silent. The quiet continued most of the morning, until the time it was customary for Bull to leave for Maloney's during his unemployment. At first both husband and wife stared at each other curiously, with each asking the same unvoiced question: what are we going to do? Bull was the first of the two to actually speak, "I don't want you to be here alone."

"And I don't want you to go alone," Joanna replied. Neither had considered Bull's not going to the bar that day. Despite the implied threat, he had been called out and somewhere in the unspoken rules of the region, it meant the only honorable thing he could do was go to Main Street.

Silence was maintained most of the ride to town. Mrs. Dukeman only broke it when she saw the condition of the road. It had been her first ride since they'd returned home and this was her chance to confirm what Bull had told her. The condition of the road and knowing why it was in such poor shape moved her to tears. She explained to her husband that until that moment she thought he might be exaggerating. The disrepair of the street proved there was a good portion of truth to what her husband had described the night before.

Joanna's tears became stronger when they reached Main Street. Her emotions started to get the better of her when she realized theirs was the only vehicle on the street. Then she saw Bull had been completely truthful about all the shops being closed. She walked into the middle of the street – knowing she was perfectly safe from being hit by the nonexistent traffic – and walked in a slow circle, taking in the lack of life. If there hadn't been trees and grass around them she could have envisioned the dirt street and tumbleweeds of a ghost town in the Wild

West. In tears, she walked over to where Bull was leaning against the car, apologized and hugged him sympathetically. He understood that the embrace was both a request for forgiveness and a search for comfort, just as he had needed the previous evening. He returned the affection and security, kissed his spouse on the top of her head and said it was okay. After a minute, they broke apart and both looked at the door to the bar.

"Are you ready?" Joanna asked.

"Eh," was all Gary answered. Hand-in-hand, the couple walked to Maloney's. Bull opened the door, but also in a show of protection went in first.

The pub was crowded, looking as busy as Dukeman had remembered it back before his adventures began. As he expected everyone looked at him as he entered, followed by his wife who slid up next to him. All the old regulars who J.R. hadn't mentioned as being dead or out of town were there. Oddly, nobody spoke or approached. Instead the occupants stared at Gary, who just focused on the closest of his former friends. Finally Bull broke the silence with a defiant "well?" The subject of his glare just made a gesture with his head, pointing to the television.

Bull hadn't realized until that moment that the HDTV set was the source of the only sound in the room until that point. He hadn't paid attention to it until he had been directed to. It was in that instance that he realized it was talking about him. Suddenly Gary was fascinated as he listened and watched and digested what it was preaching to the whole country: according to the number-one news channel in the nation, Gary "Bull" Dukeman was dead.

The crowd parted for the Dukemans to approach the bar and take seats as close to the television as possible. The report was a good five minutes long. The facts weren't all in yet, according to the reporter, but the previous evening somebody allegedly broke into Dukeman's Virginia house and savagely and gruesomely murdered the Dukemans. Even though the anchors and reporters admitted they didn't know who had killed this American hero, they couldn't help but keep hinting the attack had been carried out by some "Liberal agent:" a part of some grand conspiracy. For the first time ever it amazed Bull how much the channel was promoting a fact it admittedly had no concrete evidence of.

The time came for a commercial break and Bull was finally able to break his attention away from the broadcast. He first looked at Joanna, who had her face buried in her hands as she cried uncontrollably. Bull put his arm over his beloved but said nothing. All he could have done was try to conscle her by saying everything was alright when everything most definitely wasn't alright.

As the couple sat there stunned, the man who Bull had stared at upon entering the bar came over to them. He went by the name of Rusty, and Bull never knew whether that was his real name or not. Rusty was apparently the person the rest of the folks at Maloney's considered was in charge of the situation. However, the mob's anger had apparently been diffused. Rusty had a low, gravelly voice, which managed to belie more than a hint of sympathy. "I came here today," he said, "with everyone else to give you a piece of my mind, about the nerve you had to come back here after what you've done. About how everything going on here is your fault. About how you used us and we weren't happy about it. It never occurred to me, until now, that you were being used too."

Bull started shaking his head violently and nearly uncontrollably. He started to cry as emotion overtook him. He went to Maloney's expecting a confrontation and perhaps to be physically injured. The news that had just been reported and the unexpected sympathy overloaded his senses.

It took a few minutes for the Dukemans to calm down and their tears to stop flowing. At that point, Bull started to even feel welcomed back at the bar. Cautiously people started to tell jokes about everybody's situation. Most of the one-liners focused on welcoming Bull to the afterlife. The notion of everyone being caught in the dying town seemed to have taken hold a long time prior and was considered something more than a joke but just short of a sad truth. Bull still felt like an outsider and believed there was still a bit of maliciousness in some of the comments. He knew these people well enough to understand that while they were trying to get back on friendly terms they still harbored some bitterness for what had happened. Their anger made sense because he then understood he'd become – albeit unintentionally – the type of freeloader they all despised. However the townsfolk learned then that he hadn't planned for that to happen. He threw his own lines into the fray, but was careful to not act offended if any of the return fire cut too close to the bone.

The joking stopped abruptly within a half-hour when the station went live to a press conference in Virginia. Officials were giving their first report about what they called the murder of Gary and Joanna Dukeman. As soon as the FBI spokesman "confirmed" Bull's death, a hearty cheer roared through Maloney's. A couple of patrons slapped Bull's shoulder and shook him in friendship as the last bit of animosity slipped away among those present. It was elation for Bull, and the last moment of amusement he'd ever feel.

The FBI official at the podium described what he said were the early results of the investigation. The initial belief was that a small band of men described as "Liberal terrorists" drove up to the house, busted in and shot the couple execution style. Witnesses in the neighborhood said they first heard squealing tires, the front door to the house being kicked in and a couple of muffled shots from inside the house. Within two minutes from the start of the ordeal, the van screeched away.

Then came the dagger through the Dukemans' hearts. One witness had actually been in the house during the attack. The witness had been badly beaten and had fallen into a coma since giving a disposition about the ordeal, but had been able to confirm the events before losing consciousness. She said the attackers identified themselves as the "Liberal Guerilla Front," and claimed the attack was a demonstration of what they could and would do to "America's traitors." The witness was the Dukemans' daughter, who the FBI spokesman said had come home for dinner with her parents. She slipped into the coma after investigators told her that her parents were dead, the injury-induced sleep overtaking her sobs of pain and anguish.

At first the Dukemans were laughing at the report. A moment later the humor of the situation disappeared. At that point, the report started focusing on their daughter. After hearing what the officials claimed had happened the parents were numb. What the FBI suggested made no sense for their daughter was aware of her parents' situation. "She knew we weren't there," Bull stumbled to say the words again through heavy tears, "she knew we weren't there." As the Dukemans cried, others came to console them both, sharing tears and the pain they felt. What had been planned 24 hours before as the lynching of Bull Dukeman became a tremendous show of sympathy for the target.

What a Long, Strange Trip it's Been

Bull knew he shouldn't have been driving that evening but he had little choice. While both he and his wife were unquestionably drunk and distraught, he was still the one in far better condition. They had to drive home: there was no more hotel or place to stay downtown, no taxis or anyone else able to drive. Even if there had been, there would have been no way to get back to Main Street other than to walk. Everyone else had ridden a bicycle to Maloney's or lived within walking distance. The Dukemans didn't own bikes and even if somebody had offered them a place to stay and everything seemed to have been smoothed over, Bull still wasn't sure he trusted anyone.

The other regulars at Maloney's had been nothing but completely gracious after the tragic news knocked the Dukemans into shock. It was because of them that Gary and Joanna were so drunk. Everyone had bought the pair drinks as they all commiserated over the state of the youngest Dukeman.

He'd driven home in worse condition plenty of times before. Those times though the roads were in decent shape. If he had been sober, Bull would have remembered the tree in the road and the large pothole nearby which he'd first noticed the day before. He would have, as he had the previous night, slowed down and gone around the obstacles on the other side of the road after making sure nobody was coming from the other direction (not that there was anyone else on the road to worry about). Instead, the tree trunk surprised him and he swerved right into a gaping rift in the asphalt. The car bounced hard as the front part of the chassis hit the far side of the crack, then the middle of the car shuddered as it too hit the other side of the pit.

After the impact Bull stepped on the brakes. The car rolled to a bumpy stop. Bull made sure his wife was alright before tending to himself. She made a comment that it was a good thing they had been wearing their seatbelts or otherwise both their heads would have gone through the roof. Instead they were both just badly shaken.

After determining his body was intact, Bull tried to get out of the car. His first attempt was unsuccessful as he felt a twinge of pain in his lower back. Joanna asked what was wrong, and he replied nothing. He braced himself for the pain and made it out of the driver's seat successfully on his second try. He walked around the white sedan. At first glance the vehicle looked fine, minus a few new scratches to the lower portion of the paint. Joanna opened her door to ask him how bad things were, and he first replied things seemed okay. Then he noticed fluids of various colors running from the vehicle's underside and told her to hold on. Bull got down on his hands and knees to look under the car. What he saw added to his depression: not only was the car leaking oil, water, brake fluid and coolant but the drive shift was cracked, the rough ends of the split both touching the ground. Barring a tremendous amount of work, the last drivable car in town would never be able to roll again on its own power. "She's totaled!" he yelled out to his wife, at first with an amazingly strong and steady voice. Then he repeated himself in a wet whimper.

Bull scooted over on his knees to the front end of the car and put his hands on the side of the dead vehicle. He went to push himself up by leaning against the hood but as he started to get off his knees a sharp pain coursed through his body. He collapsed back to his knees and groaned. His wife asked him what was wrong: "it's my back again! It's given out!" The accident had jarred his back hard enough to aggravate the years-old injury and the subsiding adrenaline and his current posture brought the pain back with a vengeance.

Joanna got out of the car to try and help her husband up, but her light, lean frame wasn't much help to the muscular former miner. The attempt only depressed Bull more. He wasn't worthy of her. He had failed to protect their daughter and had just destroyed the lone possession of value they had left. He didn't want her help, but then he also didn't want anything anymore except to die. He warned his wife to stay away, then got back to his knees and leaned his hands once again against the car. His intention was to ram his head as hard as he could against the vehicle's steel skin and frame, but his back gave out again as he forced himself towards the machine. Instead of a hard impact, he ended up slipping from the car and landing on his arms on the road. Joanna tried to come towards him to help him again but he told her again to stay away. He rolled into a fetal position and started sobbing, writhing on the ground, saying he wished he was dead.

Joanna silently watched her husband for fifteen minutes when she heard a faint, distant hum. It was similar to that of a hover-car, but didn't sound nearly as loud or imposing. The source of the noise was definitely getting closer. Joanna looked up and waited. The sound was indeed coming from a hover-car which popped over the tree line. The vehicle stopped for a moment above the crash scene before descending. It then started to land on the road a matter of yards behind the wrecked surface vehicle.

Joanna stood there like the proverbial deer in the headlights. She was paralyzed with fear. According to her nation, she was already dead. It wouldn't be too hard to make that bit of fiction become reality. Her instincts told her to run, her heart told her to stay with her husband and her thoughts told her to stay frozen in place. If it wasn't a death squad coming to kill her, it could be somebody to offer assistance. Even if it was somebody out to kill her, a large part of her agreed with her husband, that death might not be a bad thing.

The hover-car touched down softly on the road and the driver ran through touchdown procedures. Upon landing, she had learned, the vehicle's operator had to make sure a number of items were in order before disembarking, similar to a plane or boat pilot. Joanna couldn't see who was operating the hover-car through the dark windshield. That notion scared her but by that point she had decided to stand her ground.

The driver completed his post-landing checklist and the gullwing door to the flying car opened. The lone occupant of the vehicle stepped into sight and immediately Mrs. Dukeman recognized him. She still wasn't sure if she should be fearful or relieved. Even though she'd met the man who was standing before her just a few times, Bull's description of him left her unsure of the man's intentions and allegiances. Joanna just stared ambivalently at him and said without emotion, "you…"

Dick Patton said, with a bit of warmth in his voice as he swept his arms out, "me."

Joanna was standing between Dick and her husband and their worthless vehicle. Patton looked past the woman to Bull. Dick brought his outspread arms back together and pointed them to the man who was still wrapped up in a ball on the road. "I don't mean you any harm," Dick said, "may I?"

Joanna nodded yes and allowed Patton to pass.

Bull had shown no signs of knowing what was happening around him since he rolled up in a ball. It wasn't until Dick said hello to Gary that the latter stopped rolling around on the side of the road. Then Dukeman looked up with wet, red eyes. He repeated the one-word phrase his wife had just used, but there was no mistaking the anger in his use of the word. Patton responded by stating in a neighborly tone that he wasn't the enemy. He asked if he could give Bull a hand. After a brief pause, Gary nodded abruptly and Dick helped his former drinking partner up.

The process of getting Bull to his feet took a long time due to the pain searing up and down his back. Dick and Joanna both helped with patience and gentle care. Once Gary was standing up, Dick instructed him to walk around. Bull was able to comply, with occasional spasms jolting him upright. After a couple of minutes Patton asked Bull if he thought he'd be able to sit down for an extended period of time. Gary said he thought so. Dick then started to help his companion into the hover-car. Once he was in, Dick asked Joanna if she wanted to go for a ride as well. At first she was hesitant, still not trusting Patton. Dick insisted no harm would come to them during the ride and that he only wanted to take them for a spin for a few hours to show them "around." Finally Mrs. Dukeman agreed, not because she trusted Dick Patton any more than she had minutes earlier, but because, as he pointed out, even if he had malicious intent, it couldn't be any worse than staying put on a deserted road in an isolated suburb of a small ghost town.

As soon as they were all inside the vehicle, Dick reached over to the glove compartment and took out a small bottle of pills. He opened the container, took out a pair of tablets and offered them to Bull. Gary recognized the pain killers but was hesitant at first to take them, "can I afford these?" he asked.

Dick laughed and said he had no intention of charging Bull for the drugs. "Besides," Patton added, "where I live they are cheap. Mostly covered by our healthcare system." With that, Gary took the tablets and washed them down with a swig of water from a bottle sitting in a nearby cup holder.

It took only a few moments for the medicine to work its magic. They worked quicker than anything Bull had used in the past, a fact he chalked up to it being a new generation pill. As the pain subsided, Bull started to look around the vehicle and its surroundings. Dick was flying lower than the few other drivers Bull had ridden with, making it harder to notice any landmarks as they sped above the tree line. Every now and then Bull would catch a glimpse of a road below, but he couldn't see enough of his surroundings to get a good fix on their direction. Bull's best guess was that they were heading east, based on which highways he thought they were passing over.

After a little while, Bull started to realize the hover-car they were in was different from any he had ridden in before. Just like the one which had brought Bull and his wife back home a few days prior, this car actually had a roof over the passenger compartment. It was also much quieter than the other vehicles he'd ridden in. Outside of the passenger cabin, he could see the wings were longer and sleeker than on the models he was familiar with. For that matter, the cars he had seen before didn't have wings. Bull broke what had been a slightly tense but totally awkward silence by commenting on the quietness of the vehicle.

"This hover-car isn't like anything you've likely seen in these parts of the States," Dick responded. The driver beamed with pride as he gave Gary a second more to look around before continuing, "this car is designed on technology which is frowned upon and scoffed at by

Conservatives. For one thing, the reason this car is so quiet is because it's one-hundred percent powered by electricity, mostly generated from the solar panels on the roof."

Bull started to get anxious, scared by the revelation, but Patton did his best to put his passenger's mind at ease: "solar power isn't dangerous Bull, and it's free. Everybody where we're going can afford to drive, whether they have hover-cars like this or electric surface cars."

"And where is that? Where we're going?"

"We're going where I live now: we're driving East along the southern border of Pennsylvania and then we'll head north along the Jersey Shore to New York City."

If it hadn't happened when Patton mentioned the solar power before, Gary was sure he turned pale white when he heard about their destination. The heart of Liberalism, the most backwards-thinking part of the country, the place where poverty was welcomed hand-in-hand with concepts of taxation, Socialism and Communism. Outside of the city, in the rest of the country, people had started using the term Evil Empire to describe the whole of New York and not just the Yankees. For a moment, the pain in Bull's back returned, brought on by the nervousness in his stomach. He felt not that he was going to the Evil Empire but into Hell itself.

Dick felt the chill from his passenger and quickly returned to talking about the hover-car. He pointed to other features about the car which made it different from the "old reliables" which those in "Conservative America" drove. The environmentally-friendly models in and around New England – and actually around the world in many technologically-advanced countries – derived their flying abilities more from true planes, gliders and old Harrier jets. The older models relied entirely on large, gas-powered fans which lifted the vehicles and smaller propellers to push the cars forward. The electric cars used a larger quantity of smaller fans which funneled the air towards the back and below the cars and used their foldable wings to help keep them aloft and moving forward. The light-weight batteries, created based on the improved technology of hybrid and electric surface cars, helped make these cars lighter than the gas-powered models which needed to lift heavier motors, gas tanks and fans. The electric flying cars also had better crash ratings then their gas counterparts. If the motors gave out, the gas guzzlers fell back to Earth like rocks and passenger and driver survival percentages were low. Between the wings and the fact most electric hover-cars had wheels to double as surface cars, they more often than not were able to glide to a landing and roll to a safe stop in the case of catastrophic engine failure.

Bull protested, saying that the dangers of solar alone made the electric cars dangerous. He'd heard for years that solar panels and large hybrid batteries were in constant threat of overheating and exploding.

"You heard that on your favorite news station, right?" Patton asked. Before Bull could answer, Dick continued, "Bull, you can't believe everything you hear on television. Remember, according to them, you're dead."

Patton's glib remark elicited a small, sad grunt of humor from Mrs. Dukemar. Gary likely would have laughed at that answer the day before, before hearing about his daughter's beating.

Ahead of the car was now a large body of water. Patton pulled the car to the left and it made a smooth turn north. The banking turn indeed felt like that of a plane and much smoother than any turn Bull had experienced in a gas-powered hover-car. Dick also brought the car up to a higher altitude. "We're out of enemy territory now, we can go higher." When Bull asked if they were ever in danger before that point, Patton answered he was unsure. "Cars like this can garner unwanted attention outside of the northeast. I don't know if anyone would've cared, but why risk it?"

The car sped north, moving faster than any hover-car Bull had ridden in. He was pretty sure he recognized Atlantic City along the coast with its themed hotels. Out in the Atlantic he recognized a line of electricity-generating windmills. Bull chortled. "I thought you environmentalists said those things wouldn't foul up the scenery."

"Of course you can see them from this height," Dick responded, "they are a lot less noticeable from sea level. Without lobbyists giving illogical reasons to block the creation of those turbines, they easily cleared all the political hurdles and were built very quickly. Nobody complains about them being eyesores, in fact, people come out to look at them through binoculars. They're more of a tourist attraction than a blemish. And the lot of them provide a majority of the power for all points within five miles of the shore. That includes the ports around Elizabeth and the city of Newark. For that matter, ninety-five percent of everything here in the 'Evil Empire' is powered by one form of renewable energy or another. Wind, solar, water and biodiesels. It's clean and it's cheap and for as much as your political darlings like to make fun of renewable energy, we haven't had a major accident caused by solar or wind in the years we've harvested them."

Bull again protested, referring to the talking points which had been pounded into him for years about all the negatives of the power sources Dick mentioned.

Patton returned fire with less cheer in his voice than he had used throughout the conversation. "Up here, we don't have to conserve our last tank of gas in case of an emergency. And I don't know if you asked anyone during your brief trip home, but you weren't going to like your first power bill, or the fact that you'd have had to heat your house only with wood in the winter."

The car quickly was approaching New York City. Dick punched a few buttons on his steering wheel and the windshield momentarily turned green. He explained that he had requested authorization to take a scenic loop around the island of Manhattan. The green signal confirmed the request was accepted.

Bull didn't want to admit it, but he was impressed with the city's appearance. The dirt, grime and smog he quickly noticed during a previous visit were not present anymore. Dukeman was less pleased with what he recognized as an abundance of solar panels on top of most of the tall buildings. Even the Freedom Tower had plenty of them at the top, something he had never noticed in the past. When he asked about that characteristic, Dick told him the Conservative stations always showed shots of the building from midtown, showing the north side of the building which didn't receive any natural sunlight and therefore was spared the solar panels. Bull thought about that for a second and realized that made sense: he hadn't seen a picture of the famed New York skyline from any other angle for as long as he could remember. It was totally noticeable once he was aware of the fact that there were no visible signs of solar farms from the north looking downtown. Patton added that it was in some ways a perfect compromise. Liberals had extreme use of solar power and Conservatives in other parts of the country didn't have to admit it.

As they continued their flight around the city, Bull realized theirs wasn't the only hover-car within sight. In fact, he became aware that he was in a line of similar aircraft, mostly of designs he'd never seen before. He was in awe that so many people drove them. There were also plenty of surface vehicles on the streets below. As they circled the island of Manhattan counter-clockwise and they flew first along the FDR Drive, the Harlem River Drive and the West Side Highway, Gary was amazed at how many personal automobiles not only still existed in the city but that life in the Big Apple remained at its legendary high-speed, frantic, busy pace. He prompted Dick for an explanation and the driver was happy to provide one. It started off simply: just as in the situation with the wind turbines, once lobbyist opposition to electric cars was dropped and tax breaks for buying environmentally-friendly cars were increased, the market for hybrid cars then completely electric vehicles exploded. All patents for low and no-emissions cars, which had been thought of by inspired civilian engineers or eager college students were returned to their rightful owners. Until President Dukeman came to office, many patents had been bought by aggressive oil and car manufacturers to keep the new generation of eco-friendly machines off the roads. The designs were given back to their creators, forcefully by the federal government, to keep the "epidemic" of progressive interest isolated and locked away in the contained stronghold of American Liberalism. The U.S. government was okay with this so long as the creators and manufacturers of such technology kept it contained in the Northeast and other like-minded parts of the country. Just as with the solar panels on an American symbol such as the Freedom Tower, the U.S. government could then disavow any knowledge of the use of such "Heathen" technology.

Soon after the patents and copyrights were returned, Dick explained something interesting started to happen: the automotive industry started to buy the rights back, some of which they had been forced to relinquish. Some had been locked up by the oil companies for fear of a decline in demand. Others had been bought up by the car producers as a courtesy to the oil producers which propelled their own business. The country's economic situation had changed dramatically and there was little money to be made on gas-powered cars in most of the country. Few people had the money to buy cars or gas west of Philadelphia and east of parts of California. Even with the government happily sending stimulus funding to Detroit, there was no way for the industry to thrive under what had then been the current business model. Sustainability became the goal in the Motor City, producing vehicles that catered to the few who could afford them. The major car companies soon realized the only way they would be able to make solid profits again would be to offer new vehicles to people who could and would buy them. Luckily, those areas of the nation which were financially strong also were the ones doing their best to divorce themselves from the oil and fossil fuel industries. General Motors was the first to buy back the best pieces of electric and flying car technology, not making an issue about having already owned some of the patents.

The decision by GM turned out to be one of the biggest and best business moves of the 21st Century, universally lauded even if some didn't want to admit it. General Motors had done its share of experimenting with both electric and flying cars at that point. Between that and no longer having to appease strict government regulations GM was able to quickly roll its first electric hover-cars off the assembly line. Demand was incredible across the Northeast. GM had trouble keeping up with consumer demand at first. The company was able to work out a deal with Metro North to reacquire its old production plant in Tarrytown, from where it could ship cars to Manhattan in half an hour. General Motors became something of a business darling for the city which remained the financial capital of the world. Besides offering a product which many citizens of the city had been wanting for an excruciatingly long time, the car-producing giant brought a state-of-the-art, employee-safe plant to the region, along with jobs. Ultimately it was one of the grand ironies of the Dukeman administration: the part of the country which had decent employment rates to begin with was where new jobs were being created. Dick could see out of the corner of his eye that Bull was about to protest again, but Patton once again played the lying television card before Dukeman could vocalize his thoughts.

The hover-car finished its loop around the heart of New York and started to head south away from Manhattan. As the vehicle approached the Verrazano-Narrows Bridge, Patton started tapping buttons again on the steering wheel. This time the windshield started flashing yellow and a transparent "SEL-1" appeared in sync with the flashes. Duke pulled the car into a westbound turn and started to weave left and right like a NASCAR driver under a caution flag. Eventually Dick brought the car around in a circle and started the maneuver again. He explained that the flashing yellow HUD in the windshield meant he was in a holding pattern for a landing runway. The symbols represented which route he should take (indicating Southeast Low One), and a semi-automated screen on the steering wheel helped Patton get to the proper height and direction. Patton pointed to other cars circling in similar fashion and was able to discern which pattern some of them were in. In a matter of minutes, the screen would appear solid yellow, indicating he should be situated in the direction of the landing field, ready for final descent. When the screen turned green and presented an approach number, he would be free to land where he was assigned. It was just like flying a plane, but simplified. The landing field in New Jersey, while the size of nearby Newark Liberty

Airport, could handle three times the amount of craft at a time because the cars were smaller, quick to move off the landing zone and didn't have enough power to create wake turbulence.

The procession between landing signals came and went quickly and Dick brought the car down for a smooth landing. As it rolled down the landing lane, the wings folded up in thirds and stowed themselves alongside the body of the car and up and over the rear, forming a large spoiler-like tail. As the car left the landing zone, Dick pointed in the distance where the gas-powered hover-cars landed. The landing for those vehicles were simpler, as they just had to float down into their parking spots. Hover-cars weren't allowed to fly over the actual land mass of Manhattan and had to convert to land-mode before driving into the city. Hover-cars which weren't conversion vehicles were parked in New Jersey and their drivers and passengers were transported under the river via a high-speed addition to the PATH system (which Patton explained was a long-serving subway system operating between urban New Jersey and New York City). Drivers of land-air craft were free to take any of the various routes into the city: bridge, tunnel or ferry. Patton chose the Lincoln Tunnel.

Once in Manhattan, the Dukemans were in awe. The tunnel had let them out near Times Square and Dick drove them as close as he could to where they could see the tourist hotspot. While Bull had been able to see plenty of cars along the outer roadways of the city earlier, Patton said the number of vehicles actually in New York was rather low compared to the city's past. That allowed the city government to close many streets to motor vehicles, especially around tourist attractions. Times Square, from what Gary and Joanna could see of it, was sparkling clean and vibrant. It wasn't at all the grimy, seedy cesspool Bull always envisioned. Truth be told, it hadn't seemed that bad when he visited in his youth, but he hadn't been given much of a chance to see it back then.

What amazed the visiting couple the most was the multitude of different faces they saw: Caucasian and Black, Asian and Middle Eastern, Latino and East Indian. They were all in Times Square and walking about the city. It was strange to Bull and his wife, neither of whom had ever been in close quarters with so many people from different ethnic backgrounds. There was the occasional outsider who visited or was passing by their small home town in the past and smallish pockets of Latinos and African-Americans who lived there but they seldom were seen out and about except when shopping. Even when the couple was moved to Washington D.C. all the faces were White, but that was what the purge had been for in the first place.

"They're mostly tourists," Patton said, sensing his passengers' astonishment, "from all over the world. This is still New York, and as you can see, life still goes on here. I'll tell you more about that when we get to my place."

Patton remained quiet the rest of the drive south. The trip was hardly silent though as Gary and Joanna pointed various items out to one another. Their banter came across as matter-of-fact and monotone, which Patton surmised was the result of the couple having already gone through Hell that day. Dick felt bad that he hadn't reached them before they received the news about their daughter. If he had, Patton believed the couple would have sounded like children themselves. However, they may have remained more skeptical if that had been the case, and that would have likely made Dick's imminent task much more difficult.

The car passed Canal Street, going through Little Italy and Chinatown. Bull seemed okay seeing the former, but his voice couldn't hide his anxiety at seeing the foreign décor of Chinatown. He went as far as saying he felt like a stranger in his own country. Patton suppressed the urge to suggest this wasn't Dukeman's America. Instead he pointed out the Holland Tunnel to the east and said while that may have been a more convenient route home, he thought it was necessary to give his visitors a short tour.

Patton drove just a couple of minutes more, maneuvering down the small streets of Lower Manhattan. The pathways seemed to go every which way but the driver handled all the twists with a keen sense of direction. He pulled into a small opening in one of the buildings and down a tight passageway. Eventually the tunnel opened up into a garage area. It was surprisingly well-lit compared to Bull's expectations but the grimy walls made up for what he imagined a New York garage would look like.

Dick parked and everyone stepped out. Bull had no trouble getting out of the vehicle. The strength and duration of the medication impressed him. Patton led his visitors to the elevator. It was one of those old-style cars, with a folding fence in the door buck and another inside on the lift itself. A defunct control lever still was in place, but the platform was operated by buttons which brought the machine to the floor requested. Dick ushered the Dukemans into the lift, closed the gates, then pressed the button marked five. The elevator began its ascent with a jerky start. The climb ended with a similar shudder and the trio got out. The host led his guests through a thin hallway. He opened the two locks on the door to his apartment and pushed the door open. "Welcome to my home," Patton said as the Dukemans walked in.

Try and See it My Way

Bull wasn't impressed by Dick's apartment. It was clean and homely and comfortable but it was very small. The short entry foyer led into a living room that was roughly the size of the Dukeman's guest room. The room also included a small kitchenette and two-person dining table. It barely had space to comfortably fit the sofa, coffee table and recliner which were in there. Dick owned a state-of-the-art flat screen hybrid computer-TV which didn't take up much space at all. Gary declined an offer to see Patton's bedroom, then asked how Dick could live in such a place.

"Hey, even though I have a job and a decent bit of savings, this still's New York," was the response. Apparently Bull hadn't ever heard the stories about the astronomical housing prices in the city so Dick regaled his guests with some of the better-known rental horror stories.

Bull still wasn't impressed with Dick's apartment or amused by the tales he'd just tried to pay attention to. Gary really couldn't care about anything at that point. For that matter he hadn't comprehended much of their conversation in the car. Bull was exhausted, physically drained and just an eyelash from being emotionally broken. The medication Patton had given him helped kill the pain but also pushed Dukeman that much further from normal cognizance. He was tired, confused and out of patience. Before Patton could go on another tangent, Dukeman asked bluntly, "why am I here?"

For a moment Patton looked deflated, having been ready to tell another anecdote, but he recovered quickly. "Three reasons," he responded, holding up his left hand, exposing a trio of fingers. "The first is to show you, in the flesh, the differences between our political philosophies.

"You see, you've had the opportunity to watch both models in action now. You've lived the way you wanted to for years and now you're seeing what I always hoped could be. We used to fight about this all the time. Well, you've lived in your small-government, no regulation, no taxation world. Tell me that you were happy there. Tell me that your favorite politicians practiced the ideas they preached. Were you living that prosperous life you expected? Was all that money being funneled to Hannigan and the other business magnates trickling down to you the way you thought it would?"

"My life has been fine the last few years," Bull answered angrily, "we lived well, we had plenty of everything. A roof over our heads, great care from our government. Yes, all was great!"

Dick gave Gary a quick quizzical look, but just as quickly realized his error. Patton gave a sarcastic, gruff snort of a laugh. "Okay, you lived well, but as a false idol who was uncharacteristically catered to so the government could show you off as a success story. You really don't think you lived an average life at that point, do you?"

Bull stared dumbfounded, not sure how to answer or if he should.

Instead Patton fired another barrage at his guest, "be honest, Bull. You were at Maloney's and I'm sure they told you how life was back home. The tree and pothole which killed your car would never have been allowed to sit there like that if the town and state had been allowed to collect taxes or had some sort of budget for infrastructure. Even in just your few days home you must've seen enough of what our town has become to know it wasn't the utopia you were promised."

Bull's anger only increased, not because he had no defense against Dick's attacks (Bull was, in fact, ready to concede much of the debate), but rather over Patton's interest in him. "How do you know so much about what I've been through?"

"I've been very interested in your exploits ever since you were freed from your prison. More or less since Armitage was ousted and Dukeman was put into power. Essentially it boils down to when the Constitution was thrown out the window and I moved here.

"For me, I saw the writing on the wall. It's like those people who bought their first hybrids when Bush the Second came into office, knowing that gas prices were going to shoot up and never come back down. They were right. It was the same thinking which drove me up here. I knew the rural or more Conservative parts of the country would be thrown into disarray and I hoped many Liberals who wouldn't be able or willing to move out of the country would come here. My hunch was correct. The government made its one smart move: it let the few Liberal strongholds govern themselves. I mean, we still live under President Dukeman, but Washington lets us do what we want, down to not forcing us to submit to the will of corporations. And those big companies are happy to let us have our way. After all, 85-percent of U.S. consumption now comes out of New England and the places where business practices and production are well-regulated. It works out pretty well for the corporate heads. We even still pay federal taxes which gives the government added revenue. Otherwise it only survives on what companies privately pay for their autonomy and the high fees the government now charges for every service it offers its citizens.

Businesses still make a nice profit because while they've lost many consumers, their losses in revenue are offset by the elimination of taxes and inspections and cheaper production and labor costs. Plus it's this part of the country which still buys things and keeps the rest of the nation from total poverty."

Dick, like a lot of other displaced Americans, wasn't happy with the condition of the country as a whole. "That's part of the difference between our views. The Democratic agenda, to steal a line from the Republicans, is to not leave anybody behind. If that means taxation and increased spending from us all into programs which protect us we're fine with that. It's like being in a union. You saw glimpses of what's here in the Northeast. We're working and we're able to support ourselves. I may rent this apartment but those who own property still pay mortgages because their houses still have value.

"But most of us who live here aren't happy with how things are in West Virginia or places which are in even more dire straits. At least our old neighbors are fortunate enough to live in an area with some natural value thanks to the coal in the land and the region is usually spared by the worst weather Mother Nature has to offer. Your source for news doesn't give you much news of the country that's not political or can't be construed in a positive light. Think of what you watched during your time in Washington. Did you ever get any indication life had stopped at home? Have you seen what Oklahoma looks like now?"

After Bull indicated he had not, Patton barked out words which turned on his television and its built-in computer. The TV quickly displayed a search engine site with pictures of demolished landscapes. There were few structures standing and only a handful of those looked habitable. There were no signs of anyone trying to clean up the area or of any human presence. The quality of the television was better than the Dukemans had seen before and the pictures clearly depicted signs of dust and weeds scattered over the destruction, indicating these ruins had stood untouched for years.

"This is Moore, Oklahoma. Remember when it was hit by tornadoes in 2013? They did a decent job rebuilding back then, but the repairs were far from complete when storms struck again in 2018. It was maybe nine months after you assassinated the President, in case you never heard about the storm. By that time the new government was well-entrenched in power, had abolished taxes and given away much of what was left in the budget in the final round of tax cuts, there was little money left for such things as emergency relief. That didn't matter much in Washington though because there was majority rule that emergency victims should fend for themselves. Throughout much of the U.S. affiliates from organizations like Habitat for Humanity and the Salvation Army were forced to close. Most people couldn't afford to donate money anymore for private recovery efforts. Every time Moore rebuilt itself, it failed to enforce new building codes which would have made the new structures more likely to survive storms. That's opposed to here, where as soon as Hurricane Sandy hit, regional planners devised ways to keep such a fierce storm from creating as much damage ever again. In Moore though there was nobody able to repair the town and no money to hire people to do the work. To be honest, even for a suburban city close to Oklahoma City, gas prices made the option of rebuilding too pricy for most. Everyone migrated, many by foot, to the city."

With a movement of his eyes, the screen started showing pictures of a city. The upper portions of the photos seemed normal enough: a number of tall, modern skyscrapers rose from an apparent downtown city center, reaching for a partly cloudy sky.

The lower half of the pictures depicted another story. The foregrounds were either parkland or wood-covered thoroughfares. In both cases, the woodsy areas were littered with shacks made of thin wood or cinderblocks or sometimes even cardboard. Dick explained the scenes, "Back in the early 20th Century, they called collections of hovels like these 'shantytowns.' In some ways, these times aren't as bad as those were. At points during the Great Depression, the unemployment rate was close to 25-percent. Now, the official figures say we're hovering around fifteen-percent, but it's probably a little over 20-percent when you consider not all the 'dead' regions like where we're from are included in the government count. Still, cities which house big businesses still have some decent employment numbers. There have even been some job sectors which have grown. Mostly in private security. In cities where police departments have been reduced to practically - and sometimes literally - nothing, people who have wealth feel they have to defend themselves. People on security forces get decent pay and benefits. These are the best jobs, because the wealthy want to make sure their protectors are happy. Content enough at least to not think of going rogue."

Patton went further, explaining how Oklahoma City's apartments and houses remained heavily occupied, mostly by management workers and executives from the companies in town and their personal security entourages. Dick became animated as he pointed out how the ruling party which always promoted small government had unconstitutionally used eminent domain to force tenants and sometimes property owners out of their homes and buildings for the sake of the businesses which claimed they needed safer accommodations for their employees, close to where they worked. Like the mines in West Virginia, the companies created or took control of the living complexes to regulate their employees. In the cities though the college-educated, blue-collar people made more money and shopped at establishments which were still privately owned outside the companies. Back in Oklahoma companies claimed takeovers were necessary because many of their employers were being relocated from the devastation in Moore. People in management contributed more to American capitalism than those they displaced.

The seizure of dwellings naturally drew anger from those who had been forced out of their homes. Most people on the outskirts of town were spared eviction because they were too far from the center of the city for the companies to feel their homes were worth taking over. Others closer to town were just plain lucky to not have their properties or rentals taken from them. However those people saw their rent fees shoot up tremendously. There was little they could do. Businesses had their small armies while individuals no longer had their firearms. Dick told Bull he'd explain that situation in a bit.

Those who were displaced not by the storms but by the affluent received modest compensation and were offered housing in tenements which weren't quite full apartments in quasi-permanent structures, but were steps up from the conditions in the shantytowns. These middle-of-the-road housing projects were closer to the heart of the city while the shantytowns were kept on the outskirts of downtown. That allowed the key streets in Oklahoma City to remain relatively clean – thanks to sanitation crews owned by the conglomerate of companies in town – and free of all traffic. The well-paid security forces sometimes made sweeps of what was considered the safety border of downtown Oklahoma City, pulling down sheds which may have been constructed too close to the so-called business zone.

The improper use of eminent domain was a recurring issue around the Continental 48. Businesses were seizing whatever property they thought could be useful, be it lodging, production facilities and even farms. In many cases there were legitimate buyouts by bigger companies of smaller operations. The owners which sold their businesses were happy with the bonuses and benefits they received and Dick couldn't argue about the fair takeovers outside the fact some companies became monopolies. Farmers seemed extremely happy with the buyouts, for without government subsidies they predicted dim futures. Patton was more concerned about the owners who didn't want to give up their enterprises. The larger companies had easier times getting their way through the federal government. All the top companies in the nation had many politicians in their collective pockets. After all, in a country which worked with what could barely be called a budget and largely on liquid assets, the governmental decision-makers were funded by those businesses. No longer did corporations just fund political campaigns through donations and Super PACS. In the Dukeman era politicians' salaries came directly from businesses. In some cases, like that of Secretary of State Thomas Hannigan, the businessman was the politician, willing to forego paying his own salary but open to taking compensation from other magnates. Elections were no longer truly elections, but instead bidding wars among business conglomerates. Rarely was there more than one candidate in any race. Collusion made public elections unnecessary, for businesses settled elections on their own, leaving little to be decided by the public in November.

Considering the state of the nation, it was probably a good thing there weren't many elections. With so many people displaced for various reasons the voting system was in shambles. Dick used Oklahoma as an example again. The majority of citizens were confused beyond what anyone had previously thought possible. With few people having permanent addresses they weren't sure if they were supposed to go the local voting precincts or try to find their election stations in their old neighborhoods, if they even had the means to get to such places. If someone was fortunate to find their proper polling station, they were regularly turned away due to the surge of Voter ID laws which were in place.

It was the loss of personal rights and responsibilities which angered Patton the most, and when speaking of the situation, moved him to tears. It was no longer considered one's duty or honor to vote when the opportunity arose. It was instead a sign of the privileged if somebody could figure out the system. Other rights had also been shelved. All homosexual marriages in the United States had been dissolved, but that didn't upset Bull at all. He did get agitated however when he learned the right to bear arms was non-existent, not because the Second Amendment was overturned – in reality the government stood by this right more vocally than ever – but because it became impossible for the average person to afford the right. With no tax income in the country, the prices for licenses and registrations became astronomical. Even if somebody gathered enough money to afford a firearm and the various permits and licenses which were connected to gun ownership, there were new fees to contend with. Due to the fear of "armed subversives," the NRA and politicians reversed their then-recent trend of advocating against background and psychological checks. Such checks carried hefty non-refundable payments to the doctors and government. There was no contesting the outcome of these tests and some people considered them shams as those few who did apply found they could be disqualified for the slightest reason. Just like so many aspects of the new American life, only businesses could get around the system. They had the ability to sponsor anyone they wanted for their security armies, allowing the subject to bypass all checks. The security people were then allowed to buy a couple of firearms, besides those which were supplied only for work. This privilege helped keep the security officers happy and loyal to the companies they worked for. As for people paying for their own guns and permits, Dick pointed out there was a clearly disproportionate number of people from families making over a hundred-thousand dollars who ended up owning personal guns over those below that threshold.

At this point, Bull told Dick to put a hold on his bashing of the supposed conditions in the country. "Just how do you know this?" Gary demanded to know.

Patton replied by saying while the majority of the country was relegated to a few government-sanctioned news sources and had practically no Internet access, that wasn't the case in New York, New England or other parts of the nation which the new regime had conceded to the remaining Liberals. While the official U.S. station was still available in the Big Apple, so were other unsanctioned stations which provided what Dick called "a more accurate portrayal of the State of the Union." It was sometimes difficult for the alternate channels to smuggle their handiwork out of some regions of the country, but when they did the government didn't seek retribution. They were happy keeping the damage contained to those few regions, the residents of which seldom made trips out of those areas. Those who did were usually business people, such as the owners of the West Virginia mines, who were mostly sympathetic to the status quo in both political climates. They lived in comfort in thriving cities, while they took advantage of the desolate conditions over the rest of America.

Bull tried once more to protest but Dick again pointed out how the government's media outlet had promoted the story of the Dukemans' deaths, knowing it was a lie.

"You've seen your hometown turned into a ghost town, you know they consider you dead and you've seen, contrary to their reports, what life is like here in a place where we embrace government regulation. Why can't you accept your politicians betrayed you, betrayed us all?"

Bull had no answer.

"There are more lies you need to consider," Dick for the first time in the conversation looked at Joanna, to make sure she was aware what he was saying now was meant for both of them. "This will be very disturbing for you and I'm sorry about that. It hasn't been shown on television yet even here and may not ever be. I received this from friends of friends who have college friends. It's a network of individuals concerned about the direction the country is headed. It was through this network that I knew you had been moved from Virginia and were probably being brought home."

Dick apologized for going on a tangent and returned to his original point, "many of the colleges open around the country are home to dissatisfied kids. That's historically the norm if you look at it: students with their lives ahead of them are often the first to stand up to the injustices they sense are being leveled at them. In Eastern Europe multiple times last century it was so, and in the U.S. in the 1960s, at Kent State and in Little Rock. Also in Tiananmen Square and across the Middle East during the Arab Spring. Well, a student filmed what you're about to see on his phone and was able to send it to somebody and it eventually found its way to me. I'm sorry to be the person to show you this but you both have to see it. Are you ready?"

The Dukemans nodded their consent and Dick activated another video on the television screen.

The picture depicted an older brick building with Greek letters attached to a white-painted wooden patio entryway. A black van was parked at the end of a short walkway which led up to the building's front door. Voices from unseen men – presumably the person filming and his friends – could be heard talking about the van, discussing the unusual scene and joking that somebody must be in trouble. One of the boys, obviously knowing that the building was a sorority house, joked about there being some bad girls getting punished inside. The sophomoric humor elicited considerable laughter from the speakers' audience.

After a matter of seconds, there was a sound of screaming and a scuffle. The unseen kids around the cameraman started screaming expletives when they heard the commotion. The person holding the phone ran across the street to get a better view of the action. The source of the sound was a trio of men pulling a young woman from the building. The captive was screaming and trying to pull away from the men in dark suits. Walking on each side of the fracas were more men, waving their arms and telling people to disperse. They warned that the situation was one of national security. Up until the point where the video shooter took up a stable position where he could film without running, the video had been choppy and hectic. Suddenly the picture cleared up, although there seemed to be little to pay attention to. Gary was about to ask Dick what they were watching and why they were watching it when he heard Joanna squeal with shock. Bull snapped his attention back to screen in time to see the cause of his wife's anguish. Most of the time the woman was putting up a struggle, trying to break away from the grasps of her captors, her long black hair and arms flailing around so much as to keep her identity hidden from the camera. Then came a moment when the woman's face was clearly visible. Despite the girls' tear-soaked eyes leaving streaks down her face and her dyed hair, the Dukemans were finally able to recognize their daughter.

The video played out with Bull riveted to the screen. The three men handling his daughter successfully dragged her into the van while the two guards started yelling at the crowd which had gathered. One of the thugs immediately reached for one of the onlookers, snatching the woman's phone and smashing it to the ground. The other man started to do the same thing, reaching for a man who was between the attacker and the cameraman who was filming the particular video they were watching. At that point the video became confusing again, indicating the person holding the phone had decided it was time to flee while his device was still intact. After two minutes of nearly-nauseating, frantic video, the picture focus finally settled down, depicting a sidewalk. There was the sound of one lone person, panting as he cooled down after his great sprint. The same person muttered something which sounded like "that's enough" and a second later the video froze on its final frame.

As wild as Bull had thought his wife's outburst earlier at Maloney's had been when they first saw the picture of their beaten daughter, it was nothing compared to the cries Joanna was emitting after seeing this film. Bull looked stoically at the television even though the current shot only depicted a close-up of a concrete walkway. Dick just waited in silence for his guests to be ready to talk again.

That moment came a minute later. It was Joanna who spoke, questioning the authenticity of what they'd seen. Patton gave another verbal command to the machine and the video backtracked to the instance in which the child's face first became clearly visible. Patton then ordered the computer to place another picture of the youngest Dukeman on the television screen. The new image was the one which the Dukemans had seen in Maloney's when they had first heard about their child's beating. The couple had been too shocked back then to realize their daughter's hair was uncharacteristically pulled back behind her head and the lack of bangs in front of her face had hid the fact that she had dyed her hair. That was blatantly obvious now that they were aware of the change. The picture taken during the young woman's abduction displayed two of the five bruises she had in the photo released by the government: a scrape on her forehead and a welt under her left eye. The bruise under her eye had grown in the "after" picture and the girl also had a severely bruised right cheek and chin and another scratch below her puffy left eye.

Joanna became hysterical upon seeing both pictures. "Maybe it's not her!" she yelled through her sobs, "maybe it's just make-up!"

"It's her," Bull responded with more authority in his voice than he'd been able to muster in what seemed like years, "that's our baby, and those are real bruises. None of us mean anything to those people. " Bull looked at the screen a little closer, then pointed out another item to his wife, "and look who's behind our baby, pushing her: Charlie." The secret service agent seemingly in charge of the operation was one of their main handlers when they lived under house arrest.

Dick was the one who answered next. "Do you believe now that things are very wrong around the country?"

Bull nodded his agreement. He wasn't sure he agreed with Patton on many things and wasn't in any real condition to think about their arguments over the years, but one thing was abundantly clear at that moment to Gary: the government didn't have his or his family's interests in mind and couldn't care less if the Dukemans were alive or dead.

"Do you believe they all played you?" Patton asked.

That was a point Bull wasn't ready to concede to Dick. He didn't answer and just stared out the window with a confused look.

Patton saw the indecision on Gary's face and pushed in for the kill, "have you ever wondered Bull, about the day you were 'rescued' from your prison? About where you had been kept, where they tortured you, where you lived for a handful of days without food or contact with anyone else?"

"What was to wonder about? Ron and the others were always very upfront about it. I was at the Marine base in Quantico."

"And your captors?" Dick had a suspicious look in his eyes as he pried.

"My captors were the Marines, the military. Ron said they were loyal to President Rodriguez and were doing all they could short of killing me to exact their revenge."

"And you never questioned this?"

"What was there to question?"

The look on Dick's face turned to an odd mixture of knowledge and compassion. "Did you know," Patton's voice sounded concerned, as though he was about to give up a painful secret, "that the Quantico Marine Base is also home to a number of FBI divisions, such as the FBI Academy? Among the Bureau's facilities there are in fact holding cells, buried somewhere down there."

"What's your point?" Bull meant for his retort to sound fierce but he was too emotionally drained to sound anything other than mildly annoyed.

Meanwhile, Patton's voice became softer with the hint of still more compassion in his words, "I mean there was no search for you Bull. There was need to search and there wasn't even a great firefight during Roberts' so-called heroic rescue. You may have been on a Marine base but you were in an FBI facility, under Roberts' jurisdiction. They wanted you to believe they went through Hell and high water to find you so you could do exactly what you did afterwards, so you would be their perfect figurehead. Bull Dukeman: the average patriotic American who had had enough and took matters into his own hands and became a hero to a boisterous minority. You had to think you had been wronged at every turn so when you spoke you spoke with authority and the rest of the Susspicious Minds would cheer for you, but more so for Roberts and Hannigan and President Dukeman."

Bull didn't respond right away. This time he did think about what Patton had said, about what points he could take away from the suggestion. There weren't any which came to mind, although that was possibly because Bull didn't have the energy or time to come up with anything. In fact, the notion Quantico was an FBI base was something he thought he'd heard way back as a child from watching shows like The X-Files. Then he remembered he hadn't had any unfiltered information since before his time in Quantico.

He mulled it over some more then asked, "are you sure?"

"Am I sure?" Dick echoed, "no. But it's what I firmly believe. I've seen emails purported to be from Roberts back during that time but I don't know that they are authentic. If they were authentic, they suggest Roberts authorized your waterboarding to help convince you that you were in trouble, and he supposedly ordered his closest aides and troops to turn the area upside down to make it look like all Hell had broken loose outside your cell. He was the architect of a special effects spectacular which made you think they had to blast you out of a high-security cell which Roberts could have easily opened at any moment.

"I do know Quantico is best known as FBI territory and that despite the verbal exchanges between leadership of the Armed Forces and Intelligence communities there were no military confrontations. I know as well as you do and as anyone who cares that Roberts orchestrated your assassination of the President. Do you really think he cared what he put you through so long as you did his bidding? Especially after these last few days, can you honestly tell me you think he ever had any care for your well-being?"

Gary again didn't speak but stared out the window again for a matter of seconds. Without turning from the view of nightfall on the Big Apple he asked again, "so what's your point?"

Dick walked over to the window and stood next to Bull but didn't touch his visitor. "What if I told you I wanted to help you do it again?"

From across the room Joanna spoke up, "What are you talking about?" Before Patton had a chance to respond, she answered her own question, "are you suggesting he kill the President again?" She gave a brief, frantic chuckle which still managed to belay sarcasm, fear and incredulity, "don't you think he's been through enough already?"

"It's because of what he's been through that he's the right person to ask. It's because they have declared him dead that he'd prove they are liars. It's because they'd have to explain to the world how a dead man killed the President. It's because I believe Gary has something to prove."

"And what about me? Can't I have my husband finally to myself? Can't we finally live together peacefully?"

"Just how will you do that? Are you ready to go back to West Virginia, live in a house worth nothing, maintain it even though his back will limit what he can do? You'll have to raise your own food, chop your own firewood, hope your neighbors really have buried the hatchet and don't blame you for their situation. I didn't bring you here to live here. I don't have the space nor the funds to support you both. Jobs are well-regulated here and there's no way Bull could find work since he's dead and all. When potential employers run a background check on him it will set off all sorts of alarms. You're welcome here for a few days but after that you're going home if you aren't willing to be part of the plan."

Joanna was angered by what Dick had told her and was about to give him a piece of her mind but Bull spoke before she could. "I want to hear more." Joanna was set to protest but Gary turned from the window and held up his hand to stop her from continuing, "he's right. My guilt has been tearing at me for a long time. I knew something wasn't right. It never sat well with me that we were still prisoners or that we were never allowed to contact our old friends. Now we know it wasn't about national security but to make sure we didn't know what was really happening around the country. I feel guilty and responsible and as if I have to make it right again. And I do believe Dick. In all these years Ron and whoever we spoke to about anything told us what was right. And when I didn't say what they wanted to hear, they quickly punished me. Dick's here now telling us things which do make sense, but he's not afraid to admit he's still speculating. Somehow I find that reassuring."

Gary then turned to Dick and asked him for more information about what he had in mind.

The Waiting is the Hardest Part

Upon hearing Bull was at least willing to hear about any action against the President, Patton reaffirmed what he'd said before that he had done his best to keep tabs on the West Virginia Dukemans over the years. He admitted that wasn't just because he was curious about his former neighbor and verbal sparring partner, but because once he moved to New York other people figured out pretty quickly that he had a personal relationship with Bull. He and those other people were probably the closest thing to being the subversive, Liberal insurgent group the new government loved to talk about. The group caused the need for the near-martial law conditions which were in effect. Patton explained the government used the situation as further reason to keep guns out of the hands of the unemployed, for fear that disgruntled out of work people could be brainwashed to take up arms against the government. However, Patton insisted his group hadn't ever planned any course of civil disobedience or violence and weren't orchestrating any so-called major, much-hyped offensive. Their plan was focused on one target and they had no desire to hurt anyone except the President. Patton didn't believe any other sleeper cells - a term Patton grinned at as he turned the government phrase around to describe himself and his group of friends - had concocted any plans of uprising, but he said he was certain other such groups existed. If they were like his group, they were concerned about their country but were happy enough with their own conditions for the time being to not consider rocking the boat.

The idea for a small, decisive attack sprouted when acquaintances of Patton learned about his connection to the Dukemans. Dick adamantly defended the group which had come up with the plan, saying they felt the odds would be in their favor if Bull joined the movement. He pointed out how, opposed to what had happened after Bull had killed President Rodriguez, there was no animosity from the Liberals against anyone else. The Liberal community would actually be angered if anyone other than the prime target or his closest allies got hurt. There would be no attempt to force Hispanics out of the country or anyone from any other race. Quite to the contrary, the country needed its citizens to return, people with money to spend, people who may want to eventually buy the Dukeman house in West Virginia when the region rebounded. It was hoped once the venomous leadership was forced from Washington that expatriates would want to return. Patton's crowd was also hedging its bets that there wouldn't be many people to stand up for the Dukeman administration. There was plenty of discontent for the U.S. leadership but not too many people who stood solidly behind it who were able to afford guns.

When Bull asked how Dick could sound so confident about his expectations for a world post-President Dukeman, Patton answered very matter-of-factly, "you might be surprised by the people who are in my group. We have a number of business owners – big-name business icons – who are ready for another change. Some had been big supporters of Hannigan once upon a time and are still perceived to be in favor of the government. They make marginal profits mainly due to the end of taxes and from large government subsidies. Their profits were better once upon time, when their income was generated by domestic sales. Those have dried up, as did, to a great degree, their international sales. While the U.S. made serious threats towards other countries about daring to raise tariffs against American-made products, those other nations couldn't force their citizens to buy items with the 'Made in the U.S.A.' label. Even people in countries which once seemed infatuated with all things American lost their love for buying products from the U.S. Many people in upper management at our most successful companies started to see the error of their ways and feel guilty about the way things were in their country, their American pride hurting.

"The truth is the support for Norman Dukeman has virtually dried up, although you wouldn't know it by watching certain news outlets. And that's just among his once-loyal base in the business sector, not the average American. And what's more, for all their rhetoric about our enemies waiting to pounce on the country, well, they know there's no credible threat. But they are oblivious to the threat which actually exists, or rather they underestimate the new opposition. We're just soft Liberals to them, holed up in our happy little backward part of the land, living along some unfortunate Conservative business owners. They can't fathom we'd all get together, Liberals and Conservatives, and talk, much less organize anything. 'Compromise' is a dirty word to the Susspicious Minds, wouldn't you agree? It's unfathomable, yet that's what we've done here.

"So what this all means is we have a small coalition of disgruntled people who, because of their prior support of the President, fly under the radar and are ready to act. We have people who get invited to Dukeman's events and speeches. They are allowed to bring whatever they want to these affairs. After all, if you have the money to afford the guns, they automatically think you must be a decent, respectable citizen, and the last thing this regime wants to do to decent, respectable citizens is embarrass them by showing any level of distrust.

"We have the means of getting you into the President's speech coming up next week. He's scheduled to announce a new trade deal with China. Some of the Conservatives in our group have been invited because their facilities have been awarded contracts to produce items to be sold in China, now that labor here is about as cheap as it is over there.

That part of the deal won't be mentioned of course, just the fact that a few thousand, much-needed jobs will be created in the private sector through this deal. We can bring a weapon to the event much easier than it was for you to smuggle one in years ago. A number of our people have been invited who are considered close friends of the party and won't be stopped for bringing a firearm. If you're the right person, you're allowed to do that as part of your Second Amendment protection. You'll go in as a friend of one of these people, and they will be able to just hand you the gun. Compared to when you shot President Rodriguez, this will be easy."

Joanna looked white as a ghost, probably the same way she would have looked four years prior if she'd known what her husband was up to back then. However she kept quiet and wept and prayed that maybe Gary would say no to the plan.

Gary looked Patton straight in the eye and asked, "aren't you playing me too?"

Patton met his stare. "I've been as honest with you as I can be. I think you know that. Do you feel that was the case the last time?"

"No, I don't," Gary said, then said he was in.

Everything That Goes Around Comes Around and Goes Around

Years prior, when giving the task of killing the President of the United States, Bull was a bundle of nerves, fear and adrenaline. That wasn't the case the day he was supposed to kill his second President. Even though he wasn't given much time to think about what he'd been asked to do the last time around, he was given even less time to reflect on his repeat performance.

The time wasn't really much of a factor as was his change of attitude. He was a different man: hardened, betrayed, frazzled and out for revenge. When he killed President Rodriguez he had been placed on a pedestal, made into a false idol. If he was going to kill President Dukeman, it was going to be personal, for his own redemption and to avenge the young love of his life, his daughter. His empathy was used up completely and he wasn't concerned about what would happen to him during or after his new mission.

The situation was also much, much different. The previous time he'd killed a President he was led to think of himself as a hero in a spy movie, set to rid the world of evil by carrying out a covert operation. The day he was to kill President Dukeman he was told just to show up and everything would fall into place.

Even that small window between hearing the plan and putting it into motion was entirely different. He was shipped to a firing range in New Jersey for a few practice rounds where, outside of a false beard the color of his recently-dyed hair and contacts, he didn't have to work in secrecy. He was quickly given a gun permit and license under a false name – Joseph Gardner - achieved in part because so many affluent partners in the operation were able to beat the system through money and favors. The same false identity had already been sent to Washington for screening for the President's advance team ahead of Dukeman's speech. He was being given the identity of a low-level manager for a major company based in New York who really existed but had never been identified with an adult photograph or fingerprints. Such people were rare, but in a city like New York where mass transit still reigned supreme, there were still plenty of people who decided not to obtain a driver's license or buy a car. Besides, the advance notice was more of a formality for people in the parties of big Dukeman supporters. They were considered friends of the state and entirely trustworthy. The person sponsoring Bull's false persona had that level of trust in the government and was known for treating rising stars with unique opportunities, such as inviting them to major functions.

Bull's limited time on the gun range wasn't as hectic as it had been the last time. He was given one pistol to practice with, the very same one he'd use for the assassination. It was a Colt pistol, much like one his father owned and which Bull had used when he was young. He was very comfortable with it and the firing traits were so familiar that he only spent the better half of one afternoon at the range before he and those in on the plot all agreed he was as proficient with the firearm as he needed to be.

There were no special plans to go over, no covert rendezvous to prepare for and no faces or passwords he had to memorize. He met his host and the person who would bring the gun to the event before the day of the attack and was told they'd all arrive together. They would be placed together in V.I.P. seating behind the President's podium. The one concern was how quickly the gun could be transferred to Bull, but even on that note everyone felt confident they'd be able to make the pass in the restroom without anyone caring once the gun was cleared by security.

The day itself was just as comfortable. Never did Gary feel alone, pushed out on a limb by himself. He, his host and others in on the plan all had taken the high-speed train from NYC to Washington together the morning of the afternoon speech and they had a surface mini-bus waiting for them at Union Station. The vehicle transported the party to the Kennedy Center where the Dukeman administration regularly conducted most of its medium-sized events. Part of the reason security at presidential appearances had become so lax was that they were held solely in the nation's capital, where ninety-five percent of the people living or visiting were loyal to the leading Far Right power. Most of the poor residents who had stayed after the war had been pushed out of the city, making the nation's capital the richest, safest city in the U.S.

Even the security check was worry-free. The line was long but moved quickly, people's IDs were checked and double-checked. Even Bull's newly-issued driver's license passed quick scrutiny. The Dukeman team and his political predecessors had worked their security procedures down to what they felt was perfection. For years they had been inviting only staunch supporters to their events. It had been especially easy in the Dukeman era, when unwelcome folks were identified with ease. The security staffers had become lazy, which worked in favor of Bull and his accomplices.

As hoped, Bull took possession of the pistol when he and the original carrier were able to make it to the bathroom at the same time. No one else was present and nobody checked either man upon leaving the facilities. The two returned to their seats together with a half-hour remaining before the President was supposed to hit the stage.

Those thirty minutes passed quickly. Being part of an entourage permitted Bull the opportunity to relax to some extent. He spoke with his companions and even cracked a smile or two. Nobody watching him would have been able to guess what he was up to. He didn't display any evidence of being scared, having burned out his emotions the day he was declared dead. Before reaching the stage he had been concerned about being right behind the President, where watchful eyes would have wondered what he was doing as he went into action when the time came. The group however was split between the second and third rows behind the stage but off to the side. The only row ahead of them was empty and was to be filled with members of the President's party. Bull was happy with the situation. He felt that he'd be out of the line of focus as he took off the beard and drew the gun.

The ceremony officially opened with a traditional flourish. The man who usually could be heard making introductions at White House ceremonies announced the arrival of President Dukeman and "Hail to the Chief" played over the theater's speakers. The President then walked across the stage, turning as he walked to wave to the people sitting on the stage and back at the people in the orchestra and balconies. Bull's heart rate didn't speed up: he felt no excitement. He wasn't fearful of what he was about to do or impressed by being in the presence of the President. He'd met Norman Dukeman many times before, after all. The luster of being close to the President had worn off years ago. Only recently had that sense of honor been turned to disgust.

He watched as the President's own entourage came in behind him. Members of his cabinet filed in behind their leader. Bull realized as these officials shuffled in how another of Patton's assertions seemed correct: many of the cabinet members were synonymous with businesses their positions were connected to. Three former high-level executives from the oil industry for instance were the nation's czars for transportation, energy and environmental affairs (the term "environmental protection" was discarded in Washington after the dismissal of President Armitage). All three were present even if there was no connection between their positions and the subject of the speech.

There were also a number of cabinet members in the group whose attendance was more appropriate for the imminent speech. A handful of people who Bull didn't know well if at all came in, introduced as the secretaries of divisions he didn't care much about, such as commerce, education, labor and the treasury.

Most of these men passed without much fanfare and Bull like the rest of his party and everyone else in the Kennedy Center served up lackluster applause. There was a brief pause then suddenly the applause picked back up. From the moment the fanfare continued it was much more raucous than it had been in the short time since the event had begun. The cheers dwarfed even those which had erupted for President Dukeman. Bull understood the cause of the excitement even if he no longer shared the enthusiasm. As most people in the theater fought to make as much noise as possible, he fought to keep his emotions in check. The last two people to cross the stage were the Secretaries of Defense and State, Ronald Roberts and Thomas Hannigan respectively.

The President stood at the podium waving to the still-boisterous crowd. The cabinet members all took seats. Bull considered it an omen when Hannigan and Roberts sat directly in front of him. The others in Gary's party also noticed and tried to show they didn't feel the same way. The person two down from Bull whispered urgently "Joe!" It took Bull a second to remember that was his cover identity and when he looked over, the person who had called to him gave him a quick, worried shake of the head.

Bull knew he had a maniacal look on his face as he returned the gesture with a large nod. If there had been any question about his intentions, the fire in his eyes left no doubt.

In the next ten seconds, Gary put his head in his hands and pulled off his beard. He would have grunted in pain once upon a time as the adhesive stuck to his cheeks and chin, but the surging adrenaline and determination to extract revenge on those before him kept his feelings in check. He then drew the gun from his waistband and returned for a brief moment to a normal sitting position. He then put his hand on Roberts' shoulder. "Mister Secretary," he whispered in a forceful, near maniacal voice, "I'm not dead."

From behind, Gary could tell Ron was confused and very annoyed with the interruption. He turned around to face Bull, ready to give the pest a piece of his mind. Despite the contacts and the dyed hair, it was obvious Roberts recognized Gary Dukeman immediately. Before the Secretary could say anything, Dukeman pulled the trigger, sending a bullet through Roberts' forehead and killing him instantly.

Bull then turned to Thomas Hannigan as his rage grew. He was yelling now, "did you hear me Tom?! You shipped me off to West Virginia and left me for dead, like you left everyone there," he pulled the trigger again, hitting Hannigan in the same spot he'd shot Roberts, "but you didn't kill me!"

After his first shot, people started scattering from the stage as secret service men rushed towards Bull. The commotion made a clear shot at Bull unachievable and the officers were forced to detain the shooter instead of risking hurting innocent, big Norman Dukeman contributors. As some of them ran to contain Bull and others rushed the President from harm's way, Gary threw down his gun and prostrated himself on the stage with his hands behind his head.

It was Charlie, the secret service officer Bull had gotten to know well during his time in Washington and the man who had been captured on film beating Bull's daughter who reached him first. "Get up!" Charlie ordered. Bull returned to a kneeling position. The last things Bull ever heard was Charlie saying "you're dead now!" followed by another gunshot.

Just like Freddy Villanueva years ago, Gary Dukeman was killed execution-style, unarmed, after he himself had carried out political assassinations. Just as Ron Roberts and Thomas Hannigan had seconds before, Bull Dukeman was killed instantly by a single bullet to his head.

Unlike Roberts and Hannigan, Dukeman didn't die in fear or shock, but with a sense of satisfaction and release.

Epilogue: Can't Cry Anymore

The course of human history can weave strange patterns sometimes. Most of the industrial, educated world expected the United States to fall into another state of civil war after the deaths of Ronald Roberts, Thomas Hannigan and Gary Dukeman. That did not happen.

In truth, there was nobody left who was willing to go to war. On the Liberal side, as Dick Patton had explained to Dukeman, there had never been a plan for all-out aggression or a desire to fight. There was no real plan for the post-Norman Dukeman era, but then again, the President hadn't been assassinated.

For the Conservatives, their base had been severely splintered along economic lines. There were still pockets of people living in poverty who felt tremendous support for President Dukeman, but even when their intuition told them to fall into order behind the Second Amendment, they had been financially forced from owning guns and therefore had no way to form the militias they believed were necessary for the security of a free state.

To own a gun was to be part of the upper echelon of the Conservative Party, which suddenly wasn't a popular position to be in. Much like after the end of World War Two, when members of the Nazi Party virtually disappeared, trying to filter into the general German population, few of the orchestrators of the Tea Party, Susspicious Minds and Neo-Con movements rushed to take credit for their parts. The common spectator would have been hard-pressed to name anyone other than Roberts or Hannigan or other members of Norman Dukeman's cabinet as the motivators of America's Dark Age.

Meanwhile the U.S. military, still mostly dispersed across the globe and feeling collectively demoralized by the second-class treatment it had unilaterally received from Roberts' intelligence coup, did nothing to come to the government's rescue. Those soldiers, airmen and women, sailors and Marines who had been shipped to other countries remained in waiting for the country they loved and served to start its repair process. The armed divisions within the intelligence community also refused to act, knowing any action would identify such a person as a conspirator for the government. Some felt guilty for what they had been part of while others knew they would likely be compared – justly – to the Gestapo for its part enforcing the questionable rule of an opportunistic few. The German intelligence machine had similarly used domestic terrorism and unbridled racism to gain a temporary hold on a world superpower. Whether because of the signs of what lay ahead or fear of retribution and potential charges of crimes against humanity, nobody who had carried out Ronald Roberts' plans were willing to maintain the status quo or allow themselves to be recognized as somebody who had supported the coup.

With its top actors in hiding, the light of the Far Right conspiracy and takeover quickly burned itself out.

Popularity for the Dukeman regime faded quickly, helped tremendously when the pro-President news network immediately turned on him. The station overplayed Bull's killing of Roberts and Hannigan, coming as close to glorifying Bull as it reasonably could and as much as it had when he'd shot President Rodriguez. Within 24 hours the news organization insisted it too had been duped by the government. The tape of the abduction of the Dukeman daughter quickly found its way onto the airwaves nationwide, evaporating any sympathy anyone had for Roberts or his intelligence machine. After the channel showed the video for the first time it apologized for its part blindly feeding the government's propaganda to the public and for not questioning the regulations which it was told to follow. Spokespeople for the network explained they did so to get exclusive access to every facet of the government. The statement given by one of the network's biggest stars was spared scrutiny: the other networks were just starting to recover and weren't given much of a chance to cover the story.

In a turn of events many called stunning and a few considered appropriate, if sadly comforting, Charlie the secret service agent was found dead, murdered at CIA headquarters shortly after the video of his treatment of the young woman went mainstream. Some called his death sickening, even though few made a fuss over it. There was no massive call for an investigation and no public report on any inquiry.

Driven by the motivation to stay number-one as well as to avoid being considered closely aligned with the government, the news network started an exposé series about the true condition of America. In trying to keep favor with some of its former allies, the segments in many bigger, thriving cities focused on what big businesses had done to take the lead in creating steady work environments and flowing economies. Little was said about New York's acceptance of taxes, Liberal politics or the embracing of solar power and the network still only used south-facing shots of downtown New York to avoid showing the vast solar farms above the city.

The pictures from around rural America were far bleaker and the stories were more or less the same no matter where the news crews found themselves. There was little to no commerce in regions which had been abandoned by big business. If there was no supply line to cities or production facilities near the town, the major companies ignored that area. Even towns like Bull's which were extremely close to industry but in the opposite direction of the flow of business traffic saw most of their financial activity evaporate. Not all those towns were fortunate enough to have major shopping marts in them like Bull's did, and even many of those had gone out of business without any paying customers around. Some of these towns and neighborhoods started group farming with each person raising a certain small crop so people could at least enjoy a variety of vegetarian items or the rare freshly-killed farm animal on special occasions. Other communities refused to cooperate in such fashion when handfuls of people proudly stated they were living in America and they would not be forced into Communism.

Electricity was hit-or-miss all over the country: government subsidies allowed some places to keep their power, depending on how close to a "productive" region they were. Still, if a power line went down in a storm that was the end of power unless it disrupted the march of industry. Wood-burning stoves and fireplaces heated most of the country, with people chopping their own wood. Houses and sometimes whole neighborhoods burned to the ground when a fire got out of hand. Firefighters were few and far between across the nation.

Without phones, Internet, postal service and all forms of modern communication outside of the handful of government-approved television stations and no viable means of long-distance transportation, the majority of people around the country remained in the dark about what was going on elsewhere. There was a sense of national shock as the crisis was exposed. With each stop the reporters made, they brought pictures and videos of a place they told their interviewees was in worse condition. This always brought the locals to tears, when they considered other Americans could be living in even more dire circumstances than their own.

After the shootings, President Dukeman remained in power for the better half of two weeks before abdicating his throne, returning the Presidency to Sydney Armitage. The media assailment of his presidency was thorough and left him without any support. In that short time, he achieved the worst polling numbers ever for an American President. Calling his association with Roberts and Hannigan an unfortunate mistake and calling their joint deception of the U.S. population and the whole world one of the worst blunders in history, he stepped down, surrendering himself to his security detail for detainment and the eventual punishment decided by the new government.

There would be no such retaliation. In similar fashion as when Gerald Ford succeeded Richard Nixon, Sydney Armitage used the first speech of his second presidency to say Norman Dukeman had suffered and would continue to suffer on his own and that the country needed to heal. As such, he granted Norman Dukeman a presidential pardon, pointing to the fact that Dukeman was as much a pawn in Roberts' and Hannigan's plan as Gary Dukeman and a good majority of people living in the U.S. had been. The worst words Armitage had for Norman Dukeman was to call him a puppet for the opportunistic, illegal regime. Armitage pointed out the true villains in this sorry portion of American history had already paid the ultimate price and it was time to help America heal and repair all the damage the old guard had caused.

Sydney Armitage continued with what was the longest presidential speech in American history by outlining his administration's quickly-conceived plan for healing. He pleaded for all U.S. citizens to return to their homeland and ordered most of the military to come back stateside. This was truly the country's most vulnerable hour and not even in the Colonial era had there ever been such a strong need for defense and rebuilding. Nobody would be subject to retribution for his or her flight.

As the President pointed out with a small trace of humor, even he had been wrestled out of power and forced to run.

The most vicious of his words, although hardly such, were directed at many of the largest business magnates: those who had unquestionably given the strongest support to the Dukeman administration and its handlers. They were the ones who helped Hannigan and Roberts orchestrate the Dukeman presidency and who, hastily-commissioned investigations already showed, harvested the greatest financial rewards since the shooting of President Rodriguez. President Armitage issued an executive order, effective as of that national address, freezing the assets of the "conspirators" and their companies for the eventual liquidation and disbursement to the majority of the American people. President Armitage stopped short of calling for a martial law regime of his own, however he made it clear that the U.S. government must step in and seize a great number of private industries in order to resuscitate a crippled national economy which was on life support.

Armitage finished his address by reaffirming his call for U.S. citizens all over the world to return to their homeland. He apologized to those who had been forced out, again pointing to the heinous, illegal coup which had finally ended after the deaths of its primary leaders. To those who had left voluntarily - even those who had denounced their citizenship - he offered amnesty. There hadn't been a more dangerous time to live in the U.S. since the first Civil War about 150 years before. It was understandable for people to seek asylum elsewhere, and he and the people he was still in the process of appointing to lead the country weren't like those they'd replaced. They didn't consider those who ran unpatriotic or un-American. "The un-Americans," he said, "were those who tried to abolish the American Dream based on skin color, ethnicity and class."

Masses of Americans heeded the President's call. Citizens in the military and expatriates alike flocked home. A vast majority of those who had left had Liberal leanings and so were in awe as they arrived back in the country in cities like New York and San Francisco and others where alternate energy sources had taken root. Even Los Angeles, which had remained somewhat neutral through the Norman Dukeman years, had seen a visible drop in smog, thanks in part to a drop in population but more so due to an increase in the use of solar and wind energy. The wind farms in the L.A. valleys had increased tremendously, with solar panels added between the large windmills. With diminished opposition to electric cars, the industry was finally in Southern California to stay and was flourishing. Cities with long-lasting reputations of having dirty streets and air were much cleaner and vibrant.

There was a complete about-face in a majority of the rural towns. People returning home to these regions returned with tears in their eyes. The rush of television reports hadn't prepared those coming home for the desolation which existed. The air was still cleaner with so many people being unable to afford fossil fuels but the streets made some of these former quaint villages look like warzones. That didn't remain the case for long however. With a resiliency Americans always showed after major disasters, all partisanship slipped away and despair turned into determination. The cleanup process started as people stopped worrying about their current situations.

Washington was quick to act and do its part. As the President had promised, the assets the government had seized were quickly liquidated and used for stipends for everyone who was doing his or her part in the revitalization process. The payments were small and it took as much as three months for payments to reach the more remote towns, but some who thought they may never see currency again considered it money from

Heaven. There came a federally-driven push for local governments and municipalities to reform. Larger portions of money which the national government had acquired was used for this. Police and fire departments were reestablished and utilities which had bordered on public and private ownership became universally public, at least until the necessary infrastructure was firmly in place.

The alternative energy sector was the single-most instrumental tool for getting the nation back on its feet. Building the infrastructure and transit lines for new power created jobs in every single big city and small hamlet. Even New York was able to expand its power grid. Besides the tremendous amount of job creation, the expansion of solar and wind production allowed the government to temporarily offer free power to all citizens, enabling them to start spending on products instead of paying for utilities. To fund the new electric endeavors, the government took a large portion of the money it seized from the oil and coal companies like the one Bull had worked for. When faced with the possibility of being charged with crimes against humanity for what they put their employees through, the mine and oil rig owners grudgingly accepted this form of punishment over potential lifetime jail terms or worse.

In general, the corporations which had pushed the nation to its knees were forced to pay for almost everything during the first years of rebuilding. In private, business owners fumed, but they made no comments whatsoever in public. Few would admit their part in what had happened and knew that to react anyway other than they did would have been suicide. They had seen their security details turn against them, not with force but by simply walking away, unwilling to protect the current generation of robber barons. The hoarding of wealth was similar to the French Revolution but the new lords didn't have anyone left to protect them. As they became more accessible to the public, they believed the only way to stay alive was to go along with what was happening. Considering there were portions of their money the government wasn't going to (or at times able to) touch, they realized it was best to take what they were being allowed to keep and minimize their losses.

The process of rebuilding the parts of the United States which had been most damaged took up to a decade, although most of the country was returning to a good semblance of normalcy within three years. The nation was fortunate to have strong international allies which helped protect it, despite the threats the previous government had issued unilaterally. The armed forces, primarily the U.S. Army and Air Force, helped not only to defend but rebuild with their corps of civil engineers and service men and women. Even among those who had put their faith in Roberts' intelligence when they looked to discredit the military there was a greater amount of respect, appreciation and gratefulness for all the military was accomplishing.

Politically, President Armitage's version of martial law lasted about a year, until there were enough municipalities able to fend for themselves. The President called for midterm elections to go on as usual in 2022. Polling would have been considered disastrous had there been many close contests around the country, but for 80-percent of the country there was a knee-jerk reaction to the Conservatives leaving few races up for grabs. In many places there were no Right-leaning candidates willing to run for fear they would be seen as too closely aligned to the memories of Roberts and Hannigan. The dominance of the Liberals was as absolute after the first elections as it had been for the Conservatives after Dukeman was sworn in. The GOP, which had been having an identity crisis even as far back as the Obama administration, would take many years before it would start to challenge the Democrats, at which point it had to reinvent itself. Items such as alternate energy, the return of healthcare and an absolute avalanche of civil rights for people based on race, gender and sexual orientation had become etched in stone as the law of the land, impervious to reversal. Republicans would eventually rebrand their party on their traditional fiscal and international relations platforms. They couldn't fight mandated insurance or convince anyone to return to unrenewable fossil fuels, but eventually calling the handouts for people who were no longer doing much to help rebuild the nation "welfare" caught on, as did their perennial call for lower taxes. The tax rate, as people started seeing money in their pockets, had started growing larger than ever. After giving so much money to the people to reignite the economy, federal interests had had to do what it deemed best to recover what it could. It would take fourteen years for the GOP to make a serious dent in the Democratic legislative machine, and in total, from the start of the Obama administration, 28 years to end the Democratic hold on the White House.

The place of Gary "Bull" Dukeman in American history became the biggest debate in American schools all over the nation for decades. He was called a villain, a hero, ignorant, wise, a pawn, a leader, a patriot and a terrorist. The incredible part of his story was that it was all true. Overall history was kind to him as most agreed his devious acts were synonymous with his being a pawn and his redemption came when he realized he had a chance to repair the damage attributed to him. "Attributed" was the way most looked at it, as he hadn't played a part in organizing what followed after his shooting of Eduardo Rodriguez.

Joanna Dukeman had steeled herself for the reality that her husband would not be returning from Washington the day he shot Roberts and Hannigan. She started crying when Gary fired his first shot that day. She whispered good bye to the television in Patton's house at that moment, then watched as her husband was inevitably killed. Dick was still in the apartment as well and did his best to comfort her, but realized the awkward embrace around her shoulders was best ended quickly.

Her grief turned to a mild sense of joy quickly when the CIA released her daughter. The child it turned out was not in such a bad condition as had been reported: her coma was in fact drug induced and not cause by any physical harm. Ron Roberts himself had ordered this, saying the girl was the best prop he could use to perpetuate their story about Liberal terrorists. With that story totally debunked and Roberts' plans derailed, the child was quickly revived by people within the intelligence committees who said they had just learned about the situation and were sickened by it. The reunion of mother and daughter started with tears of joy, then turned to drops of agony as the offspring learned about the fate of her father.

Dukeman's daughter was allowed to return to Georgetown to finish her studies while Joanna moved back to the family's house in West Virginia. The town was in the early stages of rebuilding when she returned. The people welcomed her back with pity, admiration and open arms, as it did her child when she came home for visits and eventually to teach in the revitalized school district. Dick Patton would visit the Dukemans and the town on occasion too, but remained a permanent resident of New York. He was treated well during his visits, as those who remembered him and had treated him as an outsider in the past came to accept what he had said once upon a time as near-prophecy. Even if Patton had not been pardoned by the President like Norman Dukeman had been, he and those responsible for the plot were never sought out or held responsible for the killings. Nor did it ever come to light that it was Bull who had changed the plan from killing his namesake, and in doing so had really changed the course of history. Had the two masterminds survived and President Dukeman had died, that would have given Roberts all he needed to rule unchallenged as they installed another puppet to be their figurehead.

Life in the town quickly returned to normal. The coal companies released their employees from their indentured servitude and the workers were given lump sum payments if they agreed to move back into town. That wasn't a hard sell and soon the village was full of residents who had enough money to buy or rent homes again. While some were unable to afford their own cars – surface or hover – the companies organized shuttles to and from the mines. The corporations did whatever they could to avoid financial or violent retribution, and despite a loud call to get what they could, the workers settled for the financial packages they were offered, along with higher pay rates and a return of solid benefits (some of which would become federal standards when the Affordable Care Act returned). Such scenes played out around the country and very few people on either side wanted to fight. The country was tired of conflict. Americans wanted a quick end to the pain created by the Hannigan legacy. The barracks on the mining land and company stores were immediately dismantled and people started shopping in town again. People chose to shop at the family-owned stores as they returned to business, foregoing the big chain mart further down the road. The big stores were a reminder of the big companies which had driven the area to ruin. The mega-mart was vital for many items, but everyone preferred to buy what they could at the smaller stores on Main Street. Few cared to remember the chain store as the place where Skip first approached Bull with the plan to shoot the President. Skip's fate was never determined. It was believed he probably had died while in the hands of Roberts' team, but nobody was sure, nor cared to guess if his rumored death had been from natural causes or something more sinister.

Despite that brief time when there had been calls for Gary's head, the village had for the most part been one of the places where his image was more positive than anywhere else. Anyone who said anything other than Bull had been deceived as badly as the rest of the nation was looking for a fight. Likewise, Bull's neighbors were thankful in the end for his final, fatal act. Their love for their fallen friend was recognized when the town's rebuilding process was complete. With a new government, new municipal facilities and a new chance at life, it was decided the town needed a new name. As such, it was on the two-year anniversary of the death of Gary Dukeman that Dukeman, West Virginia was born.